DETLEV'S
IMITATIONS

DETLEV'S IMITATIONS

Hubert Fichte

Translated by Martin Chalmers

The publishers thank Kathy Acker, Mark Ainley, John
Kraniauskas, Mike Hart, Bob Lumley, Enrico Palandri,
Kate Pullinger, for their advice and assistance.

Library of Congress Catalog Card Number: 91−61207

British Library Cataloguing in Publication Data
Fichte, Hubert
   Detlev's imitations. — (Masks)
   I. Title   II.Series
   833 [F]

ISBN 1−85242−167−3

This edition first published 1992 by Serpent's Tail, 4 Blackstock
Mews, London N4 and 401 West Broadway #2,
New York, NY 10012
Typeset in 10/13 pt Imprint by Setrite Typesetters Limited,
Hong Kong

Printed on acid-free paper by
Nørhaven A/S, Viborg, Denmark

Translator's Note

I wish to thank Leonore Mau, Wolfgang von Wangenheim, and friends at the Europäisches Übersetzer-Kollegium in Straelen in October/November, 1990, especially Christine Koschel for indispensable help in preparing this translation. Last but not least I should like to thank Michael Hulse for his work on the verses.

MARTIN CHALMERS

1

— We're coming from the snow into the camouflage, says Detlev.

— This is Sternschanzen Station. We've arrived in Hamburg, says his mother.

— The Alster is camouflaged too. The Todt Organisation has made a fake town out of the water. The orphanage began with eggs. Beautiful, white eggs, which are cracked on the edge of the pot. To begin with I was given egg with cognac in a little porcelain cup.

— Snow was still lying in Munich. Here a milder spring wind is already blowing. I can smell the sea, says his mother.

— The white seagulls settle on the camouflage and cover it. The seagulls aren't deceived. I stumble between the painted houses over the lake, the nets, the woods and sink into the holes, where water is beginning to soak through the camouflage.

— We've made it. It will take some time, before the documents are sent back to Hamburg from Scheyern. Until then we'll be left in peace, says his mother.

— Yes, soon we'll be with granny and grandad. But when one's achieved something that one wants, it's quite boring.

— Did you see the men who were shovelling snow in Munich? "Isn't it shameful?" a woman, a complete stranger, called out to me on the platform. I pretended that I hadn't understood or that I hadn't noticed that she was talking to me. But she stopped and caught me by the arm and said: "They're Hungarian Jews!" What courage she had. I merely uttered an indefinable sound, which she could interpret as acknowledgement and which didn't incriminate me. I took you by the hand and ran for the nearest carriage door. Perhaps the woman was an informer! She didn't follow us and didn't shout anything dangerous after us, says his mother.

— The gauleiter had sentenced me to death by hanging on the market place in Scheyern. I dreamt I was allowed to have one wish and asked for a soft-boiled egg. They let me eat it with a chipped spoon, before I had to mount the ladder.

While Detlev was still in the Scheyern orphanage, he had only imagined Hamburg in summer. There was cherry soup and granny and grandad took him to Hagenbeck. Uncle Bruno drove through the Elbe Tunnel and at Uncle Emil and Aunty Hilde's he was allowed to smell the little green bottles of scent until the inside of his nose was stinging.

"Final Victory or Bolshevik Chaos!"

— The Führer has drawn a uniform over Sternschanzen Station as camouflage. The entire hall has been wrapped up. The camouflage is fraying. I stumble over the wires hanging down from the curved roof. They're going to get me! Will they get me in the shelter of grandad's house?

— They've painted the whole town, in order to mislead the Anglo-Americans. I can't recognise my home town any more. When we went off with the evacuees two years ago, what a big, bright city it still was, says his mother. The smell of sacking.

— There aren't any taxis any more!

Detlev recognises the smell in the underground again.

The man with the ugly face is stuck to the wall here too: "Final Victory or Bolshevik Chaos!"

2

— There's granny at the window.

Grandmother twenty-four years before her death.

Yesterday she had her hair done by Mrs Mook. Her white

hair falls in waves and is burnt a little yellow in places by
the curling tongs.
— Granny has grown smaller.
He comes closer again to the smell of spittle of a woman
who is always much older than Detlev.
Granny and Detlev have difficulty understanding one
another.
Detlev says:
— Wat did you sai?
— Sais oi.
— Gawd bless.
— Hubbedy bubbedy.
— Gran.
— Oi dunno.
— Mercy.
— Sist Lissa.
— Sist Murry.
— Jeezus an Murry.
His grandmother says:
— All nine.
— Lorabove.
— It'll be awreet wi Mutha Benn, it turned oot reet wi
Mutha Benn.
— Snot i the pot, to mak thick broth.
She's a Silesian and in Hamburg no one could understand
her when she was younger either.
— Where the North Sea waves break upon the shore,
That's ma hame, that's where I belong,
That's ma hame, that's where I belong,
grandfather sings in a Silesian accent.
Detlev is there, Detlev who is to inherit the house when
he's made something of himself working for the customs,
the non-Aryan.
Now what's that coming into grandad's house again?!

3

At school they don't understand Detlev.
At every opportunity people in Hamburg say:
— Go on, cheer up!
Detlev became weaker when he was in Bavaria.
— The Prussians are always stronger then the Bavarians.
To begin with in Scheyern Detlev knocked the Weindel
boy down into the chair when they were playing dive
bombers. But the better Detlev spoke Bavarian, the weaker
he became and now he has to suffer for it in Hamburg.
Karl-Jörn sticks up for him.
Detlev and Karl-Jörn want to be friends.
Detlev is to bring him pictures of cars from the cigarette
album.

4

Detlev dreams he's sitting on the cast iron treadle of the
sewing machine in the study and Sister Appia floats in.
She bends down to him and pushes her outstretched finger
under his impurity, under the bag with the two marbles in
it. She presses there, Sister Appia, between the arsehole
and the little pipe, dibble his friend Karl-Jörn calls it, and
flies through the guest room with billowing veils, past the
potted palm, through the study, out again.

5

Grandad has retired and picks cherries during the day.
Once there's an air raid warning, while grandfather is
sitting in the morello cherry tree.
But no one goes down to the cellar.
The hum of the Anglo-American airplane is hardly audible,
high above among the fleecy clouds — Detlev can see it
twinkling — it doesn't drop anything tiny, that grows
larger as it falls through the clouds, turns black and destroys

everything, including Detlev's thought, why this afternoon and the enemy reconnaissance plane, that chases no one into the cellar, does not not exist at all.

6

Granny has a row with Detlev because he keeps putting the balls of snot from his nose into the little bottles from the toy shop and placing the corked bottles beside her armchair.
Detlev quickly takes the little bottles away. He pulls out the stopper and smells it.
What a stink!
And hides the little bottle behind the wall mirror.

7

Mummy hasn't found employment yet. She is always there: when Detlev wakes up, at meals, when he has to go to the toilet. She could wipe his arse now, as granny used to do, while mummy was sitting in the office. But Detlev is too big for that now.
His mother is making redcurrant jelly. Granny watches and, without saying a word, leaves the kitchen. Mummy's redcurrant jelly does not set right away either and when his grandmother raises her eyebrows and asks:
— Well, does it taste nice?
Detlev feels that he's supposed to choose between the two redcurrant jellies, granny's firm one, which means: wet kisses and being wiped on the toilet and never any scolding — and his mother's unsuccessful redcurrant jelly, which means: waiting for his mother till she comes from the office, waiting for his mother till she comes to the orphanage, but also: little, coloured, nice-smelling makeup pencils.
Detlev fills his mouth with runny redcurrant jelly and

looks at his grandmother and begins to cough and his
grandmother quickly lowers her eyebrows, because she has
never tormented Detlev, and quickly cleans up what has
been spat out, so that mummy doesn't see it.

Detlev's mother says to him:

— You should have had ballet lessons at four. But then
the war broke out and there were the blackouts. You
should learn piano at six. I even used to play the Beethoven
sonatas and Aunt Elli always said: With you one really
begins to understand the music properly. — When you
were six we had to move from one room to the next in
Scheyern. A piano! But at least I was able to make it
possible for you to have recorder lessons with Mother
Cecilia. I want you to see an opera, and to hear the
"Fifth," and a tragedy; we'll see *The Magic Flute*, and *The
Bartered Bride* by Smetana, and *He Wants to Play a Joke*
by Nestroy in the Thalia Theatre, and above all *Iphigenia
in Tauris* by Johann Wolfgang von Goethe. Who knows!

8

One would like to bite into it and eat it up, it looks so
appetising, the German Playhouse. Tasteful embellishments
on the walls. Cherry red and strawberry red. Oatmeal
cake-coloured plush. More solemn and something quite
different from the military hospital in Scheyern, where the
black maters transformed themselves into Jewish women
and the wounded with their white irregular elephant legs
into Herod and Joseph for the Christmas play.

The transformation took place in an improvised room,
which smelt of Uhu all-purpose glue and iodine, on beer
barrels.

Here in Hamburg it's different. Formal suits hide everything
that's a reminder of the war. No half legs, half hands,

blood-soaked bandages on ears as in Scheyern.

Mummy too is wearing something special, dark and the eight-year-old has smart short trousers on, neat white long socks, dark brown shoes and a Bavarian Sunday jacket.

Detlev is tall for his age.

The unmarried mother with the precocious son.

The son plays the grown up, mummy can take his arm, just as if he were a proper man, and his mother makes some more youthful gestures, as if she was the boy's older sister.

— Maria Wimmer is playing Iphigenia tonight.

— That they let me in despite my age.

— Perhaps even the doorman knows, how much Iphigenia means to us today.

— Yes. What?

— Beauty!

Precocious.

A word, that smells of unwashed nylon from before the war.

— He'd be better off playing cops and robbers and building model Stuka aeroplanes.

— He'll never be a proper man.

— You really are a little precocious.

Would mummy defend him against this accusation?

Granny defends him. It doesn't worry her that he's too pale and his ears are too big. Even now she still knows the "Bond" by heart and "The Singer's Curse". She reads the Bible every evening. Detlev is her dearest. He should read what he wants and doesn't have to become a proper man like her Paul, with his leather belt, his sciatica and the knife that he uses to cut his nails, if only Detlev will never again put snot in the little bottles from the shop and let them go bad.

Was mummy's husband a proper man?

If the Jew were to accompany them here in the German

Playhouse, instead of precocious Detlev, all three would not have much longer to live.

So dangerous, to go walking in this solemn cake!

And so tender the precocious arm's little caresses of the unmarried, motherly one, the dignified smile of the not quite proper little man and that of the woman not recognised by the state.

The half-public — fear does make it difficult to swallow down saliva at the right moment — attentiveness to one another. The intersecting, easily faked intimacies.

Smell of silk from peace time with makeup.

— How gentlemanly, say two blonde women.

The artificial play of precociousness and childishness.

Orestes is the most impressive:

— Which in the sacred presence of his mother had flickered low

The woollen socks don't itch any more.

— on the floor that had been washed so often/The traces of that blood so foully shed

Where does Goethe get all these words from?

These aren't just words that fit together, that follow one another without stumbling as in "The Singer's Curse" or "The Song of the Bell". And not just noble words as in Pastor Roager's Protestant church or holy, incomprehensible words from the town parish church in Scheyern. Not wild, sharp words as in Heinrich von Kleist or Hans Friedrich Blunck. Noble and wild and quite incomprehensible and moving.

Not always.

When Pylades speaks, the woollen socks itch and for whole scenes Iphigenia is so cross all the time. Yet when she says:

— It is enough

everything becomes wet and the stage swims in Detlev's tears. Because the father has had her child killed, the mother kills the husband. Iphigenia has been saved by the

goddess. But it would have made no difference at all to the father. And it's the child's fault that the mother killed the father and Iphigenia says nothing more than:
— It is enough.
And Detlev weeps out everything that's hidden behind that, without sniffing, so that his mother doesn't notice.
— Would you have killed my father, because he didn't care about anything any more?
— What nonsense you talk! It's all only a metaphor. It's an account of the development of the human ego.
The clapping at the end lasts a long time. Some cry. Maria Wimmer is happy taking her bow — at least she pretends to be. Perhaps she has to go to the munitions factory early in the morning.

9

Mummy is looking for employment. Granny cooks lunch. Grandad feeds the hens.
In the dining room Detlev pulls the tiger skin blanket around his shoulders and strides past the potted palm in the study.
— Forth into your shadows, restless wars!
Forth, forth, fo! fo! Four forth! orth, orth.
Wat did you sai?
Herod, Christ Child, Bolshe, Appia, Chao.
Horst Wessel, where the North Sea waves break upon the shore.
Zick, nick, nack, nobel, the pobel, the peoble, the pinka.
Now still I pray with Tauris, Goethe, stoal.
Flak is flak flak, flak, Oshalla and Bolona, libay, bibay.
And here my spirit finds no rest.
For oh, the star of the sea me divides the judged.
And on him not on me and not on me.
Stuka model, Greeks, bibay, mourning, muhu.
Go on, cheer up.

Uhu, uhu, the star of the sea me sticks the judged.
Mummy comes in. In August she's to take up war time
employment. Raboisen labour exchange.

10

The sponge is always on the right close to the edge. Grandad
moves it forward a little. The documents are bottom right.
Grandad unlocks bottom right and withdraws a small book
from the drawer. He opens it and puts it down right in
front of him.
He takes a stamp with Horst Wessel on it out of his wallet.
He dampens it with the sponge. But he doesn't trust the
war time adhesive and from top left of the desk, still part
of the dowry from the last century, he takes the paste,
pastes all of the stamp and sticks it in the little book.
— What's that?
— My party membership book.
Detlev looks at Horst Wessel and has the same feeling as in
the German Playhouse, when Iphigenia said: It is enough,
you will see me again.
— Who is Horst Wessel actually?
— Horst Wessel wrote "Raise High the Flag!" He fell for
the movement!
— For which movement?
— For the Party!
— Would he have talked to me?
Grandad looks sadly at Detlev.

11

Mozart was too lazy to set all the words in *The Magic Flute*
to music and Detlev wants to compose the opera once
again.

While playing in the flak shelters Karin Freier leaves him alone for a moment and immediately Detlev begins to sing:
— O Isis and Osiris!
Karin Freier has crept up and is listening. But she doesn't say anything and doesn't laugh at Detlev later either.

12

— Now it's the long holidays and I don't need to bring Karl-Jörn any pictures of cars any more.
Detlev accompanies Klaus Ostermann from school along the crooked path.
— This is the crooked path, where Mrs Apfelbach was attacked by a sex maniac.
— What's a sex maniac?
— A child molester. She was carrying the child under her heart. That's why Karin Apfelbach is deaf and dumb. She only says bits of words and she can't hear properly either.
— If you want, I'll lend you my nice shiny pencil with the rubber on it, says Klaus Ostermann.
— Although I've never looked at Klaus Ostermann.
— If you want cherries, you can get cherries, says Detlev. Have you got amerelles?
— Morello cherries.
— They're too sour for me. Bye!
— Bye!
Klaus Ostermann grows smaller on the crooked path.

13

It is Saturday evening.
His grandparents got dressed up and at eight went to an air defence demonstration in Koppelstrasse. Grandad took his good walking stick with him.
An allotment hut is to be set alight for demonstration

purposes and put out according to regulations by a new method.

Mummy makes the house tidy.

She checks whether grandad has jammed the broom handle tightly enough against latch and doorframe to guard against burglars.

Detlev is bathed.

He hopes that the gas boiler will set his mother's hair alight once again and she'll burn like a Catholic saint in the clean house in Lokstedt — between mouthwash and Nivea cream.

But the bath passes without incident and mummy wipes everything dry and shiny again.

No one is allowed into the study again. It has already been hoovered and dusted for Sunday. The study is locked.

Mummy has wiped the floor tiles in the kitchen, waxed the floorboards and polished the tiles on his grandmother's kitchen range. She takes the cheese cake out of the oven and leaves it to cool on the crystal dish in the guest room. She pulls down the blackout blind and locks the guest room.

No one is allowed into the kitchen again either.

Detlev must put his arms under the blanket, so that he doesn't catch cold after the bath.

His grandparents' bedroom has aired enough now.

His mother closes the shutters and lets down the blackout blind. She then reads something to Detlev about the goose and the dwarf who fly over Sweden.

— Hermann Goering is married to a Swede.

Then mummy prays the half room full of angels, two to my right, above, below, in front, behind.

His mother sits down in the small adjoining room and waits for her parents.

The house is ready for Sunday.

Mummy doesn't want to upset anything again unnecessarily and hardly moves.

Is she reading? Is she dreaming? Is she thinking? Is she remembering my father? Is she afraid? Is she satisfied?

Later, when Detlev is already sleeping, she will lie down in the other bed and be close to him all night.

He doesn't need to sleep alone in the small room any more. He screamed there. He didn't lie down. He slid down the wall as he was falling asleep. When his head touched the pillow, he cried out again and sat up.

The blackbirds are singing outside.

It's still light. Detlev can see through the star shaped holes in the blackout blind.

The apes in Hagenbeck's Zoo are getting their supper.

All the houses in Hamburg are now clean and tidy for Sunday and the children are lying washed and between fresh bedclothes — their arms under the blanket — and smell of mouthwash and Nivea.

The adults sit at the edge of the cleaned rooms and rinse out the glass again immediately after drinking their juice.

An allotment hut burns and is immediately put out again by the laughing inhabitants in their light summer suits.

14

The siren.

Fire brigade. Steam whistle. Weeping granny. The moon. The bones in the town parish church.

— No. You think you're in Hamburg. This isn't the dangerous air raid in Hamburg. You are in Scheyern and they're dropping everything on Donauwörth. No, don't be afraid, you are not in Upper Bavaria, thinking you are in Hamburg. You are in Hamburg. That's the beautiful Hamburg air raid warning with granny and grandad. Odel

isn't lying beside me and stinking of piss. In the other room granny is already up and collecting things together.
— Quick. Wake up. Wake up.
— So many sirens. One after the other. How many sirens there are! One in Eidelstedt. One in the Windsbergen. One at the fish pond. One in Niendorf Wood. That's where the child molesters are. One in Bramstedt, where grandad lay in the peat bog for a cure. One in Barmbek. And many more.
— Don't go to sleep again, Detlev.
— Granny has the crochet blanket over her arm. She takes the Bible and the leather book mark. Grandad goes to take away the broom handle. He unlocks the inside door.
— You must get dressed Detlev. You're falling asleep again already.
— The sirens are stopping now. I must get dressed. Mummy carries me a little.
— How can I carry you down the stairs. You are making yourself so heavy.
— Sister Silissa also brought the black candles with her.
— We're in Hamburg. We have to go down the cellar steps. Wake up!
— Should I let him sleep?
— That's mummy's voice again.
— Don't wake him up. Dragging the kids out of their sleep every night! For years on end. And most even have to cross the street to get to the big bunker.
— That's granny's voice.
— It's only a formality. A reconnaissance plane again. Let him sleep.
— That's grandad's voice.
— But I have to wake him at the all clear anyway. I can't carry him up two flights of stairs.
— I can sleep again right away. That's the wash house with the garden chairs. There are the camp beds on top of the wash house boiler, the valerian bottle and it stinks of

cat shit. The walls are six feet thick. The door has two steel levers. In front of the wash house window is the wooden board. It can be taken down during the day. When granny is boiling washing too. In Scheyern I imagined it all to be much bigger. Grandad has laid a piece of carpet over the drain. The axe is lying at the back. If we were buried! The air raid warning in Hamburg is much cosier. That's grandad's singing voice:

— Where the North Sea waves break upon the shore.

— Father, don't sing, other people are dying!

— That's granny's voice. The waves of the town moat beat against the town parish church. Uncle Bruno from Breslau stands beside the wet hydrangeas.

— Nothing's happening. Soon all be over.

— That's mummy's voice.

— If god wills, in quarter of an hour we'll be lying in bed again.

— That's granny's voice. Granny hasn't looked up from her book. I can hear that.

— The humming is getting a bit louder.

— That's grandad's voice.

— They're flying in from the north east.

— The River Paar is covered in little waves. White foam comes across the meadows. Iphigenia's white clothes become wet because of it. Now the anti-aircraft guns begin to fire.

— Hamm. Horn.

— That's grandad's voice.

— The anti-aircraft guns aren't firing heavily yet.
Granny lays the book aside.

— The aeroplane noise isn't stopping at all.

— It's passing over.

— The anti-aircraft guns are shooting loud enough now.

— Wedel or Iserbrook.

— There are anti-aircraft guns everywhere banging away.
Hamburg is much bigger than I thought.

— Now they're above us.

— But now the anti-aircraft guns at the cycle track are
starting up.
— This is no cosy air raid warning like before with guessing
games and stories about Glogau.
— Sister Silissa meets Iphigenia and Mother Cecilia in the
Paar meadows and grandad sings: Star of the Sea I greet
thee.
— They're dropping something. But it's far away. There's
no cause for alarm. Our flak is strongest.
— I wouldn't mind if it was a little less strong. The anti-
aircraft guns shake me up more than the bomb explosions.
— The flak shows the bombers the way.
Granny shakes the valerian bottle.
— Detlev, wake up, sit up straight and drink some valerian.
— Pause. Grandad comes in again and brings cold air
with him and it smells of washing powder.
— The Schwarz's henhouse is burning.
— And hens burn so easily because of their feathers.
— More and more are flying in. First they assembled to
the north east and then they suddenly changed their flight
path and headed for Hamburg.
— That's mummy's voice.
— Detlev, have another drink.
— First it hums very quietly and then it falls down louder
and louder and we're dead right away, and when it bursts
it can't be endured. It was further away. The air raid
cellar rocks each time. The air raid cellar begins to hop
up and down.
— How will Aunty Wilhelmine be taking it?
— That was granny's voice.
— Hamburg must already be smashed to pieces now.
— It's been going on for hours.
— Now the electricity's gone.
— Sister Silissa lights the black candle. But granny's hands
are trembling so much that grandad has to help her.

— We should sit on the floor.

— That's mummy's voice.

— Ach, you're always wanting to sit on the floor.

— That's grandad's voice.

— Now there's such a bang, that grandad immediately slips from his chair after all.

— Hamburg grows larger and larger. The city centre. The harbour. Always one more district that can be bombed.

— Granny begins to talk to the dear lord in person.

— Now it's falling down on top of us and then it hits us and the walls break apart and grandad is hurled against the wall and his lungs are hanging out of his mouth and my intestines are hanging in the drain and for a long time it's pretty sore until the lord takes us to him in his kingdom and the glory for ever amen.

— This bomb slides off. What does mummy do at the last moment, when she can't get any more air? She clings to her father and to her mother. And what do granny and grandad do? In the last moments I cling to my mother. What happens then? It's all so loud. Now grandad is singing again: Star of the sea I greet thee, oho Mariaha aid us. The town wall consists of the water of the Paar and of the Elbe. The whole town consists of water. The town parish church looks like a fountain. The towers consist of drops. The roof tiles consist of a thin layer of water. The whole town is whitish, blueish. Sister Silissa and Iphigenia swim in through the doors. The glass windows consist of thin pieces of water. The stairs are small waves. It's cool and the water makes little noise.

— The cheese cake has rolled through the living room. The storm throws down the roof tiles.

— That's mummy's voice.

— But it doesn't stop. It starts up again worse than ever. Now! Now! Now! Now! He's heard the "Lord's Prayer" so often now and I'm not allowed the "Ave Maria" here, because it's Catholic. At evening, when I go to sleep, fourteen angels stand by me. Two to my right, two to my left, two at my head, two at my feet. That's only eight. Now it's finished. Two at my head. If I open my eyes very carefully, perhaps one will be standing there. Not at all. The wash house is not yet broken to pieces. Granny's face is very wet.

15

Yoruba.
Ewe.
Hausa.
Bergdama.
Mande-Vai.
Bumum.
Habbe-Ashanti.
Bakuba.
Bushongo.
Mangbetu.
Dan.
Gan.
Tibor.
Fulani.
Nyakyusa.
Tahusi.
Nuba.
Korongo.
Mesakin.
Deep black. Brown.
Dendé.
Azeite de Dendé.
Malaguetta pepper.
Fire.
A whiter shade of palc.

Michelle.
Mona Lisa.
It's a man's man's man's world.
Kansas City.
Beer.
Cola.
Fanta.
Apple juice.
Whisky.
Bars, one, two, three, four.
Alcoves.
Tables.
Chairs.
Glasses.
Shards.
Blood.
Luminous paint.
Pop.
Coral face.
Naked (women).
Naked women pictures.
Loose trousers.
Women's loose trousers.
Prostitutes' short skirts.
PVC materials.
Patent leather.
Antique leather.
Chains on shoes.
Painted-on eyelashes.
Painted-on freckles.
Revolver.
Knife.
Leather arm band.
Blackjack.
Silver chain with name.

Kiff.
Hash.
Prelu.
Opi.
Hero.
Grass.
Stuff.
Blue light.
Amber light.
Siren.
Bluelight.
Dance floor.
Disc jockey.
Microphone.
Moved.
Toilets.
Mustafa.
Colaface.
Philipp.
Jeff isn't there.
The "Sahara" without temporal extension.
Sahara litany of immobility.
Are the smallest particles of movements movements or fixed?
Adjectives already assume the movement in thought from the object to its characteristic.
What are the smallest particles of time?
Is there something in time that is even more timely? Own, inherit, receive, get... given, do objects have qualities timelessly?
Or do objects without time cease to exist?
Non-presence is also a flow of thoughts.
So it doesn't work: Separating out "Sahara" as a timeless word surface.
The line "Whiter shade of pale" should nevertheless not

mean the singing of the song, but Jäcki's awareness of the
song on leaving the "Sahara".

A "Sahara" period:

The reproduction of short stories as a single sentence on
the pattern:

"During" — comma — relative pronoun — comma —
"and" — substantive "however" — dash — open brackets
— interjection — close brackets — "goes" — "apart from
that" — pronoun — climax — decline — grammatical
completion — "to the post office":

While Jäcki

is Jeff

Jeff

— Jeff

and Colaface

as Mustafa

despite Philipp's

goes, doesn't

feel

says slowly:— Je ne mens pas tellement

said: — I don't tell lies like that either, says Jäcki

by HSV Hamburg — Jäcki doesn't know anything about
football

— Are you looking for piss pots for the king's horses?

comes from the negotiations

passing through

and the glances of the others

Jeff

Theo

A gang of very pale skinned Manhattan boys bangs his
head against the kerb stone.

Philipp

Leo Africanus

Marlon Brando

as if eyeballs were being thrown after him

An the auld grandada, auld grandada, auld grandada, he
gets a pot full a, full a coo shite frae the meenister's coo
a ponta do janeiro
Obatala the sky
King Njoja, a Bamum from Cameroon
to the thoroughly normal old-fashioned Hans, who after
five years with an old crate has decided on a new Volkswagen
after all. Hans thinks Jeff's pronouncement is fantastic
from Dahomey
— My Hamburg woman has my seven-year-old boy
Philipp
dances
stands
notices
runs
marries
invents
murders
hired elsewhere
blinded
travels
now
Bild newspaper
an ideogrammatic script
Odudua, the earth
two hours behind him
that the retailers earn more from books than from any
other goods, back to the kerb stones of Manhattan and his
mammy with syph, because in the end Irma's relative
didn't want to have anything to do with a nigger.
Agunju and Iemanjá marry. They have a son. Orungan
wants to rape his mother. She falls and dies. Two rivers
flow from her breasts,
but at the moment two football mad grandads are paying
for his room, apart from that he plans — married to a

lesbian — to get into the big Palais d'Amour business,
since he's legally compelled to pay maintenance for his son
in Eilbek
— The court said: Unfit to plead. I'm not saying anything
about my dead son
for three hours and then begins to dance alone
— Jeff and Theo are everywhere
Hans would rather live in a giant imitation chocolate box
in Vienna.
— An imbecilic pharaoh, who has inherited a giant empire,
which ultimately he doesn't know what to do with.
out of her body step the gods Dada, Xango, Ogun, Olokun,
Aja, Orixa Ago, Oxossi, Oké, Ajé — Xaluga, Xapana,
Orun, Ago.
pra fazer um tabaqueiro
An auld teacher Dutch, teacher Dutch, teacher Dutch,
maks frae the udder a bacco pouch, a bacco pouch
O Bumba meu Boi, Bumba meu Boi
— Jäcki thinks anyway, that the whites are albinos!
— Jeff would be dedicated to the crocodile, would fall into
the sea, would embrace the female crocodile, both whirl
round in the foam — the white belly of the female crocodile
— Jeff's black front — his giant cock, which would thrust
between the armoured scales — black arse and the pink
soles of his feet
in Timbuktu
twisting: Divide in four. My head is displayed in the
pelourinho.
pony jerking: "Leather collar."
ska-ing: "gurgling."
broboning: "Little angel."
st bernharding: The mask is tied round me because I ate
sugar cane on the sly and swallowed earth.
alley catting: Now I'm sold as food for the journey by the
Hamitic pilgrim.

ca-sa-chocking: Now they cut out my eyeballs.

bostellaning: Now I'm seven and I'm shot down. But I remain alive and don't move, although the mercenary cuts off my hand. Otherwise he'll kill me.

sirtaking: My execution is delayed, until there's more favourable light for filming.

memphissing: I run at the planks with my head during the passage, which lasts three weeks, in order to die.

rocking: I bite off my tongue and swallow it down, in order to suffocate.

boogalooing: I swallow earth. It's an idea pregnant women have.

Philipp says

Colaface says:— Look

Mustafa says: Look at my

Jeff isn't there. — Look at my hands. Look at my

No Jeff. — Look at my hands and my tongue. Look at my

Not Jeff

— Look

— my

— hands

— tongue

— eye balls

and thrust slowly into the soft parts of his rear.

Jäcki leaves the "Sahara" in the direction of the "Grünspan".

Perhaps Jeff is there.

16

Now everything is different.

The sky is black.

The sun is red.

The bathroom window lies in the rhododendron.

Zebras run down Karlstrasse.

Poisonous spiders from Hagenbeck hang in the allotment gardens.
Elephants and buffalo in the Kaiser Friedrichstrasse.
— My mahogany furniture! exclaims Mrs Malchow.
— Poor woman, says granny.
Mrs Wichmann has to be dug out. She loses an ear and part of her leg.

Cherry soup.
The Selge's flower beds are a yellow crater.
Black silvery strips of foil flutter from the roof tiles, gooseberry bushes, quince branches; the cinder firmed paths are covered in black silvery strips of foil.
Unexploded bomb in the rabbit hutch?

Grandad takes the party membership book, the handcart and four suitcases. He doesn't look back at the light grey house against the black sky — as it says in "The Bell" by Schiller.
Grandad, granny, mummy, Detlev evacuate.
They leave behind granny's dowry, mummy's desk, the Leghorns, Jesus on Golgotha and the little bottles full of snot.

— We'll be back again at Christmas.
— Christmas.
— Christmuss.
The words feel too thick in his mouth.
Now the word "Christmas" is broken too.
A Christmas tree is something that's dropped and flares up, in order to light up bomb targets.
— It'll all be over
It'll all pass by.
After every December

There follows a May.
— Will a December follow this May?

— The home for cripples was here.
— A mine fell on it.
— Cripples and then to be killed by a parachute mine as well.

Over the Christmuss in his mouth lies the taste, which the air around the decaying cripple limbs leaves behind.
The combination of this taste and the syllables of the festival and the smell of the cripples' limbs means that for Detlev it's finished, that there will never be anything again.

Pink for hours on end. Rothenburgsort. Hamm. Horn.
No buildings standing any more. No children's play parks.
No house was solid enough.
The camouflage which frightened Detlev on the return to Hamburg has broken up into surfaces, which nudge against the horizon, of chalky, bloody pink.

The woman weeps again.

The soldiers still sing:
— Didadadada
Dadididada
Dadadadadadidada!

The panes of glass have already fallen out of the train.
Soon there will be no trains any more.
During the overnight journey the second terror attack on Hamburg.
It doesn't make any difference.
It looks like the oven from inside.

In Mölln by morning.

That upsets granny.

— Mölln!

— We've gone in a circle! After twelve hours only in Mölln!

Where is Mölln?

That Mölln still exists!

Now the cattle truck is already waiting for them.

Wounded.

Burns too.

Some can't move any more.

It's getting difficult to go to the toilet. The wounded are already shitting in torment, beside those who are eating food out of a tin. Finally the journey continues in the cattle truck.

On changing trains they're put in a first class compartment. Because everything is finished now, they're allowed to travel first class for a bit.

Granny with untidy hair.

Grandad doesn't know what to do with his hands, because here he doesn't dare cut his nails with the pocket knife. Mummy dirty with soot and a diplomat in a perfect grey suit says to her:

— You're exaggerating!

Finally mummy realises in the upholstered compartment that things here have not yet got so far, that here one still cannot say everything again for the last time, that here the war is still being won and that one can be denounced for spreading subversive enemy propaganda and that her distress appears vulgar in the superior atmosphere of the first class compartment.

Mummy's fear is greater than her shock and, after she has lowered her voice, she tells another small joke to make light of what she's said.

17

Jäcki thinks:

— What is the opposite of an anniversary? In 1968 the twentieth anniversary of the currency reform can be celebrated.

— To celebrate an anniversary!

— In 1968 is celebrated for the twenty-fifth time

— is celebrated the twenty-fifth anniversary of the

— terror attack

— that is a National Socialist expression you are using

— of the bombing raid on

— of the catastrophe of July 1943.

Jäcki takes Jürgen from the "Palette" as his model.

Jürgen, the premature demonstrator, wanking someone off at the Bismarck monument, who as a constant

— remembrance is what it's called!

of the camps carried around photographs of dissected embryos from an academic festschrift.

Jäcki wants to read everything about the terror attack.

— Who wants to reproach me for that word? The word has been rattled into my brain by some thousand tons of explosive. To me it no longer means an abbreviation for the propaganda of Dr Joseph Goebbels. To me: Zebras in Julius Vosselerstrasse. The smell of corpses at the cripples' home. The loss of the concept permanence. Dictionary of the inhuman. What is inhuman?

— Now is the style the homme or not?

Jäcki's studies always begin in the State Library.

— The Wilhelm Grammar School did its teaching here.

— For us today with a variety of beards the familiar technocratic old-fashioned backdrop — once upon a time a concentration institute for fourteen-year-old grammar school pupils.

Air raids. Subject catalogue.

The requests are done electronically now. It doesn't work for that. The little that's there.

— "Death in Air Raids"
is not sent over:
The man who's sitting at the keys sends Jäcki to the Medical School in Eppendorf.
There the cosy little death pavilions are increasingly being overshadowed by new Hamburg-uniform-Mies-van-der-Rohe-constructions.
The medical library has been moved because of rebuilding. Three lifts.
Intensive care.
— You still have to go one higher.
Jäcki has to fill out three forms again and then at last he presses it to himself, the slim little volume, published 1948. Thick quince yellow pre-currency reform pages:
Findings of pathological anatomical examinations relating to the attacks on Hamburg from 1943 to 1945. With thirty photographs and eleven tables.
Jäcki sits down in the park. Cool wind around lilac trees. In the background the cottage, tea room, piss house, around which Alster queens swarm at night. And leafs through the borrowed book.
b. The autopsy of the shrivelled corpse. Available for examination consequently were heat shrivelled corpses with the attendant effects of more or less advanced decomposition. There was no question of a section with knife and scissors in the case of these shrivelled corpses. First of all the clothes had to be removed which, given the exceptional stiffness of the bodies, was as a rule only to be accomplished by cutting or tearing and caused damage to individual parts of the body. Depending on the dryness of the joints, heads or extremities could frequently be broken off without difficulty, if they had remained attached to the body at all in the course of recovery and transport. Insofar as body cavities were not already exposed through destruction of the tegumen the bone scissors or saw were required, in order to cut the hardened

skin. Solidification and shrinkage of the inner organs prevented cutting with the knife; frequently the individual organs, especially the chest organs could be broken out as a whole with windpipe, aorta and carotid artery, with diaphragm, liver or kidneys adhering. Organs, which were in advanced state of autolysis or had been completely hardened by the effects of heat were usually difficult to cut with the knife; decomposing, cheesy, clay-like, buttery or charred-crumbly masses of tissue or organ residues were broken, torn, crumbled or plucked apart.

— Magister Graeff — the Dante of the Alster.

Jäcki phones Livio Olivieri, who is paid by his government to represent La Cultura Italiana at receptions, premieres, May Day celebrations of the foreign guest workers.

— In *Kaputt* there's a passage about phosphorus corpses etc.

— But Livio is sorry. The honest Italy-intoxicated people of Hamburg pinch the bestsellers, erotic literature of the seicento and Giuseppe Ungaretti's Collected from the shelves of the cultural institute.

Perhaps the Hamburg History Museum has something to offer.

Now it's spring. And if the smell of seeds over the Heiligengeist Field doesn't impress Jäcki much at the moment, he does see that the eternal Hamburg boys are at last showing their knees.

The reading room, very clean, nothing but straight lines — a slightly expressionist cosiness.

Old fashioned Hans would feel at ease here and learnedly rest his hand on the back of a tall chair.

— Do you know, that Gauleiter Kaufmann is still living in Wellingsbüttel?

Otherwise there's not much.

A few pages from the Municipal Statistical Office.

900,000 people evacuated in forty-eight hours.

The Hamburg air war victims July 1943 male 11,686 female 18,246 total 29,932.

A little in *Hamburg and its Buildings*.

— It must be left to a later age to describe and interpret these dreadful events.

Caidin of the Intelligence Office: *The Night Hamburg Died*.

Detlev Möller: *The Last Chapter*.

— 1,200 parachute mines, 25,000 high explosive bombs, 3 million stick incendiary bombs, 80,000 phosphorus incendiary bombs.

— Children torn away by the forces of nature

— Forces of nature

— from their parents' hands, could be seen whirling in the fire like branches and foliage.

— Such disturbances are understandably evident among the older and more mature part of the population of Hamburg. The greater part of the young people of Hamburg hardly became aware of the extent and the horror of these events.

— Karl Detlev Möller kept secret that he had held forth with anti-semitic tirades in the Nazi period and later got into a lot of trouble because of it.

— It doesn't surprise me very much with a style like that.

— Are you of Stendhal's opinion "Le style c'est l'homme"?

— Was that Stendhal's opinion?

— Now you're making me unsure as well.

In the modern landscape gardens of the former city ramparts a couple of thin titted Twiggies are marshalling kindergarten children.

— Join hands!

— Stand in a row!

— Do stand up straight!

— Wipe your nose!

— Come over here!

— Off you go now!

— Why are your hands so dirty?

— Your strap isn't straight!

— Now you're going to get smacked!

The efforts of the International Garden Show have caused relatively little havoc in the Wilhelmine botanical gardens. Jäcki enjoys an East Asia experience à la Lao: a brown bird with a red bill broods on a rotten piece of wood in the water; beside it a small turtle suns itself.

Jäcki sits down on the bench opposite and watches middle aged ladies in mink collars watching the idyll.

The Night Hamburg Died is called in the Italian edition from Mondadori *Operazione Gomorra*.

Arthur Harris, which art in heaven,

reducing the gay city to ashes with phosphorus stick incendiary bombs, come with me, Artie, we shall seek us out two Gomorrheans in New Sodom and I know a cheap hotel, where sits a seventy-year-old Rumpelstiltskin who tells how the queens scuttled out of the couple of mixi-mixi bars, which actually existed even under Hitler, into the villages in the woods, in order to wank off in mortal terror, Arthur Harris, for thine is the kingdom, and at the Hanover Station lover embraced lover in uniform

— What is the common soldier's dream?

He dreams of his Monika, Erika, Angelika!

and cried:

— You won't come back to me! I know you won't come back to me! Come on, we'll go for a piss, then you can see the seventy-year-old crying for his fallen man.

Would you like a beer, Father Harris? In the "Laubfrosch" a whisperer tells you about home leave one week before the destruction and about the gay bar, Brandstwiete, where they were more or less sitting on their suitcases, because they were afraid of getting one on the nut from you, Sir, at any moment.

— What to do, nobody felt like it any more, said the whisperer. Or come, we'll go to another cheap hotel. A

vigorous sixty-year-old is sitting there, who maintains:
There was a lot happening. During air raid warnings the
cottage at Kirchenallee was so packed that you could hardly
move. And all the things that were going on in the bunkers!
The small "Theatre Bar" was busier than our bars today.
We called the landlady the "gold pheasant", because she
had the party badge in gold. That's why nothing could
happen to her.
Come with me to Eppendorf! Along a branch of the Alster.
Chopin bubbles over the just flowering meadows. It wasn't
worth bombing here, was it?
— The tendency was to hit the work places and living
quarters of the broad stratum of workers. But it's not true
that the exclusive districts of the city were spared with the
subsequent occupation in mind and because of family ties
of the moneyed class.
Because of the disposition of the buildings along the Elbe
Chaussee and in Winterhude hardly anything was likely
to be hit anyway and if it was, then there were two dead
at most. Take a look at this collection of early Chinese
sculpture.
— Do you take milk in coffee? I've cut a couple of slices
of sponge cake
Gomorrha.
— Fear.
A single nudge could mean death. Denunciation was enough.
You didn't go to prison. You disappeared into a concentration camp, so that a court case could be avoided.
Sir Arthur, we open the hood of our car. Yes, May is cool
this year. Nevertheless the white rhododendron has already
flowered. But our sodomites' parks are empty at night. No
one is celebrating this 17th May. You understand the
subtlety: 17.5.* Since the paragraph has been rescinded,

*A reference to para 175 of the German legal code which criminalised
homosexual acts. (trans).

the Hamburg police has tripled its patrols. There's no pissoir anymore, not a single bush that isn't guarded. Hamburg's blooming parks. The green lungs of the city.

In 1934 the governor of Fuhlsbüttel prison was replaced. Instead of an SS officer, a man from the Hamburg police was appointed to the post. A heavenly time began for the political prisoners. Things went so far, that one roll-call he shouted at a sodomite who had placed himself among the politicals:

— Will you bloody queer get away from my decent politicals.

God bless the Queen, Sir Arthur!

Caidin has read Kurt Detlev Möller:

— Children are torn shrieking from their parents' hands by the wind, and flung head over heels, whirling crazily, into the inferno.

Yet another Dante. The one from the Hudson.

— A large number of the phosphorus victims were near the banks of the Alster.

— The moment they came up, however, the phosphorus received its oxygen and again burst into flames. And so began the unbelievable terror of choice — death by drowning or by burning.

Alster Regatta, the only little bit of elegance that this fog city pulls out. Death-in-Venice sons of late liberals.

Twenty-somethings in yellow oilskins, very superficially on the surface of the water, of the not very deep Alster, just grown into proper proportions, their lower parts not very well looked after, before the arse spreads out on Daddy & Co's armchair.

Crossing there, where the singed heads popped up during the firestorm.

Old fashioned Hans has a friend, who is even more old-fashioned than himself. Hans has nevertheless managed to push his way up to two thousand a month in the giant technocratic advertising agency with the very relaxed atmosphere, helping to make his view of the world, the love of choral society under lime trees, and of moustache-trainer adverts, become the view of the advertising world and so can afford journeys to old-fashioned countries in the very latest Volkswagen.

Not Peter.

Peter is the guru of the findesièclers, withdraws from the free market economy to meditate on Uhlans and daguerrotypes. Occasionally news flickers through the cream of gallery opening visitors, that guru Peter has given up his back court in Tädenstwiete and rented a shop for the production of tin soldiers.

Jäcki has taken back the slim poetry volume about the shrivelled burnt corpses from the cellar to the Eppendorf University Hospital and is strolling, with a bad conscience, because one's not supposed to do it any more, past the fish pond, where Aunty Hilde and Uncle Emil were bombed out, and wants to drop in on Peter, Eppendorfer Way.

It's very crowded there. Nothing but commercial artists with twirled beards and second hand raincoats and Peter walks palely between the dismantled fixtures of a barber's shop, alienating alienations.

The spoken words grow softer and softer.

Finally only a few typical daguerrotype movements are left. Occasionally a careful exclamatory gesture.

Once all the Archduke Rudolfs have left for the television studios, a fresh Hitler Youth imitator tells stories from the Führer's bunker.

— Goebbels said: In twenty years they'll make a Cinemascope film about the last days of the Reich Chancellery. You don't want to cut a poor figure in that do you.

Gelatinised mimicry about the collector's value of Goebbels' quotes. The Hamburg city hall was begun in 1886 and completed in 1887.

In front of it a policeman wearing a white cap looks somewhat anxiously at Jäcki's beard.

In the reading room of the State Archive lots of slips have to be filled out.

Jäcki hangs his antique leather coat on the hook.

Dr Ernst invites him into his office. Jäcki has a funny feeling leaving behind his Selbach coat in the State Archive.

Dr Ernst wants to excuse Graeff's style.

— Graeff after all only had the possibility of using a civil servant's German or a pathologist's German. Today Graeff together with other professors at Hamburg University is devoting himself to questions of futurology.

No, Dr Ernst has not heard of phosphorus burn victims in the Alster being shot from rowing boats.

Dr Ernst leads Jäcki back to Irving:

— And Germany's Cities Did not Die.

— Hamburg died.

In the Hamburg History Museum Caidin Irving maintains:

— The headquarters of Bomber Command is situated in High Wycombe, the little town thirty miles west of London. At nine o'clock exactly Sir Arthur Harris enters the big map room, which is sixty feet below ground.

His subordinates jump to attention.

The book is tastefully bound in wine-red cloth.

Large format. Swiss quality. A modern cover design: Rhythmically arranged wing bombs embossed in gold.

— And something else, says the young lieutenant-general.

— Life goes on. In Berlin always with humour.

Jäcki snaps the wine-red book shut. Jäcki takes his coat. It's already after four. The other readers have already left punctually and without being asked.

Jäcki invites Helmut to come to Michelsen's. To eat salmon. Today the deputy chief editor of *konkret* is not sitting there. Can he no longer afford the lobster now he's gone to *Stern*? Also missing is the distinguished stockbroker, who twitched his eyebrows if he wanted the waiter to shred his steak.

When it's time to pay, Jäcki notices that someone had stolen his hundred marks in Hamburg City Hall and Helmut has to jump into the breach.

The Berlin Gate Station has also been faced with bright slaughter house tiles recently. Beside it the tall police headquarters building with television aerials, and transoms in front of the windows that are intended to be artistic, but suggest to Jäcki machine guns, which could be rested on them.

Two fire engines are standing in the courtyard of the central fire station. Fifteen comical firemen are lined up in front.

— That's the practice tower at the back. There's one in every fire station. Empty window cavities. The hoses are hung up to dry on the air raid backdrop.

Mr Boje shows Jäcki the film of the terror attacks on the picture archive's cutting table.

Credits:

Silhouette of Hamburg very à la gateway to the world. Gas flames in front. Flares. Black and white. Christmas tree flares.

A family in front of a white burning house. The family runs into the flames again at silent film speed. Out. In again. Out again.

Neo-gothic towers burn.

Rescue work.

A motionless body is brought out of chalk rubble so carefully. The knees can still be bent. The rescued man raises his arm.

Colour film.

Blackblue bloated bodies. A reddish body, not bloated.

Piece of something is blown against the body.

A man with bandaged head — the nose is of plaster too — stands in the street.

Ohlsdorf.

The cemetery lawns with the rustic crossed beams on the mass graves.

Long travelling shot. Shot later. Veddel. Hamm. Rothenburgsort. Individual graves at the edge with geraniums.

Gerhard Marcks' painting *Charon's Skiff*.

Reconstruction.

The film is wound back.

Jäcki is welcome to look at it again.

The principle of Ilse Aichinger's *Mirror Story* about the mirror of the cutting table applied to air raids and cellar fire shrivelled corpses.

The lumps of wall fly from the ground up to the ruins. A man walks backwards through the rubble. The boys from the Hitler Youth march backwards by the Moor Meadow. The bombed out climb from trucks and go backwards to their burning cellars.

The motionless man is carefully bedded back in chalk and rubble.

The wing bombs are pushed back up to the aircraft. The clouds suck up the flares and the Christmas trees.

— Anyone who hasn't experienced such events finds it hard to understand that any sense of time gets lost in such situations. In the middle of a world which changes completely within seconds or minutes, there is perhaps no "in time" any more.

The Temps Perdu of Chief Fire Officer H. Brunswig (B.Sc.).

— Operational Experiences in the Fire Service.

Marcel Proust in fireman's uniform, now retired. Alban Berg records. The Chief Fire Officer has problems with the ministry in Bonn, which is exploiting his operational experiences and the pictures — the dead customs man lies

on his back on a bench. His hair hangs down. Trickles of
blood run over the forehead and into the hair — and
doesn't pay him any royalty.

— For example in some places it had become usual for
better off circles to leave the city in the evenings.

— Tout-Hambourg. The Faubourg Nienstedten.

— The trains used for that were called plutocrats' trains
by the rest of the population.

— Military theorists had already discussed such air attacks
before the war.

— Harris was only an executive.

— Jupp Goebbels, says Chief Fire Officer Brunswig.

— It's difficult to drop bombs on targets, because of the
different layers of air. Despite that they did drop them
with fantastic precision, says the fire officer.

— The whole gang sat together in Berlin and now they sit
round the same table in Bonn.

— By the third attack there were hardly any people left in
Hamburg to protect anything from the flames. So then the
houses just quietly burned out.

Proust speaks St Pauli slang.

— Irving was only earning some money with his stuff too.

— Graeff wanted to win a couple of potted plants at the
edge of the catastrophe. There are people like that at every
catastrophe. It was just the same with the big flood in 1962.

— They all copied from one another. It's probably true
that people were blown over by the wind. But the drama-
tisation: the poor little children, flying through the air...
It's all nonsense.

— But thousands upon thousands of unfortunates, covered
in burning phosphorus, had thrown themselves into the
canals, in the hope of extinguishing the fire that was con-
suming them... And the heads, as if under the executioner's
axe, blueblack with fear and pain, moved their eyes, opened
their mouths, spoke.

— *The Skin*, Malaparte — all lies, says Brunswig.

— No phosphorus was rained down at all. The phosphorus content was always only for ignition. The inflammatory material consisted of rubber and petrol. A few cases, perhaps, in which someone was directly hit by the stuff or put his hand on it. It's technically not possible to rain down phosphorus. The dust was even worse than the fire. Dust from the explosions, mortar dust, plaster dust. People were blinded and often ran in exactly the wrong direction.

— So it wasn't in *Kaputt* at all.

Jäcki phones the Istituto Italiano once again:—Have you got *The Skin* by Curzio Malaparte in your library?

— No, the book has unfortunately been stolen.

— *Kaputt* has been stolen. Please go and take a look. Perhaps *The Skin* is still there after all.

— I will go and look. But I don't hold out much hope.

La Pelle really is still there. Jäcki reads it once again after nineteen years, the book by the mirror wanker and fascist, gay hater and braggart, over which Herbert Mhe ecstatically and Axel ecstatically and radio customers of Greta Stolterfoht turned up their nose.

Diedi together with his uncle is the lord of the double sight open run for Kodiak bears, of children's play park, motorway, picnic meadow, fairy tale train, of rabbit and guinea pig village.

— Let's go to Hagenbeck.

— You followed Jean Gilbert's ringing invitation.

— We used to be friends once.

— Yes, I know the "Palette" too. That was a sort of gay place on Goose Market.

So it's not true, that old Hagenbeck shot the lions with tears in his eyes.

— Jan Schild shot the animals in the root vegetable cellar.

— The tigers were hopping up and down behind the glowing bars.

The herd of zebras arrived on Diedi's patch of ground. Diedi

locked them in Hagenbeck's hen run. But the fence was broken because of the bombs and the zebras galloped out again and down Karlstrasse past Detlev's grandad's house.
— Giraffes weren't running around the streets.
Of course it's raining, when Jäcki comes out of Hagenbeck. In Lokstedt there's Recherche-du-Temps-Perdu-pleasure only with wet feet.
Detlev's world stands on its head in Jäcki's head.
The asphalt has pressed the allotment gardens into the ground.
The oak of the children's home still looks out.
Parking lot asphalt encircles the cellar stairs from behind.
An asphalt road comes out opposite Mennig's house.
It's no longer possible to make out where Schwarz's hen house once burned.
Everything whitewashed — the ugly houses with painted roofs, pride of civil servants, the mini efforts of grandad's Bismarckian élan.
Parking lots where the bomb craters were.
Mummy sold the house with the pointed roof which she inherited.
Away with the Detlev house out of the family.
— You shouldn't have to pay off Aunty Hilde and be tied to granny and grandad's inheritance, so that I'm chained to your inheritance!
There are no traces to be seen any more of the balcony beams, which were already beginning to rot in grandad's day.
In the toilet window is the new owner's bull's eye glass.
— Faustian crapping.
And in granny's kitchen hangs a new-fashioned cane fish.
The bergamot pear, the Bürgermeister pear, the plum and the damson trees have been taken out by the roots.
— What no parachute mine can achieve, the German building society saver can achieve.
— Even the miracle tree of life — the quince.

All the neighbours could make quince jelly.

Of grandad's potato peelings Bayreuth, of Detlev's pre-pubertal smooching hut, of the fateful allotment of three generations, remains only a slightly darker mark in the grass.

— They've lopped the *Grüne Richard* too.

Lawns and tasteful uniform flower bed arrangements in the place of Detlev's cracking redcurrants.

At one corner still, some mud and charred beams, these charcoal sheds which frightened Detlev so much.

On the asphalt behind the fence a rubber.

— In the age of the pill a rubber. Potency protecting itself from potential clap.

Selge's garden with the Selge smell and lots of larkspur and Aunty Frieda's voice have metamorphosed into a not quite so deep clay hole for the foundations of a brick building.

Six feet above the clay hovers the sailor, who was always so witty and confident, who wore woollen trousers, which were completely filled out by the arse and the little pipe, whom Detlev always greeted first despite the wife with the fat stomach. Of the sailor there are left only pieces of bone washed round by the waves and half the chromosome batch and photos in chrome frames.

Or perhaps everything just went up in flames. The boy and the photographs. The letters of the words melted. Books burned. The brains which fitted the letters together, burned. There are new letters, which are used to report the burning.

Figures

70,000.

Some maintain:

— 240,000.

Is there an expression for that?

Let letters burn? Lead type melt? Cast no Uhlans from it? Should writers set themselves alight?

Or invent pictograms like Emperor Njoja for the Bumum?
Latin letters and Arabic figures only convey statements of
quantity and distance — differences.
Do pictograms convey the fire itself and the ashes?
— The cellar fire shrivelled corpse.
Do pictograms convey the feelings of the drowning sailor
Paul or the burning of his son?
Colour two pages of this book black:
— This is the destruction!
Or print a black, shining, fatty mark on two pages of the
book — in the middle leave empty a tiny, five-pointed
American star — and let syllables peep out from the edge
of the blot — ev, ma, o — or Mrs Wichmann's earlobe?
What would be very bold for literature, would probably be
pretty weak as an illustration.
Not all the letters were burnt.
Not everywhere did the brain lie next to the occiput, take
up approximately one third of the space of the skull.
Memories.
Who knows what?
Who knew what?
Who knew nothing?
Who wanted to remember?
Did you know something, Professor Dr Siegfried Graeff?
— Mr Graeff is said to have passed away.
— So with you too today only maggots in the oral cavity
and grease in the skull.
Siegfried Graeff:
— Victims of that night were available to me in enormous
numbers. To the extent that I had been able to view the
damaged areas myself, I already made a selection there.
The recovery and transport of the bodies to my examination
station took place with the support of the police and with
the help of concentration camp prisoners and convicts.

Jäcki:

— Written in 1948. Did you not talk in forty-three about the fact, that concentration camp prisoners were forced to recover cellar fire shrivelled corpses?

Siegfried Graeff:

— To submit the victims of the air raids to the most comprehensive autopsy examination possible was what was demanded of the pathological anatomist.

Jäcki:

— And what was demanded of the non pathological green-grocer, to whom the apple growers in Neuengamme* say: You should take a look round the back. You can see, how living corpses march.

Siegfried Graeff:

— This mass death was for each one of us the moment at which the eagle sent by Zeus hacked Prometheus' liver to pieces, punishing the theft of fire, the fire of active life and progress. However, was not Zeus also the god of understanding and reason?

Now Siegfried Graeff takes a rest, which lasts from the first edition in 1948 to the second in 1955:

— which should guide our will? No, it was not he. The eagle's mission therefore does not mean release for us from our own responsibility. It remains however a most solemn warning to become aware of the disharmony in the workings of nature —

Jäcki:

— Nature! Nature!

— May it prove possible for these human forces to become a blessing for humanity. Mortui vivos docent.

Jäcki:

— Concentration camp prisoners only when they're dead?

*Location of a concentration camp near Hamburg (trans).

Neuengamme had 50 outer camps. In Germany there were perhaps 1,500 camps and outer camps.

Carl Heinrich Hagenbeck:

— Completely burned to the ground or destroyed by direct hits by high explosive bombs: The main building, both restaurants, the cattle compound including aviary, enclosures and inspector's house, zebra stall (paradise), deer and goat house, entrance lodge, country house opposite main entrance, farm houses (Krohn's Farm and Kröger's Farm), baboon rock, primates' basin, rhesus rock, aquarium.

Siegfried Graeff:

— He fell down, raised himself on his hands again with his body in an approximately straight position, only his feet and hands touching the ground, head bent back into the nape of the neck. In this position he became rigid and began to burn; the bright yellow flames first burst from the buttocks.

Spokesman:

— Speech is impotent to portray the measure of the horror.

Siegfried Graeff:

— On the flat roofs of the tall blocks were positioned the machine guns and searchlights of the defence units, supported by fifteen- and sixteen-year-old air force auxiliaries, exposed to the force of the shifting storm wind, without support or protection against the danger of falling off. There was nothing more to be done for them.

But now the fire slowly rose up the stairways and shafts, it barred the descent to the ground for those holding out. The young recruits too had done their duty to the utmost of their powers. Now each one of them stood up there as a lonely human being, as a child in indescribable anguish, hopelessly set apart from the future of life. Perhaps a last searching look into the distance, towards his mother, he drowned in the dazzling brightness of the night; a final aching sob, it was lost in the roar of the elements. And then...

English spokesman:

— Speech is impotent to portray the measure of the horror.

Siegfried Graeff:

— Corpse 1.

— (Fencing position)

— The skin on the head, as of the rest of the body, felt hard as glass, is completely desiccated, discoloured brown to black and can be broken off like a thin awkward, piece of wood, still somewhat elastic in places.

— Corpse 2.

— Upon a frontal incision the heart muscle can be cut like hard cheese.

Spokesman:

— Speech is impotent.

Siegfried Graeff:

— cheese-like grooved form.

— Corpse 5 to 7.

— On tapping, the skin feels like papier mâché.

— Corpses 8 and 9.

— After breaking out the right lung its pleura displays a thick layer of mould especially on the rear surface.

— Corpse 10.

— The stomach skin can still be cut very easily; underneath it is teeming with maggots.

— Corpse 13 and 14.

— Mother and daughter? lying across one another on the bed (ill.6).

— Corpse 20.

— Aorta not to be found in buttery matter.

— Corpse 22.

— The lungs feel like air cushions.

— The scrotum together with the contents can be broken off.

— Corpse 24.

— The liver feels very hard all over, can be cut like very fatty, firm cheese.

— Corpse 27.

— The skull is sawed open.

— Corpse 30.

— The skin on the legs as cardboard-like mass.

— Corpse 32.

— Boy of between twelve and fifteen years of age.

— The tongue is firmly lodged between the right side teeth, shrivelled, hard, black.

— The heart, a small, somewhat shrunken, biscuit shaped, flattened, disintegrating object.

— The spleen is no longer to be found either, only grease left.

— Corpse 34.

— Strong growth of brown hair above the ears (bad haircut?).

— Corpse 38.

— The skull especially difficult to saw.

— Corpse 40.

— In the right hand which is clenched into a fist is a pocket knife with an open blade, held vertical to the fingers, in a position as if preparing for a thrust.

— Corpse 44.

— The skin can be cut off like stiff cardboard.

— The penis remains as a small shrunken object.

— Corpse 45.

— The skin can be cut off like cardboard.

— Corpse 46.

— A few crawling maggots and cocoons are found among the pieces.

— Corpse 47.

— The skull bones can be broken apart.

Martin Caidin:

— The city was burning well as a really brilliant jewel of flame.

Irving:
— There was never so much praying in Hamburg as on this night.
Spokesman:
— Speech is impotent.
Curzio Malaparte:
— Si alzava da ogni parte uno strepito di zappe e di badili, uno sciacquio, i tonfi sordi dei remi nelle barche, e grida subito suffocate, e lamenti, e schiocchi secchi di pistola.
Siegfried Graeff:
— The smell of roasted and burnt flesh and fat was usually strongly overlaid by that sweetish unpleasant one of the rotting decomposition of animal tissue.
Jäcki:
— Animal tissue?
Carl Heinrich Hagenbeck:
— The bull reached Kaiser Friedrichstrasse through the damaged zoo enclosure and was shot here by a police sergeant.
Jäcki:
— The corpses in the air raid shelters smell of animal fat and the red buffalo bull is shot.
Siegfried Graeff:
— Individual parts.
— Bone remnants in a pail from two houses on Rossberg. (Corpse Recovery Detail IV, formerly Section 5.)
— Corpse 58.
— As a consequence of heat attrition and secondary decomposition portions, particularly of the stomach cavity, are missing. Presence of rats at the scene leads to thought of participation of the rats in the destruction.
— Case 4.
— Corpse of a small, very powerful man.
— Brain preserved in toto.
— Case 8.

— While laying down the head the whole upper skull breaks into pieces.

— Case 10.

— Cause of death suffocation by stomach contents. All bronchial tubes stuffed with dry stomach contents (cabbage). Very plentiful content of same kind in the stomach, in the oral cavity and in the windpipe.

— Case 11.

— Corpse of strongly built man of about twenty years of age in good state of nutrition.

— Case 16.

— The hair and the face are covered with dry sand, as are all facial openings. Dried blood and bloody foam around mouth and nose. Plentiful excrement around anus.

— There is only scanty information on the melting point of human fat in the printed literature.

— The crushed fat tissue of corpses was placed in wide test tubes and heated for twelve hours in boiling water. The fat was squeezed out and subjected to hot centrifugence and after being siphoned off was filtered through a dry filter. The melting point was determined according to the official "Guidelines for the Chemical Examination of Fats and Cheeses" (J. König, *The Chemistry of Human Foodstuffs and Beverages*, Springer 1937).

Carl Heinrich Hagenbeck:

— It is notable that, despite considerable partial damage, the most essential parts of both large rock layouts have remained in good condition and the prospect exists of being able to repair these unique monuments.

Siegfried Graeff:

— In deepest turmoil, under most extreme constraint, the scientist now becomes a human being again, after he has recognised that tools of therapy and prophylaxis, possibilities of warding off such a pitiless expression of technology are not given to him as a doctor.

— Mortui vivos docent.
— Tertium non datur.
— Inferno di Dante.
— Liver.
— Hard cheese.
— Becoming cheese-like.
— Tough and doughy.
— Papier mâché-like.
— Firm cheese.
— Shrivelled cheese.
— Like hard butter.
— Cellar air raid shelter.
— Reduce the blood toll.
— Zeus' eagle.
— Prometheus' liver.
— Lawn.
— Charon's Skiff.
— Fuchsias and geraniums, thinks Jäcki and turns into Grosse Freiheit.

18

— We have been evacuated to Liegnitz.
At night the goods wagons to Leipzig, Görlitz, Dresden, Königsberg are coupled together.
— They never come here, say the people of Liegnitz.
I have an inflammation of the small toe and am allowed to wear a plaster bandage like the wounded.
Mummy can't sleep at night, because the banging of the goods wagons reminds her of the bombs.
The people of Liegnitz don't believe what has happened in Hamburg. In Leipzig, in Görlitz, in Königsberg they say:
— They never come here.
I can't sleep because of the plaster bandage. I have to lie on my back all night, because otherwise it hurts.

Granny and grandad disappear.
They visit relatives and former employers and their doctors
from childhood and the Wudkes and the Naschkes.
The Wudkes and the Naschkes too say:
— They never come here.
Uncle Ludwig is on leave from the front. There's a groove
in his sword blade, so the enemies' blood can flow away. I
run my finger along the sharp edge of the sword. Mummy
grows more and more nervous because she sleeps even less
than in Hamburg because of the goods wagons.
She doesn't get on well with Aunty Helga and Aunty
Marianne.
I tremble all day.

19

On the way back to Hamburg Detlev sings:
— Homeland, your stars,
Like diamonds light my way.
A thousand stars in that great arch,
All secretly dadum to thee!

20

— Now we're living in the storage cellar.
Klaus Ostermann has burned.
Klaus Ostermann grows smaller on the crooked path.
I have to keep the shiny pencil with the rubber on it.
Klaus Ostermann grows smaller on the crooked path.
Sailor Paul has drowned.
Why do I look at every man's arse and between his legs
at the front?
Klaus Ostermann grows smaller, smaller, smaller on the
crooked path.
The lady is always greeted first.

It would all have been grey in the garden, in the early morning at five.

Sailor Paul, I'm shivering.

What's the point of shoving one another onto the bicycle or of climbing up into the trees or eating wet redcurrants in the grey light.

He puts on the Red Indian headdress to please me and builds a cave out of peat. But really he doesn't enjoy it. An empty coffin, which they cover up again the next time with the swastika flag.

Klaus Ostermann is gone.

He wanted to go into the garden with me and pick the cold morello cherries.

In front of my eye, which feels like the marbles in my little sack, and behind the eyelid now stick Klaus Ostermann and Sailor Paul.

21

Plumber Martin comes and repairs the drainpipe.

But the drainpipe is made of lead and begins to melt, if one even just holds a burning matchstick against it.

Does Detlev not want to learn how to solder? Detlev laughs at the plumber. But the next time the plumber brings a soldering iron and soft solder and hydrochloric acid and shows him how the copper lump of the soldering iron has to be held against the tin ingot. The acid evaporates from the pot, the hole of which Detlev is supposed to solder closed. The tin melts. Detlev feels happy. He would never have thought that soldering can absorb one so much.

22

Grandad takes Detlev along to Mr Martin in Tornquist-strasse.

— Have the pots in Lokstedt all been soldered?

Detlev finds this conversation boring.

— Later he can learn to be a plumber with me.

— Later.

At last Detlev is allowed out.

In this street the houses are still whole and adorned with muscular men.

Detlev strikes the wall with one hand. The paint doesn't even flake off — and if a parachute mine comes, everything will simply burst apart and Mr Martin has soldered in vain.

— Whole, whole, unbroken is the weirdest.

— You shouldn't talk so precociously.

— What does precocious mean. I've grown up early.

Fifty years ago granny was walking around here with four petticoats and a crinoline and eggs cost twenty pfennigs a dozen.

— There's still even a bookshop open here.

— Will I be arrested, if as a nine-year-old I buy a book?

— What classical literature have you got?

— The sales assistant is astonished too and she offers him *Torquato Tasso* and an ugly yellow card edition of *Iphigenia on Tauris*.

Mummy already has *Iphigenia*.

That doesn't matter.

Detlev's pocket money is sufficient.

Grandad and Mr Martin don't know what to say at all.

Granny is proud of Detlev.

But mummy is exhausted, when she comes home from the labour exchange, and has a migraine.

She does take Detlev into her bed for a moment and tells him that a workshy woman, when she was required to appear, tried to cut her arteries, in the toilet of the Raboisen Labour Exchange.

— It's not the first time someone has tried to commit

suicide in the labour exchange. A week ago a malingerer hanged himself with his tie. All the things that go on! There are young people growing their hair long and dancing English dances and calling themselves "Swing Youth" — just so they can be like Germany's enemies. One of them was grade-one mixed race too. You wouldn't ever do anything like that?!

23

Just as if nothing had happened, mummy plays games again with Detlev on Sunday evenings. He crawls under a quilt and is a sprite and frightens his mother.

Then they play "Sir Frog-in-your-shirt, what are you doing outside?"

But best of all is always "The traveller and the landlady"! It's so nice that they play it four times. The conversation with the traveller grows longer and longer and mummy says:

— Aye, look, he's runnin away!

funnier and funnier. Detlev holds his trousers with laughter, and the landlady says:

— Traveller, sir, if you hold your trousers at the front, then Uncle Doctor will have to come.

The light is out. The roller blind down.

Detlev can't fall asleep.

The lions and apes don't cry out. The animals in Hagenbeck's Zoo are dead. Detlev touches his navel.

It's not fun.

Detlev doesn't want his mother to brush his navel when she's giving him a bath. Detlev touches his dibble. It's itchy.

— I mustn't do that.

He counts the marbles in his sack once again, the eyes.

— I don't like to touch my arse hole. There's shit there. That's disgusting.

24

Karin Freier is breeding snails between bricks and shards of glass. She collects the snails by the flak shelters. She sorts the snails into different chambers according to pattern and colour.

In the morning drops of condensation glitter on the shards of glass and the silvery trails of dried snail slime.

On the Freier's gas stove Detlev and Karin heat up a healing ointment made of vinegar, yeast, herbs, carbide, powdered lead, lemon peel for the snails that have had accidents.

Sometimes, a brick falls over or a shard of glass slides down. Karin Freier keeps snails with broken shells in a special box. Detlev treats his cut knee with their own ointment. It heals. But the squashed snail shells don't grow together again with it.

Karin tries Nivea cream, until the wounded snails are dead.

25

Detlev and Ulla Stüver want to marry.

He leads her through the allotment hut and shows her the Red Indian things and the novels he's writing, the title pages of the novels he wants to write, because he hasn't got any further yet.

He opens the little windowless attic room, where grandad used to keep chickens. Tar is dripping down. The door is mouldy, bits of wood and tar board nailed across it. In the attic flower pots, rusty wire, drainpipes, peat.

— An unexploded bomb.

— No unexploded bomb.

— Perhaps after all.

Shell limestone, nails, screws, shatterproof glass, and a little tin hen.

Detlev sings the newly composed parts of *The Magic Flute* to Ulla and together they picture a wedding ceremony:

in the Temple of Isis, white robes decorated with wavy stripes; Hitler youths in black will carry the standards of the German provinces and Horst Wessel in a sailor suit will unite Detlev's and Ulla's hands to loud organ music.

Ulla wants him to kiss her.

Detlev nudges her nose. He sees her eyes move ever closer to his eyes, blur, become distinct again, jump from side to side.

One eye-coloured stripe in it, glass or jelly.

Ulla smells.

It's hot in the attic.

She spits into his mouth. It crackles and is unhygienic.

The taste of someone else's spit — makes you feel sick.

But because Detlev almost has to vomit, he says:

— Again!

— What shall we call our children?

— Erika, Gisela, Rosemarie, Helga, Annemarie.

— Horst, Klaus, Hermann, Adolf.

— Not Adolf, Lieselotte.

— Friedrich, Amadeus, Uwe, Arno, Gorch.

26

Detlev says to Arne:

— I've become engaged to your sister. I'm giving up writing. I shall become a composer, in order to keep her!

27

Margot Schumacher is in love with Detlev.

But she hasn't got a chance, because she's as ugly as a crow.

She doesn't give up. Whenever she sees Detlev alone, she comes up and gives him liquorice pastilles.

She talks him into running away from the garden and

going with her to Christus Church, where she has to take back some books to the lending library.

Under the Sign of the Hammer, *The Heritage of Björndal*, *Abel and His Harmonica*.

Mrs Schumacher reads all day, instead of bothering about her daughter's upbringing.

Margot's unwashed hair sticks up from her head and she wears boys' shoes which are much too large on her sockless feet.

But despite that he goes with her.

What if grandad still catches him?!

The chemist holds him fast?!

Mrs Bauer from the grocer's shop calls him back?!

The milkman reports him?!

Run away altogether, for ever?

Where to?

He wouldn't get through the lines of fighting men — the Gestapo waits inside Germany, perhaps even at Christus Church underground station, in order to take him to a reformatory or a camp or a re-education camp or something for problem children of mixed race.

— Anyway I'm engaged to Ulla Stüver.

No one's standing at the exit of Christus Church station, to arrest Detlev or Margot.

Around them everything's pink.

Pink hills of rubble everywhere. Some façades pink, with flames of soot.

Detlev has got used to the colour. It no longer reminds him of a mixture of blood and chalky plaster, perhaps the pink still reminds him of that, but he has got used to this memory, so that he hardly notices it any more.

These ruins are cold. This pink has grown old. The rubble flower grows on them, violet-pink blooms, high into the air. No one walks here.

No bicycle. No car. No BDM girl.

Here there's not even the hot, freshly thrown up pink from the last air raid, under which human limbs still bleed or half a body, the squashed and buried are still alive.

28

— What does "Printed in Germany" mean?

— Sleep, as long as the English aren't dropping anything yet!

— It's the language of the enemy.

— It's English. It means: Printed in Germany.

— To eat apple and potato puree once again, till one's full up! Mashed potatoes with cream. A big dollop on the plate. Apple sauce around and right in the middle of the hole yellow-gold butter with brown onions.

— Reclam. Printed in Germany 1944.

— Sometimes I dream of roast beef.

— On my menu there would first of all be cold chocolate soup with snow balls of whipped egg white and afterwards fruit fool.

— That doesn't go together.

— Greek Classics in Reclam's Universal Library: Aischines: *Speech against Ctesiphon*. Number 3174. Aeschylus: *Dramas*. Number 988. Aristophanes: *Comedies*. Number 1119. Aristotle: *The Poetics*. Number 2337. *The Constitution of Athens*. Number 3010.

— Daddy, put something on top of the gas oven. The iron rings are jumping up and rattling.

— Or a nice semolina pudding. A symmetrical semolina pudding. With melting butter.

— Raisins, currants, cinnamon sticks, real vanilla.

— Euripides: *Tragedies*. Number 1337. Homer: *The Iliad*. Number 249 to 253. *The Odyssey*. Number 280 to 283.

Plato: *The Symposion*. Or on Love. Number 927.
— You take seven eggs and half a pound of semolina and half a pound of sugar. Stir into a paste. Add juice and peel of one lemon, bitter almonds, semolina and whipped egg white.
— Published in the second jubilee series autumn 1942: Gerhart Hauptmann: *Greek Spring.* Number 7526 to 28. Werner Bergengruen: *Hornung's Homesickness.* Number 7530. Eugen Roth: *The Fishbox and Other Stories*. Number 7533.

29

Detlev is allowed to go to Raboisen Labour Exchange.
— The staff and our manageress, Mrs Lieselotte Walter, want to inspect you.
By the Alster a battalion of singing SS men march towards Detlev and his mother.
Mummy quickly turns a corner, at the ruin of the Thalia Theatre, and begins to cry as usual.
The staff at the labour exchange are nice to Detlev and there's no hanged man in the toilet and there are no traces of blood on the benches in the corridor left by the woman who cut her veins while she was waiting, and the long-haired, insolent unGerman types have been got rid of too.
— Detlev doesn't meet anyone from the Swing Youth.
— Mrs Walter, the manageress, raises her arm in greeting and Detlev clicks his heels together and stands up straight and delivers a smart German salute and after that quickly bows too.
— A pure Aryan type, says the manageress.
Detlev feels himself turning red.
Mummy looks at him relieved.

30

In the cellar mummy reads from *Hermann*,[*] softly, because granny wants to read her own novel to the end, and grandad is only interested in philosophy. At his wedding he bought Fichte's works.

— Woe to thee, my fatherland! To strike up the lyre, in thy praise, is forbidden me, thy poet, faithful to thee in thy bosom.

When Detlev hears that, he has the same feeling as looking at the Horst Wessel stamp. Everything becomes warm and he could almost cry or he feels as if he's being tickled in the ribs. He likes the feeling.

He sees Heinrich von Kleist in front of him made of blue scribbled paper. Very small. In a yellow courtyard, surrounded by wide buildings. Kleist looks upwards and says:

— Thee!

— Thee!

— Thee!

— The lyre!

— In thy bosom!

The sun cannot be seen, but Heinrich von Kleist casts a long thin shadow.

— Lay waste your fields, slaughter

Your herds, burn your villages

So am I your man —

Wolf:

— How? What?

Hermann:

— Where not — ?

Thuiscomar:

— We should lay waste our own fields — ?

[*]In English, Hermann (the hero of Kleist's play "Die Hermannsschlacht" and semi-legendary leader of the German tribes against the Romans) is usually called Arminius (trans).

Dagobert:
— Kill the herds — ?
Selgar:
— Burn our villages — ?
Hermann:
— No? No? You do not wish it?
Thuiscomar:
— Those very things, madman, are those
That in this war we wish to defend.
Hermann interrupting:
— Well now, I believed, it was to be your freedom.
— It's a National Socialist play, says mummy.
— What does that mean, says grandad.
Granny isn't listening.
— I meant, says mummy, and says nothing for a few
seconds
— that National Socialism would be detestable if it made
use of such methods — you understand, daddy, like
Hermann of the Cherusci —
— But it sounds very nice, when you read it, says Detlev.
— If that's how you meant it, says grandad.
— Hermann of the Cherusci orders his people to lay waste
their own fields, says his mother. The Germans torture the
Germans, so that they defend their freedom better.
— I was paying more attention to your voice, says Detlev.
— Tactically that may be quite correct, says grandad.
— His mother would like to say something against that,
but then she lowers her head, turns the page and reads on.
— Hermann, looks at her:
— Arouse? Whose heart? Ventidius Carbo's?
Thuschen, pray look at me! — By our Hertha!
I believe, thou imaginest, Ventidius loves thee?
— Ventidius is the enemy's ambassador, who has cut off
Thusnelda's lock. The Italians have different customs from
us. They've betrayed us now too.

— Hermann:
Nay, speak in earnest, you believe thus?
That, which a German calls love,
With reverence and longing, as I do thee?
— There Kleist has expressed the spirit of the German
wonderfully.
— Now, you see, says grandad.
It becomes so loud outside, that mummy can no longer
go on reading. Granny puts her book away too.

31

— There's been an assassination attempt on our Führer,
shouts granny. It's been announced on the radio. I almost
got a heart attack.
The people's radio.
Detlev used to believe that dwarves live, fiddle and sing
inside the black igelite box. He looked in by the side of
the dial to see them working.
Zarah Leander sings out of the box.
The Führer's friend, says grandad.
— She sings like a bear.
Zarah, the vodka queen, at whose feet the devil's general,
O.E. Hasse, sits in 1968 at the premiere in the Operetta
House.
The whole scene is there and admires the queens from all
over the world in their brightly coloured coats.
Zarah in 1943 out of the people's radio.
Now out of the people's radio the attempt on our leader's
life. Granny says it again and again, to all the neighbours.
— I almost got a heart attack.
But for Detlev something's missing.
— She could say: With fright. — Because I'm shocked. —
Because I don't know, what will become of our nation and
the movement.

Granny says:

— I almost got a heart attack!

The neighbours want to calm her:

— But nothing's happened to him.

And granny says nothing.

32

— Detlev loves Miss Leitl. He wants to make her understand him. When the class has to write an essay on the subject "Which books would I like to own?", he doesn't lie and
write: Karl May, Fritz Steuben, Felix Dahn, *Hitlerjunge
Quex*, *Mein Kampf*, *The Myth of the Twentieth Century*.
Detlev cannot imagine that Miss Leitl has set this subject
in order to draw out the class on behalf of the party and
he writes:

Nietzsche's Collected Works and Hebbel's Collected Works.
But Miss Leitl did not understand him and gives him a
five and reads the essay out to the class and Ove Müller-
Neff now calls Detlev "noodlehead".

With the next essay Detlev is more careful.

"What kind of job shall I take up?"

— I won't take up any job at all!

— I used to want to become a boxer.

— If I still had enough time: Composer.

— Should I write "cobbler" or "doctor"? Soon everything
will be finished and there won't even be cows and pigs for
shoe leather.

Detlev writes that he wants to become king.

— Since I am not of noble birth, I have no other choice but
to marry a queen. Then I will become king automatically.
Miss Leitl gives him a five again and, as Detlev expected,
reads the essay out to the class again.

Dieter Brinkmann now calls Detlev "noodlehead, the
automatic king".

Detlev has got used to cover names, behind which he
remains hidden.

33

— Grandad patches his garden together again and I'm
allowed to pull up bog pimpernel and turn the soil.
— A philosopher thinks everything from the beginning
again, as if no one before him had formed an idea.
— Grandad doesn't listen to me. It would not be hard to
transform the garden into Böcklin's Isle of the Dead or
into not quite so hanging gardens of Semiramis.
— Philosophy has dug its own grave, says grandad. He
must know, if he says so.
— I'm to learn how to turn the soil. It's silly to turn up
the garden just for the bombs.
— He mends the chicken wire for the Leghorns.
— My Heraclitus, the worm now is sadly halved.
— I think about the spade, about the soil, the thrust of
the spade and the meaning of turning the soil and about
the juice that runs out of the half, out of the worm.
— I'm to put the worm in the tin for the hens.
— The tin is rusty and daddy, Paul, grandad uses it,
When he goes for a pee behind the pile of peat.
— You, dear friend, the Leghorns eat the half worm too,
Both of whose halves keep on wriggling,
As it flows away.
— Fat hens burn better.
— That's why I quickly want to write and sing my songs.
And be a philosopher.
— With lots of digging the spade becomes shiny.
— Why does the half worm wriggle?
— The cooked worm in the cherry soup chases away
one's appetite.
— Until mine end, Heraclitus,
Not long therefore,

Shall I nevermore eat cherry soup.
— The industrous grandfather has surely repaired the
cracks behind the bed
And screwed the wood fibre tiles back under the plaster
figure in the study.
But nothing holds. It doesn't hold anything. The next
attack will soon come!
— Like a trumpet blast!
— Yet not a single soul will be lost!
— I still want to try out everything, want to be everything!
— But again you forget to put
The worm into the rusty tin.
— But it's all too late. I'll not take up any profession
any more.
— I want to experiment.
— Clear off, you hen folk.
Don't get in the way of my spade.
— I want to try out everything now: Be poet and thinker.
Farmer and hero.
— Clear off, bird!
As quickly as possible, become immeasurably many things.
Till it's finished, geniuses!
And at the last judgement the hen folk
Groan under the incendiary stick bomb.
But I perhaps
Would still be this and still that.
Until finally there's nothing at all any more.
Not god and nothing else. Not nothing.
Everything
Would I be, ye Greeks —
As much as possible.

34

— I.
Who I?

I?

You?

You?

When I write "I", do you think of yourself or of me?

Jäcki?

Detlev?

— Now were you personally in the orphanage too?

— But Jäcki and Detlev are two figures of flesh and blood?

Figures of flesh and blood. Corpses of flesh and blood.

— Don't you think too, that Jäcki and Detlev have many features in common?

I?

You and I and Detlev and Jäcki and Jäcki's I and Detlev's I and my I and your I.

I enlarge my eyes with belladonna, draw over my brows and the skin under the lashes for a tiger look. I draw bright greasy diagonal stripes across mouth and nose, as in the advertisement for "something new from Christian Dior...", place a blond wig on my head and put on the sequined trouser suit of the transvestite who's had an operation and become a lesbian, clap the feather helmet with the cardboard horns on top of it, tie on flamingo wings, hang ducks' feet and twigs of coral from my belt, drape the veil over myself and mount the poet's pearl embroidered rocking horse and wait for the hens to be slaughtered over me and the feathers to be stuck firmly to my veil with the blood and imitate Detlev, who is imitating Iphigenia on Tauris.

— And the narrator's position?

— Perhaps Detlev has two first names?

A reference to the Old Testament added to the echo of Liliencron.

— Or is the whole thing only a play with names?

Can you decide?

Do you want to be Jäcki or Detlev?

— Hahaha, laughs Cartacalo/la the drag queen.

— Jäcki is one of Detlev's imitations!

35

— In the bookcase there's an army field edition of the
Marquise of O.

Mummy is at work.

She has locked the bookcase, because Detlev is not to read
the *Marquise of O*.

The key to the shoe cupboard fits the bookcase and it begins
to smell of mother.

Makeup. A cube of beeswax. Schiller. French brandy.
Hidden behind Schiller Dr Rudolf Steiner: *The Occult
Science*. Hidden behind Dr Rudolf Steiner: Heinrich
Heine: *The Rabbi of Bacherach*.

The *Marquise of O* lies at the front of the shelf:

— in M..., an important town in northern Italy, the
widowed Marquise of O..., a lady of unblemished reputation and the mother of several well-brought-up children,
placed the following announcement in the newspapers:
that she had, without knowledge of the cause, come to
find herself in a certain condition; that she would like the
father of the child she was expecting to disclose his identity
to her, and that she was resolved, out of consideration for
her family, to marry him.

36

— Today mummy has to take Detlev to the Hitler Youth
registration.

They walk up Schulstrasse — as if going to church on
Sunday or to the provisioning office after the terror at-
tacks. Detlev tries to cheer his mother up and sings "Wild
Geese Sweep through the Night" and "The Brittle Bones
Tremble", and keeps his back especially straight and doesn't
push her arm down when he takes it.

There are no amputees and blackened burn victims in
front of the provisioning office — today mothers with

nine-year-old boys. But mummy doesn't join the others
in the queue.

First she talks to an SS man.

— Why is she talking to him. They wouldn't have noticed
anything. I'm very blond after all.

— Perhaps she thinks: If I'm honest with them, they'll
admire my courage.

Detlev and his mother have to report to a special room.
There the SS man informs them, that they have to present
themselves at Siemersplatz.

At Siemersplatz mummy speaks to a well-brought-up BDM
girl and explains everything once again.

It's embarrassing for the Aryan girl that she's unable to
permit the racially inferior son of a lady entry into the
Hitler Youth.

But the pure blood of youth is at stake and "today Germany
belongs to us and tomorrow the whole wide world."

The BDM girl sends them to the thatched house opposite
the provisioning office.

An interesting looking elderly gentleman with the party
badge in gold is sitting there. Unfortunately he can't make
an exception either and sends Detlev and his mother to
Rothenbaumchaussee. Detlev doesn't know this area.

So in other districts of the city some houses are still standing.
Here an SS man allows Detlev to join the Hitler Youth.

— I didn't want you to be the odd one out and have
everyone pointing at you, because you're not wearing
the uniform and don't have a neckerchief and a sheath
knife, says his mother.

She takes him to Heimerdinger's Furniture Store and buys
a large picture of a blue sweet pea. Detlev thinks it's
kitsch. But mummy has it framed and hangs it over
his bed.

37

— In the art class we had to paint a ship. Otto Speck copied

from a postcard. Miss Leitl noticed and he said: I've never
seen a ship. They've all burned out. Ernst Keller painted
the harbour from his imagination, but with a ruler.
— Drew, not painted.
— Peter Hinrich painted a fantasy ship. Peter Hinrich is
a dreamer with very long eyelashes. He is a friend of Ove
and Dieter and belongs to the other group. But his ship!
Slanting from the top and red. The paper became quite
thick with it. I have never seen a ship like it. Peter Hinrich
wants to paint Kriemhild and Brünnhilde in front of Xanten
Cathedral with his pencil for my collection.
— Draw.

38

— Aunty Frieda was taken away this morning! They
were all sitting in the cellar at Schwarz's and Aunty Frieda
couldn't keep her mouth shut again and said that the
Führer... Or something about the war. And the Möller
woman went to the local party office and denounced Frieda
and this morning Aunty Frieda was taken away. Just don't
say anything. We'll probably never see her again. Anyone
who gets put inside now will never get out again. Into
prison or I don't know where to. Granny says nothing.
Grandad says nothing. Mummy is calm again too.

39

His mother quickly buys the remaining Reclam opera texts
from the stationer's shop on Eppendorfer Weg.
— *The Valkyries*.
— *Twilight of the Gods*.
— *Fra Diavolo*.
— *Lucia di Lammermoor*.
— *Tiefland*.
— *Tannhäuser*.

— *Lohengrin*.
— *Rienzi*.
— *La Traviata*.
— *Hans Heiling*.
— *I Pagliacci*.
— *The Mastersingers*.
— *Così fan tutte*.

40

— When the carpet of bombs falls on Lokstedt, mummy
sings:
— Oh that can never scare a sailor;
Don't you fret, don't you fret, Rosemarie.
And should the whole world shake and quake
And Churchill in his nightshirt speak.
Granny has already clapped her book shut and is dripping
valerian into the glass.
Grandad stops trimming his finger nails with the pocket
knife, shuts it and puts it in his pocket.
Detlev doesn't want to pray.
Detlev goes on reading:
— Highly Charged.
— Army Field Edition.
— Amusement for Every Occasion.
— Honest.
Take your tankard in your left
And take your broad sword in your right
A man should drink an honest draught
And fight an honest fight.
— The last six humorous tales are taken from the *Merry
Village in the Eifel* by Peter Kramer. Published by
Voggenreiter.
Today grandad is first to sit on the floor.

— Proverbial Sayings. (Not for those who take offence at plain speaking.)

The rings on the washroom range jump up at each impact.

Granny says the Lord's Prayer again.

— *The Wit and Wisdom of the Common Soldier* by Ernst du Vinage.

— The Underpants.

I wore them seven years and a day.

More would be dangerous anyway.

What to do with the pitiful rag?

Hang it out the window for a flag.

Mummy hugs Detlev tightly and whispers in his ear:

— Oh that can never scare a sailor!

Granny says:

— Detlev aren't you going to pray at all?

— Fortune.

Fortune is a woman's name.

Every woman loves a soldier.

Every woman's heart has told her

How to play his favourite game.

— Now it's finished.

— Fodder.

He eats all the leftovers no one'll touch,

Four helpings of everything, and still he's such

A slip of a fellow, he's so thin

His bones are like poles in a tent of skin.

— If I survive, I want to become an immortal poet.

— The craftsman has the advantage, said the knacker and set to with his teeth.

The rust on the sluice gate cracks and dirty water gushes out.

— The Hedgehog.

Where wars are fought it won't avail

To set up house.

The hedgehog knows, the ant, the snail,
Even the louse.
— A poet like Tomas Westerich: At the Heart of all Wills
— Wills or Walls — Cathedral.
— Youth.
The old die off. The young must fight,
Sure of their cause, for what is right.
Nothing of note's achieved, alack,
But by the megalomaniac.
Bang.
The cellar jumps three feet into the air.
— Lads.
They're real lads, zesty as mountain goats,
The iron girder, behind which is hooked the lever of the
air raid cellar door, is torn out of the concrete wall.
— Lord, let it end at last, whispers granny.
— Eager to fight and wanting their oats.
Quick in their loins and quick on their feet,
— Heart of all Walls Cathedral.
The smell of the corpses from the cripples' home and of
warm candles and fir trees and baked apples is drawn up
Detlev's nose.
— They don't know the meaning of defeat.

41

The bombed out families live in Ley Houses, which look
like big nesting boxes and are called Ley Houses after the
Strength-Through-Joy Minister, Robert Ley. Alfred Wöbke
eats raw frogs and ravens.
— Decent boys shouldn't play with him.
— He doesn't have a father either.
— Doesn't matter.
But Detlev does play with him. They go into Hagenbeck's
Zoo through a hole in the fence.

Even the prehistoric beasts are bomb-damaged. Now one can see that the dinosaur and the flying dragon consist of concrete and wire.

Detlev borrows money from Alfred Wöbke for lemonade. He can't give it back to him. He hides, when he sees Alfred turn up.

— I'm not allowed to play with him anyway.

42

Detlev can't sleep. He counts the eyeballs in his pouch again. There aren't any more than before. He holds his breath. Perhaps the lions will roar again after all.

If he doesn't fall asleep now, his mother will ask, what's wrong.

Detlev breathes evenly in and out, as if he was sleeping. There's more and more air. Now it's bursting... Now mummy will ask!

Detlev holds his breath and listens. His mother is breathing evenly too and is only pretending to sleep.

He asks what's wrong and she pretends to wake up, and then she admits that she can't sleep, because she's afraid, that tomorrow morning, when she goes to the labour exchange in Kielerstrasse, the man who tells her about the camp will be waiting again and that she is to be transported, with Detlev like all the race defilers and grade-one mixed race children whose orders to present themselves she types in Kielerstrasse labour exchange.

43

Alfred and Friedo and Duve and Detlev run through the allotments. The enlarged nesting boxes for the bombed out families are everywhere. From plot to plot.

Chives. Chervil. Water barrels. Bean poles.

The allotment paths stretch up as far as the horizon.

Soft fruit. Carrots.

The Anglo-Americans lay down carpets of bombs district by district.

Ley Houses and bombed out families fill the allotment gardens.

The bombed out families make their allotment huts weatherproof for the winter.

Alfred and Friedo and Duve and Detlev run along straight allotment paths.

Here there's clay under the surface and the Allies' high explosive bombs can't harm the nesting boxes — the clay absorbs the force of the explosions.

Flower beds. Hawthorn. Compost. Sunflowers. Rakes.

Rabbit hutches and flag poles.

The plots have come to an end.

Detlev stands in front of the children's home.

The zinc spoon is forced between his teeth and the pus coloured pap, tasting of almonds, slides onto his tongue.

Raspberry sauce on top.

The smell of the vomit.

The kindergarten teacher comes with the mop and the rusty enamel pail.

The children's home is empty.

A pane of glass on the veranda is broken.

Duve started it.

Detlev shouts:

— Sieg heil! Sieg heil!

Duve:

— Ribbentrop!

— Wheels roll for victory!

— Final victory or Bolshevik chaos!

Burst, burst the panes.

Stamp on the frames.

— Heil Hitler!

The door falls over.

— Dark brown is the hazel nut.
Dark brown am I, yes, am I,
Dark brown shall my maiden be,
The children's home is wrecked.
They tear off the tar board and hit the jolly red and yellow
painted little benches with bits of wood.
Sods of grass fly at the wallpaper.
Detlev hits the wall so long, that it gives way.
Here the paint flakes away with all the kicking.

44

The manageress and some of the employees arrive at the
labour exchange in the mornings without a party badge
on their lapel.

45

Make it snappy, HY!
Fewer and fewer line up for the roll calls on the playing field.
Detlev is always there first.
Arne's mother has forbidden Arne to come because of the
low-flying planes. Dieter Brinkmann isn't allowed to any
more either and when Detlev takes him to task, Dieter
walks backwards and Detlev realises that Dieter is afraid
of him.
At school Detlev is the scapegoat of the whole class; but
Harald makes him a commander in the team orienteering
game and Detlev holds his own against the enemy. Harald
praises him in front of the boys, who are standing to attention. Detlev feels: In this troop he would put Dieter
Brinkmann and his troop out of action too.
But the roll-calls grow rarer and on the last occasion Detlev
is the only one standing on the playing field during the
pre-alert. Even the unit leader has already gone into the
air raid cellar.

46

Mummy brings Detlev some special issue postage stamps.
On one is printed: "And yet you have been victorious!"
SA men with the flag.
— Fluttering at our head!
They sing beneath the fluttering flag.

47

The stamps for an extra ration of dried vegetables and
salted butter are called up.
— Now it really will soon be all over. There are no fresh
vegetables any more. The fields with the damp turnips
have been bombed and they've shot the trees with the
juicy apples and pears to pieces. A few leftovers in the
Greater German Reich have been dried just in time. Now
the Führer is having them distributed. That's the end.
The SS has stirred salt into the last butter. After the dried
vegetables there will be nothing else. Dried red cabbage.
Dried cherries. Dried quinces. Only hay left. But no German
can live on hay. Dried hay. The horses and cows won't eat
hay powder.

48

It's raining.
Duve, with whom Detlev isn't really supposed to play
either, says:
— That's the foam that's left over from fucking.
Alfred says:
— My child, why have you turned so red?
Has someone crawled into your bed
And blown a tune upon your hole?
Hansen says:
— Goethe played flute on Schiller on his diddle.

Detlev thinks:
— Will then Hector turn from me always,
When with matchless hands Achilles
Dreadful sacrifice to Patroclus brings? — Was Goethe
not disgusted?!
Harald comes out of the Thatched House and says to Detlev:
— In a heated discussion I was against the Hitler Youth
boys throwing back the advancing enemy with pots full
of boiling water.
The others run behind Harald and bawl:
— There is no point,
HY must go,
The pimps must come,
It's better so.

49

— This afternoon Hamburg is to be razed to the ground.
Mrs Wiesner shouts it out over the redcurrants.
— Who made the announcement?
— Mrs Malchow said so. A thousand aircraft have been
circling outside Hamburg for days. Tell the Selges and
the Heidas!
Grandad goes to spread the news immediately.
The neighbours' fear making information.
The radio isn't authoritative any more either.
Now only the neighbours' squashed voices. Then the end
is near.

50

The end of the Thousand Year Reich:
Running back and forward between the Schumanns' radio
and the Schwarz's radio.
— Will Hamburg be flattened? Made even flatter?

— The armistice has been signed.

— The thousand enemy aircraft are withdrawing again, because Hamburg has been surrendered without a fight.

The victors Stalin, Churchill, Roosevelt play "Hail to thee with the victor's laurel"!

Mummy begins to cry.

Willi Schwarz, who is too fat and was only to be called up for the Volkssturm at the last moment because of his glandular trouble and who broke something during exercises at the horizontal bars, so that he now gets a war invalid's pension, takes mummy courteously by the arm and escorts her out.

The enemy tanks are already driving clanking along Kaiser Friedrichstrasse.

Mummy says:

— Willi was so tactful.

— Why?

— Because he didn't ask anything.

— Why is that tactful?

— Don't ask so much today, on this day.

— But why did you cry?

— Who wouldn't cry, when one's Fatherland is defeated?!

51

    1. Yes, a new age has begun.

    2. Cartacalo/la is coming, Tyrolean hat in his hand.

  1.1. (or 1. again) The new reality has begun.

    0. (or meta-1.) Different strata of Jäcki's situation. A few incomplete remarks on the numbers themselves are intended to indicate, that there are relationships in the unnatural, not formalised language, which cannot be grasped by the formal scheme:

Fluctuations, paradoxes, lies, sentimentality, melopoeia, superfluities, antinomies, preferences, arbitrariness.

0. (once again) (I could number this and the previous section 0.1 and 0.2 and so patch up the continuity. That would be more false than the contradiction: once zero something and once zero something.) (This — the preceding — parenthesis is writing about writing, almost as I'm writing it. I can write nothing about writing, while I'm writing it, unless my writing expresses nothing about the relationships of writing to object, but writes only about writing — objectless: This is not a long sentence, for example.)

3. The "Palette" has been shut.

4.1. (or 2.1.1.) Jäcki's granny is dead.

4.1.1. The town of Glogau has been buried with her.

4.2. The house in Lokstedt was sold.

4. Jäcki is looking for a new local.

1.1.1. Around Grosse Freiheit the bedside table lamps gradually go out, next to bouncers' uniforms, working clothes, Ladage and Ölke made to measure suits. In the bars and clubs things will get wilder until three o'clock in the morning. Vikings. Fringed figures, whose contours are blown through the traffic by the movement of the air.

The wigs are still rising higher and higher and the back-combed powdery glorioles of the Afro-look.

2.2. Cartacalo/la as man wanders across Grosse Freiheit. The Roxy Bar in which he danced Robert Schumann's Träumerei 44,000 times and Atomic Death and the Tango d'Amore with his Imperial Majesty is being pulverised because now a new traffic artery is to pass through there. Carla discovers Jäcki and takes off the Tyrolean hat. A lock of hair falls over his forehead. A hairpin is bent into the lock. What is it for?

5. The hunger is so great, that you go with the only one left standing at the empty railway station. Only look, if he's got nice balls in his basket.

Oh, this satisfaction!

An older hunger comes with gratification. The hunger for excitement, when that for brutality has been stilled.

After that has been satisfied, the even older hunger for tenderness, the even older hunger for passion, for higher education, for exclusiveness.

The habituation to the betrayal of what lies deeper to what is coarser.

Until finally every chance of satisfaction has been missed and when you're lying with Marlon Brando you dream of Gérard Philippe and vice versa.

3.1. The "Palette" has been shut. Igor, spewer-up of the boot glass's contents, is giving a lecture in the sociology department about the "Palette."

Heidi has her third child. Loddl gets divorced from her. He takes charge of the children. Heidi deals and makes a tv film about her life. From the fee she puts down the deposit for an electric organ for her new fiancé. Reimar Renaissanceprince has got divorced and has a minor working for him in Berlin. Hammed has got divorced; he was a waiter in the "Palette," then in the "Oblomov"; when the "Oblomov" was closed because of drugs and minors, he was a waiter in the "Grünspan", went to another psychedelic place because of higher wages and is a waiter in the "Grünspan" again.

The Flower of Sharon has committed suicide. He entered suicide. Walked around in it. Laid himself down in suicide.

He only succeeded at the second attempt. Stiff and blue.

Enoch comes back from Zambia and with hepatitis.

Schusch lives in a commune with four other couples. He's publishing an underground newspaper. But he can't stop fascism in Germany any more either.

— This time we'll be in the concentration camp!

His wife has bought a little house in the North of England, to which they both want to emigrate.

1.1.2. — I would not hesitate to fall in the storm.

1.1.3. The enemy is called Adorno, Mitscherlich, Grass, Rowohlt and Kiepenheuer and Witsch. It is necessary to abolish *Der Spiegel*. *Die Zeit*. There's nothing worse than the German Playhouse.

3.2. (3.0. is better or — since that isn't possible — 3.0.1.) The "Palette" was the non plus ultra of pluralism. There irrepressive tolerance put up with repressive intolerance.

— It will never get better than that, thinks Jäcki.

There the Hanseatic fascist wept on the paraffin bosom of the Hanseatic transvestite. Today an abyss of fundamental differences would divide booth from booth so deeply, that only with a sense of vertigo could one speak from one chair to the next, still less stroll from one to the other.

1.1.3.1. We know what's right.

6. (or 1.2.) A Nazi is chancellor who says the Nazis are not National Socialists, because he hopes that the Nazis won't say that he is a Nazi. The Socialists say nothing, because they hope that the chancellor doesn't say which of the Socialists is a Nazi. The FDP says nothing, because it hopes that the Nazis of the CDU or SPD will prefer to join up with it rather than with the Nazis of a party which only lacks the letters SA to make up NSDAP.

3.1.1. It's got very dangerous in the Wilfredo Bar. When you go to get cigarettes out of the machine, there's blood in the drawers.

1.1.4. Fear.

The new reality.

Fear of displaying the white deformed body. Fear of the wage-earning family with lots of children. Fear of being lynched as a traitor. At last fear again in Germany!

Someone who invites three New Leftists to his home insures the apartment and the collection of antiques; places the warning shot pistol ready to hand and unscrews the glass pepper pot. Could it not be that he has invited the wrong Leftists or Leftists who have spoiled overnight, gone bad?

1.2. (or 6.1.) The architect votes FDP because he wants the SDP to get in. Uli votes CDU, because Senator of the Interior Schmidt put him in prison. The son from a good home believes, now that the SPD has helped do away with paragraph 175, it's possible to vote CDU again. The queen from Marrakesh votes NPD with all her friends, just to get even with the young louts. Loddl votes SPD, because he wants the SPD to get in.

— If I vote SPD, the CDU will get in. Perhaps I should vote CDU, to strengthen the FDP. If one wants a socialist Germany, then it's only logical to vote for the Nazis.

1.3. Heine, Schwitters and Rimbaud shout boo! during a platform discussion with Goethe, Thomas Mann and Borges. Johann Sebastian Bach is politically more reliable than Wolfgang Amadeus Mozart. Sappho leads the Greek composer Theodorakis into a cell, so that he hears the cries of the tortured. Whereupon Lord Byron interrogates Sappho in his turn. Arnaut Daniel hits out at the passers-by, till the mud guard gives way.

Luís de Camões goes from prisoner to prisoner and shakes one after the other awake, if they fall asleep after seven sleepless nights. Camões constantly repeats his round. Hardly is one closing his eyes, than Camões strikes his ears with a cudgel.

Marcel Proust hasn't signed the appeal at the Frankfurt Book Fair.

0. (chronological)
1944:
Razed to the ground.
Roll.
Degenerate.

Hard.
Blitzkrieg.
Aryan.
Labour.
Exhort.
Shades.
1945:
Peace.
Freedom.
Construction.
Original cause.
Ration card.
Labour.
Exhort.
1950:
Fin de siècle.
L'art pour l'art.
Home comfort.
Axiom.
Labour.
Exhort.
1966:
Irma says:
— Fritter.
Igor:
— Fucking is the best landscape.
Maximilian l'Allumeuse:
— Horkheimer.
Heidi:
— Maciste.
Reimar Renaissanceprince:
— Jail.
Lausi:
— Game.
Schusch:

— Syph.

Lydia:

— Dortmunder.

Jürgen:

— Spring wind.

The commercial artist:

— Booby.

Loddl:

— Gays.

Do you know Basel:

— Do you know Basel?

Enoch:

— Germanic.

Hard.

Blitzkrieg.

Labour.

Exhort.

1969:

Sensitize.

Aporia.

Hard.

Roll.

Degenerate.

Razed to the ground.

Labour.

Exhort.

6.1. (or 4.2 or 0.1)

Le style c'est l'homme!

Le style ce n'est pas l'homme!

Le style ce n'est pas d'homme!

Le style ce n'est pas la femme!

The style is the paddle!

3.1.2. (3.1.0.1. is better or 0.0.1.)

Irma says:

— Informant.

Igor:
— Early capitalist.
Maximilian l'Allumeuse:
— Digitalise.
Heidi:
— Frustrate.
Reimar Renaissanceprince:
— Healthy.
Schusch:
— The eleventh hour.
Lydia:
— Scene.
Jürgen:
— Marcuse. But the right one!
The commercial artist:
— Ché.
Loddl:
— Tertium non datur.
Do you know Basel:
— Surplus value.
Enoch:
— Reproduction.

6.2. Roast lamb with the art loving businessman, the defender of United Fruit, which finances the house, in which we eat roast lamb. The roast lamb remains juicy, if it's pushed into the oven wrapped in tin foil.

It's supposedly cynicism, when Claus R. says:
— You mustn't forget, that two thirds of humanity is starving. Or three quarters.

4.2. I enjoy the garlic cloves stuck into the red saucy fibres. Rosemary is caught between my teeth. With sauces she's the best. The mixture of mashed potatoes and sauce, sauce made from Madeira, cream, Spice Island herbs drips onto my beard. The lamb juice spatters the hair on my chest. Those slowly going blind fall onto my knees. The bodies on the embassy lawns are swept into my armpits. Chicken bones, skeletons pile up around my lap. My calves, down which the lamb fat trickles and congeals, rise above the deadly silence of kraals.

4.3. Jäcki just about gets by. Sometimes an experimental radio play. Trip. Disc jockey. The intellectual reports on the workers.

Who wouldn't get his passion fruits together at the post office?

1.1.5.1. In *konkret* Peter Hamm establishes the commodity character of what Peter Handke writes. Thereupon Peter Handke establishes in *konkret* the commodity character of what Peter Hamm has written in *konkret*.

0. (and 4.4., possibly 1.1.1.4.1.) I cannot speak about the deformations of our language without the deformations of our language.

I cannot change our society unchanged by our society.

4.4.1. Chemical analyses for psychology.
Nicolas Bourbaki for sociologists.

6.3. — Seventy per cent, says the black American soldier between Cologne and Hamburg, of the conscripted Americans would carry out torture, without rebelling. First burn a finger, then the hand, then the arm.

Cut off a finger, the hand, the arm, a toe, the foot. Cut open the abdominal wall.

Make a statement with the intestines in full view.

4.5. Jäcki believes that it's boredom. Not Venus

and its phases. Not progress or reaction. Not
the course of history.

Fashions.

The war had become boring. The New Look
was called peace. Non violence and democracy
were worn long. Gradually the skirts are becoming as short again as the skirts of the women
flak auxiliaries. Peace has become boring.

— When war comes.

— What kind of war.

— War. Some kind of war.

Buckles and epaulettes and corpse identification badges dominate the boutique windows.

1.1.3.2. — Protest must be fun too.

4.2.1. It's easier to move from misery directly to
revolution. "I had the opportunity to become
reconciled." Yellow with jaundice outside
Paris in a cold October, it's easier to despise
Racine and the repressive statements of the
Pre-Socratics; with rats behind the pillow it's
easier to give up the longing for sensitivity
through Ming vases.

4.2.2. Of course I'm for...

Of course I'm against...

Of course I'll sign it too...

...against...

...for...

But usually everything is different.

And if I make myself a little better informed,
I'm still for...

but of course I no longer want to

sign it

too...

And of course I'll sign.

7. The mothers twist the foot of the new born
child round once in the joint, in order to

go begging with the deformed limpy Dan.
Does Maria Callas as Medea inflame Pier
Paolo Pasolini?
Jason as double of Oedipus.
The Queen.
Love of one's mother?

1.1.5.2. — R. is unpolitical, therefore right wing.
— G. is a fascist. St. and H. are fascists.
B. is fascist.
— The novel is dead.

4.2.3. Is the suffering of the young Detlev suffering,
measured against the suffering of the infants
of Djakarta?
Weigh up?
Six pounds of suffering per terror attack?
How many pounds of suffering for slowly
going blind because of vitamin deficiency?
Who wants to refuse Jäcki the right to show
his cracks? Who?

1.1.3.3. — Nevertheless we have to thank Hitler and
the concentration camps for half of Germany
having a socialist government today.

1.1.5.3. Join American Express or not!
Pangs of conscience.

4.3.1. (if one interprets it more leniently 4.2.4.)
Do you want to miss the boat?
At fourteen you performed in a Sartre premiere
in the presence of Jean-Louis Barrault.
You wrote nouveau roman before the nouveau
roman.
You were the first beatnik.
You already knew in 1954 that two thirds of
humanity is starving.
Two telephone calls, three articles, four plat-
form discussions and you're there, where you
belong — right in front!

Go and do a little bit of mixed media as well
and quote Mauthner and Fourier more often.

1.1.3.4. It's supposed to have struck the fountain pen
out of their hands!

It's supposed to have made them speechless!
Their hearts are supposed to have stopped
beating!

1.1.3.3.1. — Gustav Heinemann as President of the
Federal Republic is dangerous precisely because of his integrity.

4.3.2. Sign a petition against the defence minister
with the right hand; with the left take the call
from the Ministry of Overseas Development.

1.1.4.1. (and 4.2.5.) Jäcki experiences it for the first
time: no longer daring to think, what one
would like to think. To doubt every feeling.
Finally repress thoughts and feelings.

2.3. Cartacalo/la was drag queen in the Roxy Bar,
an allotment gardener, who came cycling up
on his bicycle in the afternoons and transformed himself into Dali's giraffe beside the
urinal downstairs.

Cartacalo/la comes towards Jäcki without
makeup and without forty metres of black
tulle. Pigskin, Tyrolean hat and the grey hair
of the resting actor, subsisting on elocution
lessons.

4.6.1. (or 5.1.) You will give Jeff thirty marks and
he will be passionate and tender.

That's the worst.

How many futile non-financial rendezvous!
Tenderness between causing a public disturb-
ance, party jokes, jags for the clap, syphilitic
shakes and sailor's knife.

The practical experience, to be able to corrupt

the perfectly normal horn with a couple of
hard earned notes, to see them spread legs
wide and open lips for the kiss of love, discreet,
honourable, unspoiled with school leaving
certificate — Hermann Hesse, Orff, Franz
Marc, Grass. Dreams still corrode social
position, everything familial.

8. — I'm mad about money, he says.
Liberation under the pretext of money.
To dissolve one of society's deformations:
family life with another: finance!

5.1.1. Hygienic money. No pollution by feelings.

4.6.2. Just don't do it then.
You state:
— I can stop, whenever I want.
Well, stop then!
To try everything also means to be able to
do without everything. Can you give up the
formal circuit, which you disguise as a health
walk. "In every case it is the consequence of
a strenuous thought process, which exhausts
you and to which you devote yourself with
only the greatest reluctance."
You can no longer free yourself of it. If you
did, you could no longer live.

4.6.1.1. Quickly make somebody. Quick, quick! So
that you've done it and can avoid him the
second time.

4.6.1.2. Today you mustn't go with any blacks.
Today you mustn't go with any whites.
You must never go with someone twice.
Today you mustn't go with any Moroccans.

4.6.2.1. Wailing after the fulfilment of the obsession.
Let the obsession go: Wailing after it.

4.4.2. Because of the way Jäcki thinks about his

repression, more and more repressions arise.

Is there anywhere at all in the world a house that Jäcki would like to live in?

The architect's fairy tale about tower blocks. How many architects live in tower blocks themselves?

Jäcki wants to live by the sea.

Why should Jäcki repress his desires from himself?

Sense of duty.

Conscience.

Bad.

Good.

Demands that split Jäcki into accuser and accused. The accused goes underground and the accuser looks for employment and indiscriminately forgives his neighbours.

The natural — what a compulsion.

The masses.

The simple life.

The undistorted.

The avant garde.

Clothing.

Advert.

Bircher-Benn müsli.

Adjectives and all of spelling.

But what kind of compulsion would it be, to liberate oneself from spelling with every word and from grammar with every sentence!

1.1.5.4. "He considers roughly this: that the position of the liberal publisher, as he had tried to occupy it till now, is no longer tenable."

1.1.3.3.2. Frantz is supposed to have been buried by the CIA.

Dany is supposed to be working for the CIA.

Herbert, Dany is supposed to have said, is supposed to have worked for the CIA.

In short:

Paul the Sixth is an agent of Mao.

4.2.4. (and 1.1.4.2.) Am I afraid of no longer being able to buy at the international newspaper kiosk? To have to do without lamplighter, packets of French books, as well as Italian shoes and men's clothes made in

Puerto Rico?

"I am he" who slept in garages, was a scape-goat, has a pigeon chest, cleaned out the stall, taught loonies how to milk.

I should have got used to it?

I am no longer to be trusted, because I'm over thirty?

4.2.5. Am I lying?

4.2.5.1. Whose lie am I lying?

4.2.6.1. (and 1.1.4.2.) Slip in the bath tub. Let the bottle of Youth Dew fall to the ground. Accidentally scratch the Brahms record. A nervous impotence. Coughing. Hardly is the coughing over, than the headaches start again. So one's always swallowing something. Recently the Vitamin-B complex has been attacking the heart. Stuttering and fumbling.

4.7. Were the concentration camp guards so bad because they played Bach on the cello?

4.2.7. In order not to use force, I would sleep in the little allotment house again, and in shanty towns, even in a Persil carton. Walking through the spring drizzle.

Gandhi demands abstinence. Perhaps he's right after all.

4.8. I'm on the side of the con-men.

2.4. Cartacala's eye, the eye of a prophetic goose tried by adversity. But he talks differently from before. Conversation in French is no longer the pretext for digressions into Sudeten German, digressing digressions.

Depressant psycho pills for the hermaphrodite seer?

Did the Capitoline oracle get electric shock treatment?

The shaman on the analyst's couch?

Underwater gymnastics for the drag queen?

5.2. So the gestures of affection are transformed into the gestures of hate. Instead of a kiss, lips pressed tightly together. Twisting and tearing at the nipples.

Push away rather than penetrate.

Spit out.

9. At the parties it's always the same people. The gentlemen from the Press House. The rising generation at Rowohlt. The lady from Milan or Düsseldorf. The professors from the art school and from Eppendorf Hospital.

— Didn't we meet yesterday?

— No, it was five years ago and at the same host's.

— But tomorrow we'll meet at Anette's with the Kampen cranberries.

4.6.3. Do marriages break up because too many partners participate or too few?

4.6.4. I could easily go without speaking.

With a mean frequency, as Kinsey calls it, of three times a day, difficult to realise.

4.6.5. (and 5.3.) To lie on Irma and scream. Scream louder than her whimpering. The feet fly apart! Expressionistic feelings of the exchange of bodily fluids.

4.6.6. (or 7.2. against 5.) You are my friend and your arse swells towards me.

What could my childhood have been like, if we had both grown up together and watched the edge of the waves under the Chiquita banana bunches and our black bodies; we would have gone to the girls together and a tourist would have invited us to drink a glass of Chacassa, and read Stefan George, Oscar Wilde and André Gide to us.

2.5. Push on to the stage:

Cartacalo/la as the most oppressed. Cartacalo/la as the most revolutionary.

Oh yes, gay plays are in fashion. No old Nazi who doesn't turn human in a gay play now.

No, mine shall get under the skin. Art as tribunal! Several levels. Kafka and operetta.

First scene:

Carla arrives with his bicycle. Male striptease. Investiture of the transvestite. Newspaper life. Indictment.

Boogie woogie.

Second scene:

Through an estate agent Cartacalo/la acquires on permanent leasehold a small, solidly built house on an idyllic plot of land.

Third scene:

The allotment gardeners and the gentlemen from the local council prevent Carla from putting up a fulgurite garage.

Carla writes to the President of the Federal Republic.

Fourth scene:

Aggravation. John XXIII. Mayor Nevermann.

Fifth scene:

Cartacalo/la is made a ward.

Sales outside newspaper publishing houses.

Sixth scene:

Carla plans to open a dance studio and the production of an Apocalypse of the Atomic Age.

Carla gets engaged to a hippy. They are violently separated.

Eighth scene:

Carla turns to a legal adviser of the Springer publishing house and asks him to become her guardian.

Ninth scene:

The audience is compromised. Gentlemen have to go on stage and are undressed.

Carla predicts the world revolution of the homosexuals and unmasks the abolition of paragraph 175 as an insidious establishment manoeuvre.

Tenth scene:

The Springer publishing house gets into ever greater difficulties, and so things look bad for Carla too.

Eleventh scene:

Carla flees into the Thalia Theatre and since he is starving appeals by registered and express letters to personalities all over the world.

Twelfth scene:

Revolution in Germany. Cartacalo/la appears on the barricades and reads out a proclamation on changing the hormone level.

Climax of the play. Very majestic!

Remodelling of man and woman.

Life's task. Party office.

Carla philosophically:

In the negro, the white man hates his father; in the gay, the orangoutang, his grandad.

Total permanent revolution of society through operations.

Mixed reception for Carla's proposals from the revolutionaries.

The end:

The press barons keep the upper hand. Cartacalo/la's guardian wins back his influence and provides her with a two room flat. Delightedly Carla moves into an apartment crowded with albums and cauchemars.

4.2.6.2. I can hear everything. Every aeroplane. The higher it is, the less I can sleep. Pillows don't help. Or saliva soaked Kleenex. I twist Earex into both ears till it hurts and in the suburban silence hear the people in the next house breathing.

1.1.1.1. Lil complains from New York:
— Everything is so different now. It's the turn of the very young hair boys and girls and art "decays". All my hair boys are under twenty-five. Are you ever going to come here, before the porno wave disappears too?

0.1. The difference in speech between Gotthold Ephraim Lessing and Gustaf Gründgens is less than that between Enoch in 1967 and Enoch in 1969.

4.9. (or 4.4.3.) There is as much to be said for deciding, as for not deciding.

1.1.3.4. Tertium non datur or perhaps non dabitur. Hic et nunc etc and:
Taedium Vitae.

4.2.8. 8.4.1. (or 2.1.1.) 18.3.2. (3.0. is better or —
since this is not possible — 3.0.1.) 23.1.2.
(or 6.1.).
4. (n^*.) Jäcki:
Bisexual.
Grade-one mixed race.
Monsieur Ouine — Herr Jein — Mr Yessno.

52

— Now everything is different.

Now it's peace and the bells that have not been melted down for cannon will ring for a week.

Now all the SS men will be executed. Dieter, Ove, Miss Leitl will go to jail and the Möller woman, who had Aunty Frieda put in jail, will be laid on the strappado, killed, liquidated, razed to the ground.

Never again will there be an air raid warning!

Never again will anyone have to report to the HY!

No one will have to shovel snow any more!

No one will ever again lay down a carpet of bombs!

Everyone can say what they think, without fear of being overheard!

Those of mixed race and the persecuted receive offices and medals from the liberators, their hands are piled high with honey and black chocolate and real coffee!

Will it last for long?

53

Detlev sees the first enemy soldier. His arse is so round that the material of his trousers is stretched tight across it. More than anything else Detlev would like to crawl between the halves of the English arse. He imagines that in there it must smell of smoked sausage.

— But you can't crawl into his arse.

— Against your breast I'd like to cuddle;
Up your bum I'd like to shelter
mummy heard people singing in the twenties. Detlev
admires all the round arses of the occupation soldiers
tramping past.

54

Aunty Frieda comes back from jail.
Most inmates were shot before the liberators marched in.
Aunty Frieda had to wash the open sores on her legs with
her own urine.

55

Granny:
— I already felt the end coming in '44. When they tried
to assassinate the Führer, I almost had a heart attack with
happiness.
Grandad:
— These are the king's elite troops. Their behaviour is
impeccable. Hamburg has never been able to regard the
English as its enemy.
Mummy:
During the attacks the villas in Harvestehude were left
unharmed for the occupying forces.
Granny:
— You can complain! We handed over our bedroom to
you. We had to make the study and the guest room into
a single room. If the big room upstairs really should be
requisitioned for the refugees, our dear Silesians, you and
your child are entitled to use our kitchen.
Grandad:
— Ilse. Just like an ordinary person. Like our niece. Ilse.
Ilse Koch!
Granny:

— Who would have believed it?!
Mummy:
— And if we had believed it, what could we do?
Granny:
— They deceived the whole nation. Ilse Koch. A camp
commandant. The unnatural woman.
Grandad:
— Satan! God's scourge!
Mummy:
— Now you can't say it loud enough.
Grandad:
— Was I the one who wanted to get the boy into the HY
at all costs?
Mummy:
— Because you were afraid of being thrown out of the
Party!
Granny:
— Dad, don't start quarrelling again!
Go and pick some parsley!
Mummy:
— Don't let the child get hold of the newspaper!
But the adults hide it so badly, that Detlev discovers the
newspaper the following day on the coal shovel.
Pictures of piles of corpses.
Piles like those he had imagined when people talked about
the victims of the air raids.
Thinner than Mrs Wichmann, like bones.
In a photograph it looks worse than in the imagination.
But the photos don't move, while thoughts move forward
and jump back.
Children's skeletons too.
Not skeletons — skeleton-like corpses.
— Don't let the child get hold of the newspaper!
A pile of the thinnest child corpses, who were gassed be-
cause they didn't fit into the party programme.

Photos of corpses smell of printer's ink and not of Christmas
and the cripples' home.

— Christmuss.

— After every December there follows a May.

— Yes, it's true. In reality everything's already finished.

Granny surprises him, although he's had practice in keeping
secrets: Occasionally he steals little flakes of fat from the
meat broth in the food cupboard.

Granny presses him to her and kisses him wet:

— Put it away, don't look at it any more. Just forget it
again. A child doesn't have to know everything. Now we're
living in peace time!

56

— German soldier brave and true

German women big fat whores, writes a smart English
occupation soldier on the side of the Robert Ley house
on the crooked path.

57

The Rüter family are allocated the large room, upstairs, in
which granny and grandad slept until the evacuation and
in which mummy's black mahogany desk now stands.

The Rüters also occupy the small room.

I and my school-age son inhabit a half room with sloping roof and chimney, mummy writes to the housing
department.

Mr Rüter helps grandad at the back and the front.

— Legacy hunter!

Mrs Rüter has Parkinson's Disease and when she crosses
the hall, she scratches the wallpaper.

Hannelore Rüter reminds mummy of BDM girls.

Hannelore talks about their flight:

Grandparents died on the trek. The horse collapsed and died. The women left behind were something by the women.
— First they said in Pomerania and Silesia: They never come here! and now they all owned an estate.
— The Poles wash potatoes in the WCs and keep chickens in the bathtubs in the farm houses.
— Those are the lies told by people who have millions of Poles on their conscience.
— No one killed millions of Poles.
— Not all alone.
The Rüters are dealing on the black market.
They melt down illegal fat till late at night. Mrs Rüter holds one pot after the other in her shaky hands and cooks fatty meals for hours on end, to bind her husband to her.

58

His mother takes the part of the elite soldier.
It's true she doesn't have a round arse like the English do
— even her bosom has become quite thin because of the war — but it's funny the way she sticks her hands into the track suit and chews chewing gum!
— What shall I say?
— Goot moaning — if it's morning. Goot ehvening, in the evening.
— Goot moaning.
But the elite soldier doesn't even look at him.
— Goot ehvening!
Now mummy taps her curlers and says:
— Hallo!
— Du yu hev schoklett.
— Mummy pulls a piece of cardboard out of the breast pocket of her track suit and gives it to him.
— Senk yu!
— Mummy taps her perm again and says:

— Bei! Bei!

Detlev never does it, when he really meets an elite soldier. He is afraid of making a mistake. Perhaps they would have a good laugh at him.

He doesn't, like the refugees, run after the cigarette ends that are dropped in the street by the elite soldiers. The cigarette ends of the foreign-smelling cigarettes are particularly long and the elite soldiers are pleased when the thin enemy children and the refugees run to snatch a butt. Detlev is hungry. But not for chocolate. Apart from that he prefers, when mummy plays the elite soldier and he can speak to her and she, chewing chewing gum — which she hasn't got at all — gives him a piece of cardboard.

59

The Rüters want to have mummy's furniture.

The black desk. The Viennese-style chairs that mummy bought when she went to the state art school. The round table. The one good-looking easy chair, table lamps, flowerpots and odds and ends like that.

— I'll make you a generous offer: Three wholemeal loaves. Proper black wholemeal loaves, not yellow ones.

— 1,000 gram loaves or 1,500 gram loaves.

— 1,500 gram loaves. Three of them.

A week later Mr Rüter says:

— You must make up your mind! I want to live with furniture that's my own. Either you sell me your furniture for two, three 1,000 gram loaves or you must remove your stuff, so that the rented rooms are entirely at our disposal, in accordance with the regulations.

— Where shall I put it?

— Perhaps I'll add on a small liver sausage, says Mr Rüter.

— But I want a decision immediately.

— Go and take them to an exchange office. Perhaps you'll

get a heavy woollen coat for them or a camera.

— What am I going to do with a camera?

— We must know by tomorrow.

The black desk stood in Heim Way, when Detlev was still small and mummy had fallen out with granny and grandad. Grandad had had a fit of rage, because mummy had visited Uncle Emil and Aunty Hilde again.

Uncle Emil wasn't a party member. Grandad had joined right away.

The two green iridescent metal tins full of makeup pencils were kept in the desk.

— Those old moaning minnies! Three thousand-gram loaves and a liver sausage. We'll fill ourselves up with that and won't give anything to granny and grandad.

— As I said: Two thousand-gram loaves and perhaps a liver sausage.

— Three.

— Yes. Sure. It's difficult at the moment. There are lots of raids. In Thalstrasse maize bread now stands at ten to fifteen Ami cigarettes.

Mr Rüter knocks and says:

— Can I bring the loaf now?

— Two at least.

— I've only been able to get hold of one 1,500 gram loaf.

— Two.

— No. It's not possible.

— One and a third at least.

Mr Rüter begins to smile and says teasingly:

— One! One!

He brings an underbaked 1,500 gram loaf.

— Liver sausage is completely impossible nowadays. We'll see.

The loaf is still warm. Mummy cuts it open. The baker lives inside too — a big bubble.

They scratch the soft part out of the bread. As Detlev does

when he buys on tick from Mrs Stuhdt. Then he comes home with a loaf that's been eaten empty.

Detlev and mummy break the crust into pieces and eat it after the soft parts of Rüter's loaf.

— Now we're full. The desk wasn't mahogany at all. And the screws are sticking out on the Viennese chairs. The Rüters will tear their black market clothes to bits on them. And the chairs could fall apart at any moment under that fat guy and his BDM daughter.

60

The grocers' shops sell flavourings and flour made from rose hips for which ration stamps are not needed.

With his pocket money Detlev buys:

Bitter almond flavouring.

Rum flavouring.

Plum flavouring.

Cherry flavouring.

Egg flavouring.

Butter flavouring.

Maraschino cherry flavouring.

61

The leaves of the yew tree if one pulls them off in passing stick to the fingers.

The aluminium pot is too wide. The lid rattles. It only lies loosely on top.

— But we don't have a bigger pot.

He makes his pocket bulge.

Mrs Wichmann with her single crutch and the damaged ear helps her husband to repair the house.

The Königs don't do anything to their ruin.

The hawthorn smells in the heat.

Craters are filled up.

The cloth covered cardboard bag bumps against his naked legs.

It's cooler on the crooked path.

The bombed out families have planted tobacco beside the Ley houses.

No wind.

The unripe blackberries don't move.

Lutterothstrasse.

Methfesselstrasse.

The fins of the perch in the pet shop stick to one another. Detlev's friend Karl-Jörn kept perch and guppies. Well before the terror attack, and the aquarium didn't leak even during the air raids. The warm water fish didn't flop about on the dusty carpet till they died. For a while Detlev had an aquarium too. But the perch perished one after the other and in the mornings Detlev had to scoop them from the surface of the water. It always started with stuck together fins. In winter it was too cold for the exotic animals and in summer they got too little oxygen. Finally Detlev kept a fat black fresh water beetle, which could also live outside the water. One day it had disappeared. Perhaps it had run away. Presumably it had become entangled in the algae and had suffocated in the green stuff.

The Church of the Apostles.

Faberstrasse.

Bleached ruins.

The aluminium pot is too wide. The stiff card of the bag rubs the skin on his legs raw.

In a grocer's shop there are big jars full of rhubarb without. The pale pink lumps in the piles of rubble dissolve and dye the air and make it heavier.

No cars.

The tram cars aren't operating here again yet.

Slow cyclists.

Opposite the crooked path and the little park with the allotments — where tonight the legalised 175'ers are having it off and threatening to offend public decency — is the Kielerstrasse Labour Exchange.

The former party comrades, who had already thrown their badges away before the capitulation, allow the grade-one mixed race boy to fetch lunch from the employees' canteen in the aluminium pot.

Sweet oatmeal soup.

The whole pot full to the brim with calories. The lid is placed loosely on top.

Mummy gives him a quick office kiss.

Slowly over the street. The pot is too wide. There's no traffic coming. Past the parks. As far as the grocer's shop. Detlev decides to buy another jar of rhubarb with his pocket money. He carries it in his arm.

Dull pink air and rubble flowers the whole length of Faberstrasse.

The oatmeal soup slops over.

— Tomorrow the rhubarb will already be sold out. Rhubarb contains calories too. The sun begins to dissolve the Church of the Apostles. It twitches in the heat.

The oatmeal soup soaks through the shopping bag. Now it chafes less badly, but it can tear apart at any moment. Methfesselstrasse.

On the surface of the water, the perch try to snap oxygen from the pet shop. They use the floating bubbles like a lung. Lutterothstrasse.

The crooked path.

A thread is being spun across the plant beds.

Now it's no longer far. Just take a rest every fifty steps. Just every ten steps. Single strands of jute still hold the bag with the aluminium pot together.

Change around with the glass jar full of rhubarb.

At home Detlev mixes maraschino cherry flavouring into the oatmeal soup, to make mummy feel happy.

She enjoys eating it. At supper time he has to vomit, because he dripped some more maraschino flavouring onto his plate again.

62

Everyone's back again and Detlev searches in his grandfather's desk for the party membership book.

Ove, Dieter, Miss Leitl.

The chemist sells mummy Camelia sanitary towels again, as if he had never said the word "Gestapo".

At the labour exchange the former party members no longer greet one another with the German salute, but with:

— Hau du yu du?

Detlev has taken the key to grandad's writing desk out of its hiding place and opens the filing drawer bottom right and pulls out the documents that start with the year 1875. He can no longer find the party membership book.

Detlev wanted to know, if one can tell from looking at Horst Wessel.

Mrs Möller is running around Karlstrasse again too, pale, and all along the fences. One could almost feel sorry for her. But she did go to the local office and reported:

— Last night Mrs Frieda Herzog expressed doubts as to the final victory!

so that Aunty Frieda was put inside, had to wash the open sores on her legs with piss.

Even Peter Hinrich's father, who rose higher and higher as a pastor with the Nazis, is back again. He shoved Peter Hinrich's head into a full bathtub as a punishment, until he couldn't breathe any more. Now the pastor hands in a form as a victim of National Socialism and writes to Thomas Mann. Mrs Möller, still a bit shaky on her feet, but back again.

63

Granny and grandad have gone to Bayers for a birthday party. Granny took ersatz coffee and sweetener and milk powder with her and a little bag of potato flour she made herself as a birthday present.

Next door Mrs Rüters clatters and melts down fat.

Detlev searches the shoe cupboard. But he doesn't find anything there that will fill him up. French brandy for hair. It only burns in the throat. Rose hip flour. A piece of turnip. Something for a hot drink.

Detlev takes the shoe cupboard key and opens the book case with it.

The *Marquise of O* lies on top of the army field edition of *Matteo Falcone* by Prosper Mérimée.

— In vain did the marquise cry for help to her terrified women, who went fleeing back through the gate, as the dreadful rabble tugged her hither and thither, fighting among themselves. Dragging her into the innermost court-yard, they began to assault her in the most shameful way, and she was just about to sink to the ground, when a Russian officer, hearing her piercing screams, appeared on the scene and with furious blows of his sword drove the dogs back from the prey after which they lusted. To the marquise he seemed like an angel sent from heaven. He smashed the hilt of his sword into the face of the last of the murderous brutes, who still had his arms around her slender waist, and the man reeled back with blood pouring from his mouth; he then addressed the lady politely in French, offered her...

A Franco-German, not a Russian who speaks French, is the main character of Detlev's novel. It will consist of three volumes. Detlev has already written the three title pages. He hides them under the Red Indian things in the allotment hut.

Detlev notices that the *Rabbi of Bacherach* by Heinrich Heine is in the front row of books again. The volumes by

Dr Rudolf Steiner are no longer hidden behind the others.
— A new age is dawning.
Detlev finds a singed lantern stick.
The stick is as long as the canes in Bavaria. Will Robert
be hit on the arse with such a stick?
Detlev sucks at the charred wood.
It tastes of ham.
As the period of the occupation continues the elite soldiers
grow ever smaller and darker haired and less pink in the
face and less smart.
The charred wood tastes of smoked sausage.
Detlev is hungry for smoked sausage and bacon and eggs
and semolina and roast beef.
Detlev closes his eyes and continues sucking the charred
end of the lantern stick, till his mouth is full of wood fibres
and the taste of smoked meat products grows thinner and
thinner, finally he only remembers it with an effort and he
pulls the stick, chewed white, out of his mouth.

64

After the office closed mummy and Guschi Mahler went to
see an old film with Olga Tschechowa and Wolf Albach-
Retty which had been licensed by the military government
again.
They sang:
— What the good Lord brings together, man should
not sunder.
Following which Guschi Mahler and mummy got engaged
to one another.

65

This afternoon has already lasted an eternity and it will
never end.

There has never been any change and nothing will never stop and be smashed to bits.

Mummy is keeping watch in the Kielerstrasse Labour Exchange and I sit with her in front of the covered typewriters and the new rubber stamps.

Where are the old rubber stamps for the compulsory detention of persons of mixed race and of women guilty of defiling the race?

Paper clips and glue that smells of bitter almond flavouring. The street is empty.

The cars are saving the wood gas for week days.

But there will never be a Monday again.

Mummy has been reading *Easter* by August Strindberg to me for years and there will still be enough pages of the slim little Insel edition left for years and years of reading aloud. The words "red lead".

Sadness.

The creditor is wearing galoshes. Squeetch! Squeetch!

Easter was always and for ever.

Joseph Haydn should be played before each act.

I look through the window of the labour exchange over to the grocery shop.

My two eyes melt into a single one and I'm drawn towards the brick house with the shop window full of pictures of foodstuffs.

It's equally bright everywhere. But I can't make out where the sun is coming from.

Mummy's voice behind a pane of frosted glass.

66

Robert has stolen cigarettes from his father and shares them with Detlev in the old flak shelter. It's something new. Robert says that in the Dörnstrasse school he locks himself into the toilet with the girls.

Detlev thinks it's going too far, for a big boy to piss between girls' legs in the toilet.
Smoking is more grown up and it's not true about diarrhoea.

67

Mummy takes Detlev to the Altona Savings Bank, where the German Playhouse is performing *Nathan the Wise* by Gotthold Ephraim Lessing.
— Lessing was forbidden too and the Lessing memorial on Goose Market was unscrewed and below "Softly singing measures wing/Sweetly through my mind" by Heinrich Heine they wrote "Poet unknown" in the reading books.
The dervish cries:
— Oh a fool! Fool of a fool am I!
and:
— No man needs must, and shall a dervish, then! What must he?
The Master of the Templars poops on stage.
He is wearing a knight's suit of wire mesh and a loose white cloak with a red Maltese cross, that falls in majestic folds.
The Master of the Templars delivers a stirring speech, pauses impressively, walks imperiously up and down and poops into the silence.
— That's terrible and destroys the illusion.
— Don't allow yourselves to be robbed of your illusions, said Hermann Goering. Who is now eating from a mess tin in Nürnberg.
Lessing pooped too.
Mary Stuart.
Goethe.
Orestes. Hamlet. Medea. Oedipus.
Churchill.
Adolf Hitler.
Horst Wessel.

Ludwig the Second and Richard Wagner.
Zarah Leander.
The bishop in Scheyern.
Adam and Eve.
Ilse Koch, the devil.
Our Lord Jesus Christ, who became a man for us all.
Sister Appia.
The Marquise of O.
Even Uncle Emil.
Gandhi.
— Is it reassuring or forbidden, to think something like that?
— One mustn't say it out loud. It's too embarrassing.
— The Master of the Templars has eaten nothing but turnips for months too.
Boiled turnips, turnip soup, turnip cake, stewed turnip, turnip jam.
— But it's very funny, when the Master of the Templars turns round in his fluttering cloak and suddenly goes "proops", "proops".
— Is that all you remember about *Nathan*?!

68

Detlev's future father introduces his fiancée and her eleven-year-old son to his brother-in-law's family.
The new aunt is wearing a modern turban hat and offers real black coffee wearing her turban hat and egg liqueur and a very successful ersatz cake made with real coconut butter and real chocolate and Leibniz biscuits.
Mummy would rather not drink any alcohol.
— As a matter of principle.
Mummy has the feeling that she looks very thin.
The aunt and the uncle think that Detlev's jacket is very chic.
They have never heard the word "anthroposophy".

Mummy smokes a cigarette and her eyes begin to water.
During the conversation mummy mentions that our house
will be paid off in ten years.
— Your garden here must be 500 square metres at most?
— Are we going to keep on being so formal? On the other
hand this is a first rate part of town to live in.
— When the underground has been extended as far as
Hagenbeck, then of course the value of our 2,000 square
metres will shoot up.
The new aunt dabs mummy with French perfume.
— My Eric brought it back for me from the Seine metrop-
olis when he was a soldier.
She pronounces the river wrongly.
All in all Guschi is very satisfied with the course this visit
takes.

69

As she is only a temporary war-time employee mummy is
dismissed from the Kielerstrasse Labour Exchange by the
liberators and now has to go to Besenbinderhof Labour
Exchange every Friday, to collect unemployment benefit.

70

His mother is sun, moon and stars. His mother is happiness,
beauty, the rosy dawn breaking, warmth, star of the sea I
greet thee, Iphigenia, Cassiopeia, Vega in the Lyre, shadow,
bigness, the best father and guardian, the future.
Mummy can't ride a bicycle.
Robert has a fat vulgar mother who deals on the black
market and rides a bicycle. Robert has had a father all his
life now.
Robert doesn't obey his mother.
He calls her:

— You old woman, fatty, you fat cow, you've got a screw loose, come on give me some money now, I want something to eat, you old cunt.

Mummy never hits Detlev and he's never locked into a dark closet.

Once Detlev pushed his mother to the edge of despair and she took the soup ladle and struck him twice on the shoulder with it.

In the evenings Robert is beaten by his thin, weak father. Then Robert doesn't defend himself. Sometimes he's kicked his mother, when she wanted to give him one.

His father fetches a supple stick from behind the wardrobe or the mirror or he cracks the whip in the air or he unbuckles his belt.

Detlev imagines, the stick must smell of smoked sausage. Robert begins to beg and plead. But it's no use. He knows that he has to let his trousers fall and lie across the table with his white arse and, if he were to poop with fright, his father would probably beat him to death. The following day Robert is just as nasty to his mother as before.

Detlev begins to imitate Robert.

Mummy has done nothing to him. Detlev is tormented because he behaves more and more repulsively towards his mother.

But when she asks him to do something, he says point blank:

— No!

Going shopping he forgets half of it.

He says:

— Go and do your own shite!

because it doesn't sound quite so bad in Low German.

He sulks all the time.

He says:

— If I'm not allowed to go to Hagenbeck, I'm not getting the shopping.

When he's supposed to give an account of himself, he simply doesn't answer.

He greets her with:

— Well, old woman.

Sometimes he stops copying Robert for a moment. But then she doesn't notice right away, and he notices that she has changed under his treatment:

An unemployed, unhappy mother who can't see a joke any more and doesn't feel like doing anything at all in the evenings any more.

She's not pretending.

71

It used to be worth living in Hamburg, because of the "Palette".

Why is it worth living in Hamburg now?

Because of the "Sahara"? Because of the "Grünspan"? Because of Jeff?

Must it be worthwhile?

The view of the Elbe from the harbour hospital?

(The Elbe as medium of huge displacements of space — cargo space displacements.)

The sobbing of June nightingales in the Elbe suburbs?

— I'll go up and see Wolli first.

Jäcki rings the secret sign.

The buzzer buzzes and the door clicks open.

Jäcki climbs over the iron cover of the dungeon.

Underneath voices, practice shots, laughter.

Jäcki mounts the stairs which have become antique from millions of delinquent steps.

What kind of Wolli awaits him upstairs?

The apprentice in a boiler suit bought somewhat too large?

Wolli as beatnik, tramp, circus clown, flower child? Is he

patching up a set of dentures for Cartacalo/la because he
ruined her teeth in the Lily of the Valley Allotment Gardens?
Are his boots full of blood, after kicking in the face of a
competitor?
Is he forcing Christina, the Gold Hamster, to commit
suicide in the dungeon under the iron cover?
Christina puts the revolver to her temple, pulls the trigger,
pulls the trigger — but Wolli hasn't loaded the revolver
and stands there and laughs himself silly.
Gold Hamster faints with humiliation.
Is Wolli taking care of her now?
Is he coming out of the bath, is his hair lying flat, does the
water look like brillantine?
Wolli with a pimp's head?
Are his features slightly smoked? A charming expression
in his amber eyes? The grass face?
Or the thin face of the sick Wolli with the symptomatic
hollow cheeks, lips and lines?
Wolli stands at the top of the stairs and waits for Jäcki.
He has back-combed his hair a little. His face is powdered
white. He has emphasised his eyebrows with the derma-
tograph and put iridescent green on the lids.
A flower pattern suit from Kashmir.
Jäcki thinks of the transvestites in trouser suits, who get
themselves operated on in Casablanca or Neumünster for
twenty big ones, that is twenty thousand marks, so that in
their trouser suit they can feel attracted to butch femmes.
Screwing with lesbians as artificial women.
— Come in, says Wolli tenderly in a Thuringian accent or:
— Well! or:
— Well, my dear!
and shoulders the submachine again, that he had levelled
at Jäcki.
Reimar Renaissanceprince introduced Jäcki to Wolli.

The "Palette" was shut down and everyone in Hamburg was hopping restlessly around looking for something to hold on to.

This fitted kitchen. This bedroom with these two portraits of father and mother. This television. This rubber plant. This green sofa, its plush worn away by Eros Centre negotiations, playing cards and preparing hash.

Christina sits naked in front of her makeup box. She's smearing a syrup between her legs that dyes her pubic hair black for business. Her tits — Wolli is quite mad about her tits with the almost hand sized nipples — nipples looking so disproportionately exciting on the completely smooth, firm, white body as if they were stuck on. A sheath more supple than plastic over bones, veins, sinews, flesh, tangled up bras, foam rubber. Gold Hamster is tired and Jäcki can see where her face will begin to sag and turn puffy. Wolli fetches chewing gum and chocolates, hashish, a bottle of High C and caviar.

In the mezzanine opposite the lesbian is poking a customer with a rubber dildo.

From the Freiheit below the sound of feet, sounds of a fight. A police siren. "Help!" The porter on the other side bangs on a copper door. A horse rides an advert. The crackling of the neon signs.

Wolli says:

— I regret, that my work as a film projectionist and manager of a girls' hostel, the guerrilla warfare with the competition, procuring material, that is picking up women, do not allow me to devote myself more intensively to reading Marcel Proust's *Remembrance of Things Past*. Moreover, at the moment the distraction of a good book would do me more good than anything else in the world. I'm surrounded. They want to liquidate me. My pursuer is advancing towards me bar by bar. I have to think about every gesture.

— My nerves are overburdened too, replies Jäcki.

— I'm looking for Jeff and don't want to meet him. In order not to love him and to preserve our love, I first of all make love with two others, so that I meet him more lovingly. I've known him for three years now. He indicated from the beginning that his commitment was tied to monetary considerations. If these were satisfied, I was overcome by a mood out of Baudelaire and Querelle de Brest, which occasionally overpowers me again and would destroy my life, were I not artificially to remove myself to cooler conditions. Exotic raptures in a plastic food bag. But aren't they really more valuable than the whole collection of gonorheoid blackmailers of the middle class, who are waiting for me in the usual bars and to whom I flee, if I'm honest, so that Jeff can't hold a knife at my throat.

Wolli:

— My dear, Jäcki! All day I hear about nothing else except sexual intercourse. Now you have to talk continuously about it as well, as if the whole world consists of nothing but it and as if the abnormal is the normal. I would so much like to know something more about Proust and Pound.

Jäcki:

— But dear Wolli, all day I hear about nothing else except Proust and Pound.

The doorbell rings.

For the instant that Jäcki's eyelids tremble, Wolli is motionless.

Wolli touches one of his green painted eyelids with an index finger. Jäcki could swear: Wolli turns pale.

In the mezzanine opposite the butch femme with the rubber dildo has still not managed to finish off the customer and the butch femme is getting impatient and reflecting that in this perverse hour at 120 marks he could have knocked off three normals at 60 marks a time at least. Wolli takes the submachine gun out of the desk drawer again.

Christina sticks on her second eyelash and digs out a revolver

from the Helena Curtis, Estée Lauder, Helena Rubinstein
in her vanity case, tears off an eyelash with the exclamation:
— Que cela m'embête!
Wolli presses the buzzer and goes into the passageway with
the submachine gun.
— I've only got one chance. Even before he's quite stepped
through the door and knows where I'm standing, I have
to put the hand with the gun out of action and then shoot
him if necessary.
It was only the man with *Bild* newspaper. Wolli shoves the
submachine gun back into the desk drawer.
— You see, I don't even get round to talking about Proust,
still less to pursue his recherches any further. Because of
Proust I'd like to learn French, even though the translation
by Eva Rechel-Mertens is very skilful. She doesn't strain
to put every expression into homely German. The text
becomes very light because of the many Frenchisms. And
that after all suits a work so full of fun —
— Irony?
— humour rather, very well. I could have rolled about
with laughter, when as a child the narrator imitates the
aristocratic Swann.
Jäcki:
— I don't know anything about Jeff. I know far too much.
Every sentence is a lie. Of course that's informative too.
Is he a guerrilla or an agent of United Fruit? How many
queens have been living off him in Eppendorf Hospital
for the last ten years. As a child was he brought up by
Jesuits or by the couple from Carinthia in the Sera. Did
his father beat him half to death and force him to kneel
on the lemon press till he fainted, or was it his aunt, who
suffers from lung cancer, anaemia, bowel cancer or bilharzia.
The movements of his well-proportioned, ebony coloured
body are lies. He lies when he groans like a deceiving girl.
I sometimes think he's only pretending to have an erection.

On the other hand of course the situation is ideal.
Wolli:
— "Nothing is as mysterious as stupidity!" — roughly,
says Ödön von Horvath, I believe.
Jäcki:
— But he also expresses ironic aperçus like: Je ne mens
pas tellement. Or: Je suis dans le doute. Il y a des moments,
je ne crois pas en Dieu.
— Not only funny. Reading it also produces a solemn
mood. When will I be in a position to free myself from
the whole shit and write a book of my own in appropriate
surroundings. I would like to study Proust by candlelight,
fresh from the shower and combed, wearing a little makeup.
— Not only solemn. Clear too. No complicated nonsense,
where complexity is only intended to conceal a lack of
experience and the inability to write interestingly.
The doorbell rings again.
The two false eyelashes, which are now straight and firmly
fixed, enlarge the movements of Gold Hamster's eyelids.
Wolli doesn't take the submachine gun out of the desk
drawer. He presses the buzzer.
— You have to write for the man in the street. Simple
and exciting. Is there a more prodigious joke than Odette
de Crécy as Madame Swann?
Christina calls:
— The guy's coming up the stairs.
Jäcki reflects that no one will let a journalist live after the
settling of accounts with Wolli and Christina. He wouldn't
get out of here again. Through the window down the neon
sign is impossible. Couldn't he have taken gym a little
more seriously at school?
Jäcki:
— Do you know the Life History of Mr Jonathan Wilde
the Great by Henry Fielding? Do you remember the first
conversation between Jonathan and the Countess La Ruse?

Wolli:
— No.
Christina has mislaid the revolver and looks for it, her black
dyed pubic hair almost dry, among wigs, hair extensions,
Youth Dew, Je Reviens and eyeliner and Green Water.
Wolli:
— I refuse to read, what is incomprehensible to me.
The door opens. Christina looks at the door. Jäcki looks at
Wolli. Wolli looks at the wall.
Reimar Renaissanceprince walks into the room.
— No, it's not the hired killer.
St Pauli swims away. Just for a moment the "Palette"
rules again.
Relatively unbloody ambivalences of the early sixties instead
of the hard conditions in the district after the "Palette" was
closed down.
Reimar Renaissanceprince with his lighthouse shaped prick.
Wolli:
— You may object that that is Morgenstern's Mr Meyer's
point of view: Who's your art for, if it's not for me. So
what! I maintain: There is no experiment that you cannot
make exciting and comprehensible to the most simple reader.
Gold Hamster is completely ready now:
She carefully rinses off the green black gel and the jet black
hair glistens through her nylon tights. Patent leather shoes
with stiletto heels round the legs off.
— That's how the customers like it.
Bladder, liver, spleen, pancreas, bowels are hardly warmed
by the handkerchief wide miniskirt.
Her tits stretch the meshes of the woollen pullover.
The evening mask shining white from inside. Eyes accen-
tuated with marten hair no longer look at anything under
the infra red heater in the contact yard of the girls' hostel,
but are only to be looked at, exaggerated eyes, to entice.
Reimar Renaissanceprince has grown older too.

Wolli:

— Let's go for a walk.

Christina:

— With the guns?!

Wolli:

— No. Just for a little change of scene.

Christina:

— You've got a screw loose, if you risk going out without your pea shooter!

Reimar Renaissanceprince, who worships Gold Hamster, whose eyes flash back, to Wolli:

— We all still need you!

Christina:

— Wolli, what will happen to me without you?

Outside on the Freiheit Wolli gives Reimar two blue banknotes.

Reimar:

— Thank you very much indeed!

And shoves off with Gold Hamster Christina.

Wolli:

— Amuse yourselves. Reimar plays the love clown and imagines Christina feels something important for him. She assured me only yesterday: Reimar is great at cuddling. But he's not someone to get married to!

72

This is the rococo:

Mummy's salmon coloured face. The glittering green colour in her eye sockets. The little flakes of red makeup on her lips.

His mother has put on another age — a white rococo wig with corkscrew locks.

Around mummy girls are running back and forward with makeup — another age — on their faces.

Sparkling dresses with trains, frills. One can see mummy's bosom peeping out at the top. It's not made up.

The girls say about Detlev: — It's an egg! and powder his nose white.

— I lisp. Most of all when I say the word "lisp." "Lisp" is a foreign word. That's not true. I haven't been lisping for long. It started with mummy and me imitating lispers and stutterers. I only lisp. I don't stutter yet. Erich Schellow is an officer at the court of the English queen. He wears tight, cream coloured trousers and one can see that his legs are quite a lot thinner than the legs of the English occupation officers. Erich Schellow walks through the darkened auditorium and speaks nothing but words with a clear, sharp S. There's almost nothing but S in the German language.

— On stage a boy, who's hardly any older than me, is allowed to carry a chair from one side to the other. I want to become an actor. I want to. And I shall do it too. No one really knows how long it will still be possible and whether bread coupons will soon be required any more. Who knows who will get through the winter. Germany is to become a meadow and a shepherd is to wander across it with his flocks. We'll all be put down the potash mine. I want to try it out before then: Actor!

Mummy and the girls enter chattering. Queen Anne sweeps in. The ladies of the court make the deep curtsey, which mummy has already been practising for more than a week in Lokstedt.

A lady of the court says:

— Your majesty, oh!

The director, the old Nazi, isn't satisfied and shouts:

— Do it all again!

Mummy and the girls enter chattering.

— You have to put a cork in his mouth. Then he has to recite poems for hours on end. Then the lisping will stop. Forth into your shadowth rethtleth treetopth,

Into the anthient, thacred, verdant grove.

Goepe pliep ploop on Schiller on hith diddle.

Detlev dreams that Erich Schellow is expecting him in the
Besenbinderhof Trade Union House in a tower above the
stage. Detlev is allowed to audition with Orestes. Every S
comes out clearly.

73

At Möller and Weseloh in Spitalstrasse all the stage managers with plucked crows in their briefcases, which they
want to sell as Christmas geese on the black market, Su-
sanne von Almassy, Jews, with yellow fever, Alexander
Hunzinger, profiteers, with hunger swellings, émigrés,
SS men, with berets, de-Nazifieds, with a knight's cross
buried in the garden, camp guards, Peter Ahrweiler, refugees, the famous, with holes in their socks, prompters,
child stars, Will Quadflieg, anthroposophists, the bombed
out, dialect actors, who have left everything behind them,
poets with second and first degree frost bite, Werner Hinz,
who had been raped by a whole company, lighting men,
walk on parts, extras, the opera chorus, with artificial limbs,
dysentery, half and single legs, Walter Giller, with ruptures,
Gisela von Collande, property men, Benno Gellenbeck,
Willy Schweissguth, hairdressers, Erich Schellow, makeup girls, with shell splinters, producers, directors, Maria
Wimmer, cleaners, those of mixed race eat barley soup,
turnips, jelly and drink hot drinks and Mr Möller and
Mr Weseloh distribute extra coupons and are pleased that
everyone is enjoying the food.

74

The money that mummy earns with walk-on parts in the
German Playhouse is not enough. Two marks fifty per
rehearsal and five Reichsmarks per performance.

Apart from that mummy sews dolls.

Mummy makes the skin out of the last pre-war stockings. She seams up the fingers and toes and fills arms and legs with sawdust, which Detlev fetches with the handcart. Mainly the sawdust is used for heating. If Detlev is lucky, he discovers a couple of solid wood offcuts in the sawmill.

Mummy seams up arms and legs and stuffs the rump, embroiders the nipples, little pipe, dibble, doodle never.

The head is stuffed, hair made of unravelled dish cloths threaded through, eyelids embroidered, lashes, eyebrows, eye buttons sewn on.

The mouth red wool.

Mummy takes the remnants of a raw silk dress from the twenties and makes petticoats and panties out of it. Granny gives a worn out duster for a peasant dress. The shoes are made from the oilskin table cloth, which was with them in Heimweg before the war. And the Ukrainian peasant woman is ready for Mrs Schulenburg's handicrafts shop.

— Cost price twelve Reichsmarks.

The customers have to provide cloth remnants and stockings for new orders. Mummy will continue to supply buttons, sewing materials and sawdust herself.

75

Two old people froze to death in a Ley House in the Lily of the Valley Allotment Gardens.

They woke up in the morning and were already quite stiff and speechless. They could not sit up any more and could no longer move their mouths either. Then their eyes froze. They had to be carefully carried out of the Ley House by the Red Cross nurses, who themselves have nothing to eat and are freezing at night.

When something breaks off and falls to the ground, it

shatters into a thousand pieces and blood lies on the allotment plant beds as red ice.

76

On a violet Christmas morning Detlev sets out for Kielort
Allee with a particularly successful "Master of the Hunt"
and a "Tyrolean Peasant Woman" and a "Don Cossack".
Mrs Schulenburg's handicrafts shop is almost comfortably
warm from all the thin genteel Hamburg ladies.
Everyone is taking a deep breath and shuddering. It's the
first free Christmas after the war.
Detlev looks at the wrinkles around their red made up lips.
Masses of lipsticks in every shade are on offer in the
chemists' shops.
The wrinkles of the genteel Hamburg ladies as they say:
Democracy! and: Peace! and: We are guilty — but what
could we have done?
The wrinkles which are still left around their mouths
from the words Final Victory and Final Solution of the
Jewish Question.
Mrs Schulenburg does good business selling artistically
designed dishcloths, ash trays, table mats, mittens, tasteful boxes, tins, chests, little chests, containers, handpainted,
made from wood shavings, waxed, decorated with poker-
work patterns.
Once, twenty years ago at the state art school, mummy also
contributed to the awakening of the new art, thinks Detlev.

77

The Christmas trade is over and Mrs Schulenburg sits in
the cold among the remaining antimacassars and distinc-
tively designed toothpicks.

Accompanied by Detlev and her fiancé his mother is de-
livering new dolls.

This time Mrs Schulenburg is far from enthusiastic. She
remarks curtly that the "Finkenwerder Fisherman" had
been delivered too late and the "Spanish Bolero Dancer"
had been lacking a petticoat.

The curt remark by a genteel Hamburg lady, a figure such
as granny could also cut, though with a Silesian accent —
when grandad became a customs inspector, granny was in
charge of an elegant five room apartment and gave instruc-
tions to maids — mummy recognises the refined, established
tone again, which has survived the phosphorus and the
mountain of gas swollen bodies and mummy feels that she
has been put in the position of an employee, of someone
just reprimanded and she exaggerates the gestures and
expressions of this role, to prove that she isn't going to
humour anyone any more and throws the "Colombine"
and the "Young Volga Boatman" at the feet of the chilly
Mrs Schulenburg and screams:

— For twelve marks!

Guschi, the cashier, doesn't understand the point of his
fiancée's proletarian behaviour and remains silent and
refined, when mummy looks as if she needs support
from her man.

78

— My engagement finished tonight. And Aunty Hilde has
just written to me, that now I would certainly sail safely
into the harbour of marriage. I've brought you up without
a man. What do I need one for now, when we've got the
worst behind us. I'm not used to love any more either. I
always have to cough. But you don't understand that. He
wanted to persuade me to stop working at the Playhouse
as a bit player.

I see myself no longer knitting ear muffs and melting down black market fat. I've never dealt on the black market and profited from the misery of others.

He simply climbed into the garden of a ruined villa and sawed down a fruit tree and brought it home with grandad's handcart. Something like that would never have occurred to grandfather.

— You pay for your high-mindedness with the child's bones, said Guschi.

In his opinion, people like Dostoyevsky should be in the lunatic asylum.

Waiting in the evening, until Guschi comes from the office, making sure that the gooseberry jelly has set and the kidneys are not too hard. I burnt all the photos from when I was young because of Guschi. Thorsten and I on the heath with dance costumes we had made ourselves, Tyllmann and I on the speech drama tour.

— Was there a picture of my father with them?

— I don't know whether I only burnt it now or back then when you were born. What on earth made me get engaged like that? When everything began to crack up, he was the only one who went to see the old films with me and when the Thousand Year Reich fell apart, I thought: Now you must become decent.

He had strong hands; but I always burn cakes and I want to be there when the new art begins!

79

Mr Thiessen, the extra, reads *Medea* by Grillparzer and tickles Detlev all over in the wings.

Medea kills her husband and her children.

The stage hand with the curly hair tickles Detlev all over too. Mr Thiessen and the stage hand take it in turns.

They don't tickle him too much, not so that he loses his

breath, but so that it's still just about enjoyable to laugh.
Clytemnestra kills her husband.
Medea kills her husband.
Orestes kills his mother.
Medea kills her children.
Mummy doesn't like to see Detlev being tickled all over
in the wings. She says so to the curly haired stage hand
once and for all.
Antigone's father is supposed to have killed his father and
married Antigone's grandmother.
She has a serious word with Mr Thiessen too, when she
takes him by surprise as he's tickling Detlev all over, his
head red with the effort.

80

The stage director has cast mummy in a small part as the
nurse in *Volpone or the Fox*. A German émigré is return-
ing from Hollywood for the production. It will be a completely original, musical staging and mummy has to appear
several times with a giant rectal syringe, execute dance
steps and warble in chorus with Mr Volpone's servants.
Detlev is not allowed to admire her, because the play
is not yet for him. He's only allowed backstage to collect autographs.
Mr Sartori comes offstage. He has pressed a thick flesh
coloured cap over his hair, drawn two thick lines under
his eyes with lipstick. Gauze ribbons are stuck unevenly
all over his black suit.
Mr Sartori writes in the artistically designed notebook
from Mrs Schulenburg's shop.
Climb high, climb far,
Your aim the sky,
Your goal a star!
Mr Sartori has to go onstage again. Detlev sees how the

flesh coloured bathing cap is transformed under the spotlights into the bald head of the Venetian usurer and the
lipstick under his eyes make it look as if the bags under
his eyes were turning over and the bloodiness underneath
was coming to the surface.

Under the spotlights nothing is left of the gauze on the
black suit except a shininess — of a worn material. The
usurer doesn't buy himself a new suit, which he could have
done in the Renaissance.

Mummy pulls Detlev from the stage, because the next
scene is also not for him.

81

Hamburg-Wandsbek, 7th February 1946.

Dear Elisabeth!

I herewith send back to you the little blue travelling alarm
which you lent me once, before our engagement, although
I would very much like to keep it in memory of an all too
brief, but happy time.

Such an object is nowadays much too valuable and perhaps you can exchange it, if you don't absolutely need it,
for some fat.

Our two worlds were not to be united in the long term!

You cannot accuse me of not doing what I could to make
a compromise possible. Was I not even prepared to regard
your son as my own!

A boy needs a father, if something proper is to become
of him. I hope and wish that, despite your theatrical view
of things, you succeed in providing for him and being an
example to him. That sort of thing does not correspond to
my idea of an ordered family life, even though I see quite
clearly that nowadays I could not make a better choice
than you. Which is why I'm giving it up altogether. But
regret with all my heart, dearest Lisbeth, that at this time,

when so much is falling apart, you have not remained true
to your intention of laying the foundation of a permanent,
solid existence. But you're not to blame for that.

There remains nothing more for me to say, except to thank
you once again for the kind loan of the travelling alarm
and to wish you and your blond boy a healthy and un-
clouded future.

Your sincere Guschi.

82

Mr Thiessen is not Erich Schellow.

But Mr Thiessen sits there in the half room with the sloping
roof, opposite Detlev and his mother.

— I am Orethteth.

— Despite the cork your S is still not ready for the stage.

Mr Thiessen will perhaps be engaged as a small part player
at the Thalia Theatre.

— Moissy lisped too, says Mr Thiessen.

— That's not true. I heard Moissy myself, says mummy.

— All our liberators lisp.

— The English language has just remained stuck at a much
earlier stage of consciousness, says mummy.

She will perhaps be taken on at the Thalia Theatre too —
as a prompter.

— Orestes kills his mother, because she has killed his father,
whom Orestes loved very much, because she loved Iphigenia
so much, whom Orestes' father wanted to have killed.

— Oedipus kills his father and marries his mother.

— Medea kills the father of her children, who didn't want
to kill any of her children. Medea is not killed by any of
her children. Medea kills her children.

— On the day on which the couthin fell, Electra
Hid and thaved her brother. Thtrophiuth
Her fatherth father-in-law willingly took him in,
Raithed him with hith own thon,

Who Pyladeth by name, tied the fairetht bondth
Of friendthip round the thtranger.
— At the word "Pyladeth" Detlev lets his voice soften
while turning to Mr Thiessen, as if he was the Iphigenia
in the third act.
— I am Orethteth.
— I am Orethteth! and thith guilty head
Thinkth down unto the grave and theeth death;
Be it welcome in whatever form!
Occasionally Detlev even lisps in his thoughts.
— I am Orethteth!
— Why must my child play the matricide and read him
in front of me, exclaims mummy and lisps a little herself.
— Ith only meant figuratively. Ith about the ego devel-
opment of the human being. You thaid tho yourthelf!
He is afraid of Medea. He is afraid, that she could hold his
mouth shut and he begins to hiss the next lines very softly,
as far as it is possible for him to do so, becomes louder,
has to pause, because he's got no breath left and wedges
Clytemnestra between shoe cupboard and bathroom stool.
　　　　　— Unckthpected, dithguithed,
They reach Mythenae, ath did they bring
The mournful tidingth of Orethteth death
The mournful tidingth of Orethteth death
With hith asheth. Kindly
— Kindly
　　　　　　　　　— doeth the queen
Rethieve them; they enter into the houthe.
Detlev remembers his clean S.
— I am happy! I am Orestes! Am I happy, to see my
mother in front of me, her face full of fear, of her son,
who is tearing out her heart? I'm acting it. Since the de-
struction of the cripples there are no lasting, binding feelings
any more. But how happy I am at this moment as Orestes.
　　　　　　　　　— Orethteth
To recognithe thee.

She fanned the flameth of vengeanthe
That in hith motherth thacred prethenthe
Had flickered low and thmall.

Detlev is dizzy. He can't jump, otherwise the heater with
the copper boiler will fall over. His lips tremble so much,
that the words that are produced between his teeth and the
tongue thrusting too far forward are cut short and sound
like the cries of the animals burning under phosphorus in
Detlev's imagination.

          — Thilently she leadth
Him to the plathe at which hith father fell
Where an old faint trathe of the rudely
Thpilled blood thtill thtained the oftwathed floor.
She forthed the anthient dirk upon him.
Which onthe in Tantaluth houthe did furiouthly rage,
And Clytemnethtra fell by a thonth hand.

Detlev sags with exhaustion. Iphigenia is dumbfounded.
Medea is weeping.

The flamingos flutter phosphorously in the night.
Herds of burning lions, inextinguishable crocodiles fall
upon the detached house.
Mr Thiessen says:
— Sweet!
with an S that isn't so very clean either.

83

There was something about the Gestapo at the chemist's
shop. But Detlev can't make any sense of it any more. With
his pocket money Detlev buys soaproot, milfoil, worm-
wood, sage, juniper berries, arnica, lavender, camomile,
mugwort, elder blossom, lime blossom, hips, cut rhubarb
roots, Iceland moss, bearberry leaves and a pamphlet on
the preparation of stimulating, soothing, sweat inducing,
invigorating, cordial, refreshing, warming teas.

Detlev prepares a warming tea for his mother, when she comes home chilled from the performance.

But he means too well, and the drink is so bitter that she can only warm her hands with the chilblains against it and then, despite the cold, pours it down the lavatory.

84

Now Klaus Hansen starts on about it too:

— You have to stick it into the cunt and pull it out again and stick it in again and in the end you piss on it and so then the children come out of the woman out of her arse.

— Bet that my wife gets children without all that!

— Everyone does it.

85

Spring is coming.

Detlev rolls cigarettes from the warming teas and smokes them with Robert in the flak shelters.

86

It is ten o'clock in the evening and still quite light.

One can tell that it's night only because there are no people passing between the ruins any more.

The blackbirds again.

The red hawthorn again.

As if everything was just continuing.

Detlev was allowed to fetch mummy after the performance. She wraps around Detlev the elegant, somewhat worn, brown coat from before the war, which is far too loose on her now. Because of the wind.

— When can I see *Volpone*?

Mummy doesn't hear in the wind.

— Why am I not allowed to see *Volpone*?

— Keep your mouth closed, otherwise you'll catch a chill!

— When will I be allowed to read the *Marquise of O*

— Klaus Hansen says you have to stick it into the woman and piss on it. Then the children come out of her arse.

— Detlev, how can you use such coarse words to talk about the most mysterious and complicated thing in all the world?

— So! I bet Klaus Hansen that my wife would get her children without that.

— What a thing to have a bet about! says mummy.
That's something else that's new.

— Is that why I'm not allowed to see *Volpone*?

— Love should be carried out in mutual harmony, completely undisturbed and with very great tenderness.

— What does Volpone do?

— Volpone tries to rape a girl.

— Can I see it now?

— A child should not see how man becomes an animal.

— Well which is it? Is it like an animal or is it the most mysterious love?

— The Marquise of O is also almost raped by an occupying Russian soldier and then a young officer saves her at the last moment.

— A German?

— No, a Russian, but an educated one, who speaks French. But as he sees her lying in front of him — unconscious and desirable, then he indulges his pleasure.

— But she doesn't notice.

— She doesn't know the father of her child.

— I don't know my father either.

— Your father was a cynical man. He wanted to have lots of girls and when he laughed he showed his little pointed teeth.

— How does one rape somebody?

— I wasn't raped. I was just not very happy and your father was living under the constant threat of the National Socialists. Till he fled to Sweden, and I can tell myself that we were parted by politics.

— How does one rape somebody?

— One threatens her, one beats her to the ground. A woman is forced to surrender herself. One violates her.

— How does one violate a woman?

— By raping her. By forcing her to surrender.

— How does one surrender?

— You're talking in circles all the time.

— Have you done it too?

— The man's sexual organ becomes very stiff and red and stands upright. The aroused man puts his sexual organ into the woman and moves the lower part of his body back and forward.

— A grown man!

— Until he discharges his semen.

— The officer in the *Marquise of O* too?

— Yes. And Volpone would very much like to as well.

— Can I read it now?

— If you want to.

— Why shouldn't the curly haired stage hand tickle me?

— There are men, who feel themselves drawn to the same sex.

— Goethe too?

— For heaven's sake!

— And where do they want to stick it?

— It's forbidden and is heavily punished. And harmful. It's called homosexual. Even though it is also said of Patroclus, that he's a man's whore and lies with Achilles.

— What is a whore?

— A woman, who does it for money.

— There are all these things I had no idea about. Homersexual!

Will then Hector turn from me always
When with matchless hands Achilles
Dreadful sacrifice for Patroclus brings?
— Marvellous!
— The cork helped after all! Have you noticed that you're
not lisping at all any more? The nut tree and the rhododendron bush in the front garden. Hagenbeck already has
a few animals again, which cry at supper time and later
too. The rhubarb. The quince. Lettuce and forget-me-
nots.

The feeling, which the lettuce and the allotment and the
gooseberries arouses in Detlev has changed. Now there
probably won't be any more surprises.
— Now I understand the Marquise of O.
While pissing Detlev thinks:
— So from out of that came granny and grandad and
mummy and the stage director and the blackbirds and the
worm and Sailor Paul.

87

Stiff, aroused, rigid, firm, thick, round, aroused, taut,
long, wide, aroused, aroused, aroused, torn jeans.
The crumbly bag, dots.
Muscles.
Men, men, men, men.
Smelling, strong, juicy, meaty, brutal, bull necked.
They all have the same face.
Nipples of metal —
Grey speckled super penises.
Varnished arses, perspectivally flattered.
Many.
Shining aroused.
— or of dried ball point ink.
Crevices slit open.

The threads, the hair motionless for eternities.

Glans as broad as knees, balls as big as children's heads, eternal erections.

Finns — Negro albinos.

Jeff bleached, wallpaper thin on the wall.

(The magician with the antlers, neolithic Thessalonian Sesklo, Hans Licht, History of Greek Customs, Supplementary Volume.)

Pubic hair in chains.

Cropped leather over Nivea cream gleaming leather.

Mouths smashed in, peaked caps, pointed costume stars.

The impalement kept up continuously at the unbearable moment, without feeling, completely still.

Queen's sistine without colour.

Willy building.

The wet looking dots, cream made of lead.

Stiff for eternities in an atmosphere of lead.

— with dot to dot leather bikers and sweet sailors done in pencil by an ugly menopausal Finn. Photographed drawings. Huge lifted up stuck on: The decorations on the walls of the "Loreley" Bar.

The movements in the rest room of the Palais d'Amour girls' hostel subside, before they have been carried to a conclusion, between tower and contact yard. The girls come back from their tower; the customer makes as if to give a farewell kiss and says something that he doesn't mean, and runs down the steps as self-possessed and as quickly as if he was coming from the managing director. Before he had shiny wide-open eyes, into which could not be fitted anything like enough clefts and white balls and rods spread wide covered in white yielding stuff. Afterwards the annoying thought of the second fizzy wine, the superfluous one. The girls make the movements which they won't carry to a conclusion, and which have only just begun to speed up, slow down:

— Squirt it out quickly! Go on! Aren't you finished
yet?! Don't touch me there! Lie down! You're hurting
me like that!

Now — even the concept "now" moves only slowly and
limply from the keys to the refrigerator — the cigarette
moments, the coffee moments stretch out before the girls
go down to the contact yard again under the infra red
heater, and from there waddle cheerful salesgirls up the
mosaic covered steps waiting for business, the customer, in
the tower. Stretch out the sitting with the feeling of labia
parted by bank notes and willy rubber gloves — calcareous
water, Fa soap — sinking into the synthetic fabric of the
settee during the break, half warm, shivering. Down in the
contact yard it's the wig that gets most of the heat and the
face, from the mini-skirt downwards cold and draught.
The tower upstairs is pleasantly heated and before the
customer wants to begin, the girls cross their arms over
their breast and quickly rub their shoulders. Under a compulsion to maltreat, they unwillingly maltreat the customer's
cold thing, with the drop of cold fluid at the tip, smelling
sweetly of the aftermath of gonorrhoea. Above all they
tell themselves:

— I'm not going to be aroused! I'm not going to enjoy it!
His tongue smells of schnapps and Peter Stuyvesant. The
heating has hardly warmed me up a little — the shower.
The limpness of the chocolate in the rest room. Even the
striking of a match could happen less abruptly and swell
up the interval further. They circle slowly round one another
with their first rate lustful legs, cup and saucer and cigarette
in their lustful right hand. Here they carefully put on their
lustful stiletto heels, lean against the radiator, against the
juke box, against the poster, against the easy chairs covered
in imitation leather and their lustful breasts stick out. The
girls hang on to one another, sink down with their hips at

the head of the other one who's lying down. The long black artificial lashes clap against one another protruding from the smelly mask of makeup. The wigs of those kneeling down reach up between the lustful thighs of the one pushing past with the cup.

— And then they rub their hands all over your body and slobber all over you.

With voices that stretch out like sponges the others in the rest room add:

— Lick your whole face wet. How nice you are. Oh, you're wonderful! So exciting. For me you'll go down five marks. Oh, you randy girl you. And then you're sticky all over with their spit and then they start with their finger. It drives me round the bend.

The rest room is crowded with the slack, fumbling bodies of the shivering girls having their break, slowly washing down pills, sheathed in thin nylon and spun hair constructions and coloured face creams, from whom soft cries swell out, which provoke no response in whoever is nearest — till the manager says to them:

— A customer has just torn up a thousand mark note in the contact yard, because not a single woman was standing downstairs!

and they make their way down over the mosaics and in the paternoster.

88

One of the patriarch's altar boys has had an accident on the railway line while stealing coal; Detlev is to stand in for him in *Nathan*.

Detlev will tread the boards on the temporary stage of the German Playhouse in the Altona Savings Bank.

He rubs Nivea cream all over his face.

— Nivea cream contains the urine of pregnant women.

— When I look at the starry sky at night, I doubt, that god exists.

— Youthful red? Number 4? Number 2? Red-brown? Red Indian tone?

Detlev applies number 2 in thick stripes.

In the mirror the face of a leper, of a peat bog corpse, of a mummy.

— To the hills lift thine eyes!

Detlev rubs his face all over and the eyebrows, the eyelashes and the lips disappear under fingers full of makeup.

— Daughter of Zion, reeeeejoice!

Detlev powders himself and his whole face, with the tiny white enamel and sapphire imitation eyes, is covered with dew or frost.

— Mendelssohn-Bartholdy.

— Father, thou!

Detlev wipes and taps around the blunt stump, fixes the cheek bones again, paints in eyebrows and lips and cuts larger slits for the eyes with the dermatograph.

— Now I'm stepping into the history of world theatre. Without a name of my own, but still the altar boy is listed in the programme in very small print and at the Last Judgement I shall be able to say: I was Eugen Klimm's altar boy on the temporary stage of the Playhouse! and the audience will have to call out: Yes, he was! He was!

— While the millions of genuine altar boys from all the parish churches in the world turn green with envy. When I was in the Scheyern orphanage, I wished I had an alb. Now I pull on the powdered white vestment and put on the red collar. I fetch the censer from the property man and on top of that I'm earning my living with the appearance.

— And if there's no more Last Judgement at all? Then there's no difference at all between me in the Savings Bank and the unartistic and genuine altar boys.

— Perhaps the end already came a long time ago and it makes no difference at all, if my name is going to be in the programme of the German Playhouse even once.

— I have to step onto the illuminated stage floor. If I let one go now, like the Master of the Templars, then I enter the history of world theatre as a pooping altar boy. I would automatically cause an earthquake with my flatulence. All Jerusalem would be destroyed by my wind.

— The way I swing the censer in the ruins of Altona. Crooked building box pillars, white glowing Christmas trees, celluloid window panes, the starry sky over Jerusalem, which the stage hands take down again afterwards, because tomorrow *Lumpazivagabundus* with Alexis is being performed. Jerusalem smells of makeup dust, Jerusalem's, Golgotha's horizon, which stretches from one wall of the Savings Bank to the other. Jerusalem's star, which trembles, boxes of building bricks in bed, when one's ill, it could be Venice too, from the property store for *Volpone* or the Russian steppes and I the Marquise of O., I mean, the educated French speaking officer in the *Marquise of O.* instead of the altar boy.

— I marched past the eyes of the audience, without falling. There's the fireman standing in the wings.

89

Which porter here is engaged to a transvestite? Who here has blown five North African freedom fighters to bits with plastic explosives?

In the "Yoshilambodu"?

Who was in a concentration camp at twelve years of age and slept for three months with a burning electric light bulb in front of his face every night?

Albert was in a concentration camp at twelve years of age and was locked in a dugout cell for three months and slept, didn't sleep, because an electric light bulb was burning in front of his face day and night.

Fraternal kisses, kisses on the cheek exchanged by Wolli and Albert.

Wolli's dialect and Albert's art language (Maurice Sachs performs his translations of Villon into Low German):

Albert's story of his annual journey to the French Minister of War to have his concentration camp inmate's pension renewed.

Albert mimes a deaf and dumb, crippled, blind stutterer and Wolli accompanies him with sympathetic foreignness through the offices from questionnaire signature to questionnaire signature. Monsieur Miser Sacer and Herr Jabberer at the Place de la Concorde.

In the "Yoshilambodu" Albert offers a very dry Veuve and throws in a proposal.

For a couple of thousand Jäcki is to write a night time show for him. Jäcki is going to think it over.

Wolli advises against. Albert is an artist himself and would reshape Jäcki's nude show after all; apart from that the top class performers always run away from Albert after a fortnight and then the show becomes provincial because of the second rate performers. Albert's current sex festival:

First act:

"The dollar!"

Bang: Spot on tit!

Bang: Spot on arse!

Bang: Spot on cunt!

Bang: Dollar note!

Bang: The American president's face projected onto the tits! The tits are the eyes.

Bang: Spot on tit!

The more his eyes are supposed to be deadened by the abrupt alternation of spots and darkness, the more clearly Jäcki recognises where the round white skin is beginning to sag and beside the nipple the reddish crater of an eczema.

Bang: Spot on arse!

— A face like an arse is in many cases an insult to most arses.

— Really?

— Darwinian raptures!

— The plastic primal experience!

— The two ugly wrinkles, which fall away to right and left at the lower edge.

— At what point of swelling does the Boucher feeling give way to gas chamber associations?

Bang: Spot on cunt!

Since Jäcki was allowed to witness a birth in Athens, he can no longer look at a cunt calmly. He forces himself to look at it in the spotlight. An irregular slit with hair on it. Jäcki senses a programming gap in himself.

Bang: Dollar note!

Bang: The American president's face projected onto the tits. The tits are the eyes.

The brownish, shivering, especially protuberant, cracked knots of skin are enveloped by the projector light as if by egg white. They thrust out white from the eye cavities of the American president — white pupils in the grey eye white — the American president is a little cross-eyed. She rolls her breasts.

— Yeah, give them a big roll, Natascha!

The American president rolls his cross-eyes with the white pupils.

Second act:

"Jungle!"

The trembling art student, naked, five centimetre diameter nipples, school nativity play stage fright.

Then Jeff bursts out of the jungle, roars and throws his leopard skin onto the speakers.

Jäcki doesn't long to be Dr Benn's clod of slime, but to be black with big hands.

The art student who is shivering again is now raped for the third time this evening in front of the four hundred mark Veuve drinking medical probationers from Heide.

Jäcki sees between the overwhelming flesh columns of Jeff, who is not Jeff, a kind of black-violet trunk hanging; up above they mime joyful orgasm and underneath the giant willy with the giant balls swings like mad and looks on too and shakes its head.

Third act:

A castrated transvestite as Catherine the Great with a large rubber cult object. Albert on tape pants something spiced with Russian vowels as accompaniment.

Catherine the Great touches the erector with two black gloves and finally stuffs half a yard of pink rubber sausage between her fresh scars and squeezes it out again in front of the champagne glasses of the expensive guests.

Fourth act:

A clueless girl from an approved school lets a real anaconda curl round her twice, rolls over the boards, which signify the world, with the anaconda and imitates a picture by Franz von Stuck which became modern again a couple of years ago. The light goes on and the waiters pull a part of the anaconda out of the minor's genuine vagina.

Fifth act:

Cartacalo/la steps onstage. Albert lets her work in the toilet and appear once an evening as Blanc de Blanc and turn the customers off before the high point of the show:

— A number from the Arab-Israeli Six Day Races.

Carla curses and prophesies as usual, and as a novelty adds on the story of the seer in the underground scene.

In flight from protective custody and warrant orders moves from the Lily of the Valley Allotment Gardens to the cellar of the Thalia Theatre.

Jäcki sees Wolli staring at Carla's smile. Carla's upper teeth flash through the room in the spotlight; substitutes for the

teeth Wolli once knocked out, when she let him live with
her in the temporary house as a wild gypsy.
Cheap false teeth — a white rib of artificial material, smooth,
not even divided into individual teeth, a leg for the members
of the health insurance fund turned into geese to chew on.
Sixth act:
Slides from the Six Day War.
Casualties.
Bombers over Cairo.
A mother with a mutilated son.
At the same time Maria Magdalena, as Albert calls her on
the tape, a Viennese disguised as a parachutist, takes off
her clothes.
— Why doesn't she undress more skilfully.
— But that's just the joke.
— How would I do it:
First act: A rococo lass and a beau in top hat. Striptease.
A hairy man appears from under the rococo lass. The beau
in the top hat turns out to be all woman. Both dress again.
The point is the dressing. Second act: Children. Hunch-
backs. Dwarfs. Third act: A negro, who with a donkey,
who with an old man. Fourth act: Photos of tortures.
Together with intestines. Bleeding headless poultry. Mice.
How could Albert get away with it in his place every
evening? The police usually think they're dreaming and
after every rubber thrust Albert whispers: It's art, sergeant.
My piece will be a revue put together around Cartacalo/la.
Numbers on top of one another. Circus. Trained animal
act. Subculture. The arrogance of the artist: Now I make
use of the entertainment genre. And everybody yawns.
Now we're disc jockeys. Why not on the trapeze for once
or as jugglers! At the moment there's only one disc jockey
— a woman — who can do it. What does the artist want to
add to Carla emerging from the toilet and talking about
his letter to the students' union and the SDS, which calls

on the SDS to struggle against the transvestite being made
a ward of court and against the Lily of the Valley Garden
Allotments Association? What else can the artist add to
the pictures from the blitzkrieg, which after thirty years it
can at last be called again in the headlines, to the desert
foxes, to the completely Germanised desert foxes, who
torture prisoners of war and take families hostage — and
in front of that a clumsy daughter of Mary Wigman, Eva,
removing her parachute costume, New Israel Dancing,
with a bosom two pounds above the average?

90

I am a child of the suburbs and look through the
paper palings.
Gustav Knuth sets the fairground swing going and Gustl
Busch makes flippant remarks.
Later mummy and I in shabby clothes follow Liliom's
corpse.
I look intense and very threatened.
Every evening Gisela Collande brings us to the edge of
tears again simply by not doing anything. She is just there
with her harsh voice and leaves everything out.
My colleagues say that I convey innocence and misery very
genuinely too and I'm innocent with the same intensity
even at the subscription performances.

91

If there's coal, there are three kinds of school meal soup:
chocolate soup,
pea soup with peas of uniform size,
pink biscuit soup.
If there's no coal, school is cancelled and rations are distributed and homework:

Cadburry, which some parents exchange for cigarettes,
biscuits,
Mars bars,
peanuts,
"The Adventures of Susie the Snowflake!"

92

Rolf Lüders, a half starved production assistant at the
Thalia Theatre, engages Detlev as the Christ Child in
Frau Holle. At the end, when everyone, half starved,
stands on the stage with joyful faces, Detlev has to leave
the day labourer's house and return to the silent, snow
covered forest.
Gerd Madsen, who has already performed sexual inter-
course once, sings softly:
— When it's springtime the songbirds bring back a memory
Of a night in Capri when he met his sweet Marie,
There were stars in the skies and love in her eyes divine,
It was heaven to see, but heaven could not be mine.
while the Christ Child walks past giving his blessing.
In the dressing room Frau Holle deals in smoked sausages
and white woollen carpets.
The Christ Child blesses the cheerful poltergeist draped
with icicles. He is homosexual and in the last year of the war
denounced another homosexual to the Gestapo for revenge.
Detlev arrives behind the cardboard firs.
The well-fed stage manager, who sometimes brings mummy
Bismarck herrings, gives the signal for the curtain.
Detlev doesn't feel like taking a bow and is already taking
off his makeup

93
— When we're marching side by side
— Truruderu truruderu!

— In the morning dew to the hills we go, fallerah!
— Hussassa, fiderallala!
— Valerie, valera and juchheissassa!
— From the waters we learned it
— I came up and I went under,
This and that on my way I found
— Juja, juja
Jujajajajaja
Juja, jujaja, juja!
— And the old songs we do sing
— Tayterray, juchhu!
— And we know, that we shall win
— Halli, hallo!
— Hollahiaho!
— With us marches a new age
— Odulallala, odulallala!
— Fallerah!
— Truruderu, truruderu!
— With us marches a new age!
— Taytterayttayttayttayttayttayttay, tayteray!
— As we walked out, to catch the sun
— Root, root, root
— With us marches a new age
— Emil Nolde, Hermann Hesse, Hermann Claudius.

94

Detlev sees Creon's willy in the mirror, when the actor playing the Theban king believes himself unobserved in the dressing room of the Thalia Theatre's temporary stage and takes off his long underpants. Grey, like a stone, were it not in itself mobile. The bag hangs on ropes and stretches over the glass eye shaped balls.

That's what's hidden behind men's homely trousers, the rounded woollen cloth of Paul the drowned sailor, the protruding slits of the elite troops.

The thin actress playing Ismene has difficulty understanding what it means, to be afraid and not stand by her sister.

— Antigone wants to act in defiance of the official regulations. Would you have removed the brother who had been beaten to death from the camp, in order to bury him in the family vault in Ohlsdorf?

Then she looks at him with Ismene's eyes.

— You must look like that onstage. Not in the green room! The most beautiful and tenderly felt thing in the world dependent on the grey length of hose. It hangs down, long with veins like macaroni. I can see that the king's pubic hair is turning white. It's a tragedy by a modern Frenchman. The Greek heroes wear postwar Hamburg clothes. At the beginning a speaker stands on stage and elucidates the figures sitting around. It is very original and everything should appear very improvised; but the speaker has been grinding away at his lines for weeks and still doesn't know them by heart at the premiere and one can hear the prompter calling out eternities, whispering the improvisations from the cellar.

Creon is in no hurry to pull on his state dress. The bag draws up in the cold and shrivels into a violet plum.

Creon parades up and down in front of his page, who watches him in the mirror.

The white calves. White hair on the pale thighs of the powerful.

Executions:

— I order, that you shall be walled up!

— The marine is shot three days after the armistice for refusing to obey orders.

— So! The law — and do it now!

— Lift the sixteen year old delinquent higher, so that the noose can be placed around his neck!

Now the judges with the white calves blubber and the

prominent pastors with grey macaroni between their legs
have to comfort them.

The homosexual producer gives Detlev sweeties.

Detlev doesn't dare suck the sweeties, each one of which
the old man in his lust has perhaps handled indecently
before he gave them to the child of the same sex, and
throws the paper bag with the calorie rich confectionery
into the snow.

The greenish pictures are doubled in the mirror of the
temporary dressing room and the speaker and Creon step
towards one another. The mould coloured sexual organs
rise up, become red and redder, blood spurts from the
tongues of the informers.

Detlev walks from Lokstedt to Gerhart Hauptmann Square.
Gerhart Hauptmann loved Hitler so much and lamented
Dresden so much, that Detlev cried in bombed Hamburg
over bombed Dresden.

In the tramless streets tears fall from Detlev's eyes from
the cold and freeze into milky spots on his coat. Detlev
is the page.

Detlev has to support Creon as he whimpers about his
judgements.

Creon presses him close.

Turnips, egg liqueur, American cigarettes, home fermented
tobacco, hunger swellings, boils, bad fillings too.

The page cheers up the king with childish sentences.

Then Oedipus in his own mother begat Antigone, who
in another play guides her father who has been damned
by Creon.

So as not to see his bag any more, Oedipus cut the balls
out of his head.

If one wants to let water, one has to hold it firmly. A pink
piece of the more delicate, sensitive skin peeps out at the
bottom end. The longer Creon hesitates, to cover himself
again, the more distinctly the smell, of which Antigone

in the tragedy exclaims that it's the smell of men, strikes the mirror and from the mirror Detlev's face.

95

What do mummy, Aunty Hilde, granny, Mrs Selge, the grand dame do in the toilet?

Women sit.

They go in two by two and one can see them gossiping through the crack in the door and when they come out, they smell of very cold water.

At the premiere of *Antigone* mummy spoke to the director of the chamber theatre in the toilet.

— It's my son, who's playing King Creon's page. A couple of years ago he wouldn't have been allowed to.

— He has very large ears. A couple of years ago I wouldn't have been allowed to be in charge of any theatre in Hamburg.

— My son has no greater wish, than to be allowed to act once in your theatre.

The director can't hold it in any more or the toilet attendant pushes her into a cubicle that's become free.

When she's pulled the plug, the director says:

— Perhaps I can use him in the *Post Office* by Rabindranath Tagore. First rehearsal is on Monday morning at ten o' clock precisely.

Then she doesn't want to gossip with the prompter in the toilet any longer.

Mummy is also glad now that she can get in and adds through the door:

— Hopefully it can be fitted in with his engagements.

96

— Rabindranath Tagore, says the director in front of the whole cast at the first rehearsal.

— A poet of the Indian subcontinent. The most important thing, which we must never forget, not during the period

of the rehearsals and not for a second during the performances: Indians put their toes down on the ground first and
roll the sole of the foot to the back, towards the ball of
the foot!

97

I have to strip down to my gym pants. They have set the
figure of cane, seaweed, jute on its hind legs.
Two men lift me up and with my naked feet I feel my way
down into stiff, crossed cane tubes and by sitting down
push my legs into its legs. The curtain man and the property man have let go of me; my head and arms stick out
of the beast's neck opening. The two men pull and tug at
the front legs, till my arms fit into them and I've grasped
the cane supports, which will bear the weight of my body
when I'm walking. Before I'm completely laced in, I look
round to the waiting dinosaur. It's easier to climb into it
than into the baby mammoth.
Now they bring the rustling head with trunk and ribbons
and tie me in completely, my breath can only escape through
the eye cavities and beside the tusks. The papier mâché
face in front of my face shuts me in.
Gandhi, who was highly regarded even by Hitler, has
been murdered. Hundreds of millions of Indians have
left their homes. Millions of Indians are dying of hunger,
millions of Indians of cholera, smallpox, fevers. Millions
of Indians who lived in the north, move to the south to
their friends, the Hindus. Millions, hundreds of millions
of Indians from the south move to the north, into the new
land of the prophet Pakistan. Where those on the move
meet, they become hostile, beat one another's limbs with
plough beams and rocks from the fields, tear flesh from
bones with their teeth, drill one another's eyes out, nail
tongues to trees.
— And it's true! They all put their toes down on the ground

first and roll the sole of the foot to the back, towards the ball of the foot.

— Not exactly, replies the producer's wife, who speaks with an English accent, when she's asked:

— Are you English?

Mr and Mrs Human got away by the skin of their teeth. The professor of film in the Third Reich got away by the skin of his teeth.

Hilde Krahl. Moses. Plato. Cain.

During a carpet of bombs mummy was in the cinema and saw *Romance in a Minor Key*. An unhappy love affair between Marianne Hoppe, Paul Dahlke, Ferdinand Marian. A pearl necklace against a shiny lacquered grand piano made a big impression on mummy then.

Veit Harlan and Christina Söderbaum got away by the skin of their teeth.

Helmut Käutner and Marianne Hoppe and Paul Dahlke. Not Ferdinand Marian. He killed himself, because he had acted in *Jew Süss*.

— Veit Harlan and Christina Söderbaum want to make up for everything now and shoot a new film: *Der süsse Jude — The Sweet Jew!*

We represent the Ice Age.

Mr and Mrs Human allow me and the dinosaur to enter their house in Brooklyn.

Moses comes. Cain is four thousand years old. Hilde Krahl improvises insincerely to the audience, as the text prescribes. The wheel is supposedly invented. The epochs get mixed up. But it has an artistic significance. Cain complains, because he has to wait at street intersections, until the red light has turned green. In Germany there are no traffic lights at the street intersections.

At certain points I call out:

— It's cold.

I am afraid of sliding from the stage or rolling onto my back. I would roll from one side to the other and move my

legs quickly like a bug and suffocate in the steam of my
own body.

An iceberg is hoisted up in the background.

The stage manageress makes weird noises on the percussion.

The extras wear bright summer suits made of paper.

We got away in the nick of time again actually *The Skin of
Our Teeth* — a modern play but thoughtful nevertheless.

Basically a play about a lovable American average family
with all its failings and its virtues.

How cheerfully a writer of the victorious nation reflects
our situation!

— It's cold. It's cold, says the baby mammoth.

— I'm sweating.

98

In *The Trojan War Will Not Take Place* Detlev plays the
part of Peace.

It's meant to be symbolic.

Detlev has to appear almost naked, bony and white, in
front of Cassandra and Helen.

He has to trail a fake palm leaf behind him.

The makeup girl blows gold dust into his hair.

99

During the gym period Uwe Lütkens puts glass cherries
into Marion Böge's satchel.

Kurt Schietzel, Peter Jörg Jacobi tease Marion.

Every morning Detlev waits, until Helga Fuchs passes the
petrol station.

Dr Bahlmann succeeds Dr Storch as form master.

Every pupil has to write down on a scrap of paper, whom
he wants to sit beside.

Dr Bahlmann works out the seating order.

Presumably Kurt Schietzel, Peter Jörg Jacobi and Uwe Lütkens wrote down Marion Böge.

Detlev writes down Helga Fuchs.

Ove Müller-Neff wrote down Helga Rose, he says because she always wears such nice pullovers.

Dr Bahlmann puts Uwe Lütkens beside Gisela Bruhns.

Dr Bahlmann puts Helga Fuchs beside Ove Müller-Neff.

Dr Bahlmann puts Detlev beside Marion Böge and everyone envies Detlev. She opens the Bible at the indecent passages, to make Detlev laugh.

Uwe Lütkens finds it out: Marion Böge wrote down Detlev.

Detlev doesn't dare ask Helga Fuchs, why she wrote down Ove Müller-Neff.

Now Uwe Lütkens brings in glass cherries for Gisela Bruhns.

100

The English military government let the actor Brackebusch starve to death.

Oedemas are boils, in which one can press holes.

The body dissolves into water.

Mr Brackebusch had hunger oedemas. But he wanted to do his duty to the last in *Now They Sing Again*. It is a moving play by a Swiss architect, who has a deep sympathy for our situation.

Mummy is especially impressed at the point where a man is shot by the National Socialists and doesn't fall down — but goes on speaking.

— That expresses in a profound way the transition to the world of the spirit, says mummy.

The actors, Mr Brackebusch too, wanted to build their theatre themselves in a ruin by Dammtor Station. But then the Munich Hofbräuhaus got its way.

Now the "Young Stage" plays in the assembly hall of the

Emilie-Wüstenfeld School.
— The actor Brackebusch died of his hunger oedemas on the assembly hall stage of the Emilie-Wüstenfeld School, while he was acting in the Swiss writer's moving play, says the stage manageress.

101

After the physics period Ove crushes Detlev in a sweatbox and messes up Detlev's hair. Ove shouts:
— Verdigris!
— Detlev has verdigris on his head!
Detlev wants to get out of the sweatbox.
So the gold dust for the part of "Peace" is not real, sticky and can't quite be rinsed out of his hair. Ove has a tight hold of Detlev, who flails around, and the whole class comes and admires Detlev's flaky verdigris scalp.

102

— Just imagine, Detlev was within an inch of becoming the victim of a sex maniac!
Before his appearance as "Peace" Detlev performs gymnastic exercises with the stage manager.
Back bend, shoulder stand, revolving round the horizontal bar, splits, somersault.
What he's not capable of doing at school at the parallel bars and at the horizontal bar, he manages at the ear, against the unshaven, at the thigh, on the arm of the stage manager.
Detlev doesn't particularly like him. He's too fat. But he's always there.
He talks to the almost naked "Peace" every evening and lets the Greek warrior, Detlev, do gymnastic exercises with him every evening.
Back bend, shoulder stand, revolving round the horizontal

bar, splits, somersault — and once again now! Splits, splits, splits, splits, ah, once again, right?! At night the manager of the extras puts Detlev behind him on the bike and cycles with him to where the location shots of *In Former Days*... are being filmed.

— Perhaps I'll get you a film part.

— Shall I buy you a knackwurst at the fairground?

— I don't have any meat coupons.

— Don't you worry about that.

— Thank you very much.

— Take the fat one.

The manager of the extras calls the knackwurst the fat one.

— And when you're finished, wipe your diddles on my handkerchief.

In the dark they go into a ruin together and stand at the blocked up cellar stairs to piss.

The stage manager stands behind Detlev. Detlev is near to being frightened, but then he thinks it's so cosy with the fat old man who calls fingers diddles, and while he's pissing Detlev leans lightly against him.

At every performance the stage manager brings Detlev four slices of bread and butter, sausage and mayonnaise, because "Peace" is too thin for him.

The stage manager talks about a street in Buenos Aires where boys wait.

The stage manager carries the almost naked "Peace" along the fire escape outside the auditorium. In the dressing room, after the makeup girl has sprayed the gold dust on Detlev's hair, the old, fat, thirty-five-year-old stage manager kisses Detlev's shoulder.

Detlev doesn't resist. It tickles. But what does it matter? Detlev is reminded of Paula Wessely and of: I kiss your hand, madame, and think it is your foot!

Mummy as legal guardian has the duty to know everything exactly.

His colleagues intervene.

Detlev doesn't say that he called fingers diddles.

Nevertheless the stage manager who can count himself lucky to be allowed to keep his job, no longer dares to bring Detlev bread and butter and mayonnaise and sausage.

103

Even grandad wants to buy books. Detlev must take him along, when he invests his 7.50 Reichsmarks pocket money in *Treasures of World Literature, Little Treasure Box, Short Stories from Around the World, Prisma, Art Work*.

For Detlev the book shop assistants go behind the curtain and fetch selections from Eichendorff on coarse paper, cycles of poetry by Hans Leip and Beheim-Schwarzbach, de la Motte-Fouqué; but when the grandson appears with the customs inspector (retd.), they become suspicious and only show silly children's books with artistically worthless illustrations. Grandad is looking for something philosophical.

There's a stationer's shop in Hallerstrasse or the English wholesaler at Sternbrücke — grandad can't speak any English — Blencke at the town hall market place.

Criss-crosssing the city for books.

Eventually grandad buys one that's printed like a newspaper. At home grandad is a little ashamed because he hasn't acquired anything more durable — in leather or at least with cloth binding. But it's thick and has small print and is philosophical. Grandad leaves it lying around and hopes that Aunty Hilde and Uncle Emil will leaf through it, so that they will realise that the party membership book was only forced on him, at the last moment, temporarily, really he's concerned with the fundamentals:

Rowohlt's Rotations Romane series. Rororo. Hans Zehrer: *Man in Our Time*.

104

The darkness expands from the direction of Eidelstedt. There are no street lights working. In the evening there are no cars.

The dynamos on the bicycles make a reassuring noise. The murderer in the ruins doesn't appear on a bicycle. The lamp swings back and forward behind Jürgen and Detlev. Now both are lit up and the cyclist can steer past them.

Detlev isn't afraid as long as Jürgen is walking beside him in the darkness, he can tell him about the premieres in the Playhouse, about *Mourning Becomes Electra*.

— The performance lasted until midnight. There were no trams any more. A couple brought me home. I talked to them, because I was afraid, of walking on alone.

— Yet it's illogical. Jürgen would run away immediately and hide and watch, while I was being killed. How would I defend Jürgen? Defend Jürgen? Him? Help him? Run away! Defend myself! Scream! The murderer could easily wring both our necks with wire string.

Jürgen says:

— Bye!

and walks away through the front garden. Some carbide light is visible through the curtains. Behind them it's warmer and preparations are being made for Christmas. The turnips bubble in the box cooker. Mr Rühl has put an apple on the iron stove, the ugly old thing, to roast.

Now Detlev still has to go down Karlstrasse for between five and seven minutes. Past the empty telephone box. He can't make out what's written on the boards at the entrances to the garden allotments. At the lemonade kiosk under the horse chestnuts there's a rusty Coca Cola sign, which has survived the war, and a Mauxion Chocolate sign. In winter no one lives in the lemonade kiosk. Everything around it rattles. It's completely damp and the fungi are forcing their way in.

Lemonade in the happy days before the war. Detlev with white galoshes. Tasted of raspberries. Sneeze with pleasure. Oh, giraffes

— Gee-raffes, says granny.

what long necks they have!

Detlev tells Jürgen to wait and keep on whistling, till Detlev is past the lemonade booth.

Detlev senses how Jürgen is trying to follow him with his eyes. Detlev whistles and in doing so pays less attention to his surroundings.

Jürgen whistles and as he listens Detlev's eyes become less accustomed to the darkness.

That's the murderer standing there.

— Sand paper!

The murderer in the ruins can hardly be recognised yet. Then his arm becomes large and distinct, then there are bubbles in front of his eyes and coloured rings.

Detlev would have walked past him whistling, without recognising him, if the murderer in the ruins hadn't snapped his briefcase, as he laid out the wire ready for use. He's sitting under the sign of the Lily of the Valley Allotment Gardens.

Jürgen Ruhl has now gone in to the box cooker and to the tin stove and his father.

— Anyone can overtake me. Apart from that my legs are very heavy and I'll fall down.

Detlev slowly turns towards the Lily of the Valley Allotment Gardens sign and walks to within five steps of the crouching murderer in the ruins. The murderer makes himself smaller and smaller, and with the wire tries to draw his arms and his legs in under the American nylon stocking, which he has over his face.

The allotment gardeners would perhaps take the law into their own hands and cut the murderer in the ruins into little pieces with the handsaw.

— Can the bombed out families in the Ley Houses hear me? They're doing fretsaw work and preparing potato flour. Those who can hear me are perhaps just about to freeze to death.

The murderer in the ruins begins to crawl under the white palings of the entrance gate to the Lily of the Valley Allotment Gardens.

Detlev doesn't turn his face away from him, but forces himself backwards step by step.

The murderer in the ruins crawls through the allotment garden plots.

Detlev thinks he can hear the noise of him crawling away.

105

The HHA* House for example is still there, in a city pink with rubble flowers and pink chalk and brick dust, very solid, square, long, tall, grey.

It reminds Detlev of the sculptor Arno Breker who created very solid, square, long, tall, bodies of fighters for the Thousand Year Reich, heroic, bellowing with manly courage, falling in the east, Aryan — Guschi Mahler as titan.

Electricity is in short supply.

The paternosters don't go up and don't jerk down.

Detlev runs up the stairs, the arteries of the titan. To the right and left corridors with offices, iron stoves.

— Outside Beethoven, inside arch files.

In the garret, in the low brow of the HHA House with the mammoth Greek columns, a married couple, Dr and Dr Sello, has opened the "Gallery of Youth".

Detlev would very much like to get to know modern painting. Mrs Sello lets him in, without asking his age. The new

*Hamburger-Hochbahn-Aktiengesellschaft (Hamburg Elevated Railway Company Ltd) (trans.)

modern painting of today's youth is hanging there on cardboard walls, in niches, stands piled up in a store room.

Tom Hops, Herbert Mhe, Professor Metzel, Carl Hofer,
Otto Müller, Ernst Barlach, Gerhard Marcks, Christian
Rohlfs, Pechstein, Skodlerak, Kronenberg, Spars.

Detlev looks at it all very carefully and remains hidden
in the closet for a long time.

The Sellos assume he has fallen asleep and surprise him
with a cup of rosehip tea sweetened with artificial sweetener.

— Does the artist, says Detlev, not have a responsibility?
Must he not show the way for mankind as an example?
Transform the big questions into eternal ones? Render
comfort and cheer like Thornton Wilder in his plays? No,
Mr Sello, this cannot be the painting of youth: sloppily
painted harbour views and gypsies, lovers, whose mouths
and eyes are somewhere or other, crippled bodies in repel-
lent yellow colours. Eccentricity! Not one of them a beacon!
Barlach yes — Barlach is a great prophet.

— At the moment a lot of money can be made with Barlach!

— If a painter, to make himself famous, paints interestingly,
is that art?

— You should write it down.

— I've thought of doing that myself already.

— Artist, what does it mean, after all? Who is going to
tell someone, how he should paint! I'm not.

— Every dot in a picture must have a significance, says
Mrs Sello.

— And all the messiness and the dirty colour tones?

— Dirty — in your opinion.

— Who decides, that every dot really has a significance?

— When Cézanne was told that his mother lay dying,
he replied: I have found a new blue! and went on painting.

— Who is Cézanne? Do you believe he would have lost
the new blue again if he had gone to his mother on her

death bed? And you would tell me: when Cézanne was told that his mother lay dying, he went up to her bed and said: I have found a new blue.

106

Crooked paths and alleyways are particularly suitable for astonishing theatrical experiences.

One is afraid, because boys are being murdered even in daytime.

September midday is nowhere so sad so sad, as in the alleyway or the crooked path. White coolness develops under the leaves and the fruit grows fatter and redder.

Fear:

— Clytemnestra, Rosencrantz and all her Eumenides

Don't lie in wait, by, for, behind, in!

Don't smoke me up!

Ah, wot! Ah, beside.

Ruins à la *The Man Outside* or *Napoleon is to Blame for Everything* by Meyer-Marwitz.

Detlev sweeps in over the iceberg of *The Skin of Our Teeth*, plunges along the slope of *The Trojan War Will Not Take Place*, enlarges his eyes, his eyelashes grow up into the gold dust in his hair, displays his white pigeon chest and clenches his fist in the paper toga.

Detlev looks round quickly once, in case Mrs Schwarz is looking and tugging at his jacket.

— Oh! Oh! Oh! Out and outwith, with and within, by, towards, opposite, near and next, together with and since!

Pleading:

Detlev kneels down beside a puddle.

Noble submission:

— Duke, take for thyself, what thou desirest.

Contempt:

— I don't hate Ilse. May a human being! Through, for, without, at, around, against. I don't hate Ilse Koch!
Timid advances:
Shy sideways glances. Astonishment over the shoulder.
Natural voice:
— With that tyre, Mr Wiesnagrotzki, you risk not getting the mother's milk, butter milk to the Kruppcripplecorpses.
But the explosion! The big explosion:
Detlev looks round wildly in the crooked path.
— Revenge, retribution against, over, under, before and between. You want to steal my ladies' shoes? You pitiful, weak, homosexual willyfucker, who wants to draw in tribute from me my mother's holy lady's shoe, Mörike's and Jocasta's, whose blind, hung by the neck, selfbloodied, it can Franz no and never ever will.
More! More! Oh! Oh!
Leave the mouth open for a long time.
Take in a lot of air.
Calmly show them how the mouth opens and stomach goes up and down with excitement.
— But you.
Pause.
And now go!
Up onto the stairs, to the balcony, up the tower, up to the top, round about the flagpole and bellow it down!
Detlev's teeth tickle. Everything turns black in front of his eyes. Up into the hawthorns!
— You dare, base fellow, at, on, behind, in, beside, over, under, before and between the starving Ley House.
— Never!
Pause.
— Never!
Curtain! Applause! Bravo! Bravo!
— They should just let me!

107

On the remaining empty sheets of army field paper Detlev
writes an essay about painting, in which he also summarises
the conversation with the Sellos in the HHA House.
He himself begins to paint watercolours:
Sunset. Landscape in the snow. Ice. Mourners. Vase. The
Mother. Despair. The Dead City. Lonely Man in the Rain.
Lost! The Bluebell. Lovers. Niobe. Lads on the Beach.
He shows Jürgen the exercise book with his watercolours
and Jürgen says:
— There are too many Jews!
Jürgen leads Detlev into the shower room and says he
must remove his rings and undress. Jürgen takes charge of
the property, the beginnings of the novels, theatre pieces
and the Bavarian jacket. He gives Detlev a piece of soap
which has been rubbed smooth and a towel. Jürgen seals
off the washroom, in which Detlev and his unclothed
mother and his unclothed grandparents and hundreds
of others wait unclothed for the water to gush from the
showers and the gascocks are turned on, until the tongues
are black and squeezed between the lips.
— Why do you say Jews?
— We've always said that. Jews are the white spots in
your watercolours, where there's no colour. You have
to eradicate the Jews.

108

Curtain up!
Spotlight on!
America, the land of unlimited opportunity.
Johnny Sonnyboy sits in the sun.
— What to do with my strength?!
Jump! Do cartwheels! Headstand! Hupp! Happy! Joyous!

That's how the writer Saroyan imagined it.

Detlev is rehearsing it.

The colour swallowing spotlamps of the rehearsal lighting.
At the first rehearsal entrances are worked out:

— You come from the right! You from the left! To the
left round the father's chair in a wide circle. Look. Stand
still. Look. Off to the right at the front.

The colourless stage floor becomes covered with loops,
streaks, the steps worked out — the Indians put their toes
down on the ground first — scene by scene, overlap like
cut out pattern sheets, which Detlev traces with his feet,
clumsily, getting stuck.

Then come the run throughs.

Not only are Detlev's steps — standing leg, trailing leg
— led by rings, the height of his arm movements is also
fixed, the radius of a gesture of the hand, the opening of
eyes and the duration of a smile.

Hair thin, thread-like algae invisible to the eye, which
entangle Detlev like a water beetle, grow to fill the whole
cube of the stage.

Headstand.

Detlev can't do a headstand.

But in the text the author has written:

Headstand!

So the producer and the director and the dramaturg and
the overweight hero, who's already cross anyway, because
his name will come second in the programme behind Detlev,
and the stage manageress and the prompter all demand
a headstand:

Expression of an exuberant joy at being alive.

Detlev can do shoulder stand or polka.

Dances joy at being alive. Forgets that it's a stage and for
a rehearsal. He forgets thread-algae to camouflage the whole
world, dances his grade-one-mixed-race-liberation-dance

and it's so embarrassing, that they would all rather not look, but then do look, because it's so enormously embarrassing, the tumbling splayed out Detlev, his terrible joy at being alive bubbling up over the greasy pattern sheets.

It's got nothing to do with Johnny.

It says headstand in the text, because it's all supposed to appear so light and easy.

His mother takes Detlev to Lola Rogge's Dance School. There his body is rhythmically loosened up and two weeks before the premiere Detlev can go round in a circle expressively and call Abraham a Santa Clara — but he can't do an American headstand.

Detlev goes to Käthe Kahl's Gymnastics School.

There his stomach muscles were made stronger. The calves are relaxed. A headstand is built from the bottom up!

A week before the premiere Käthe Kahl has prepared everything and transmitted to Detlev a new awareness of his body as it were — but he can't do an American headstand.

Detlev is bound in, rinsed out, another head is stuck over his own head. His eyelids, his rainbow skin merge with the eyelids and the rainbow skin of the American boy.

The camouflage becomes frayed. Detlev stumbles over wires. Threads of glue hang into his mouth.

The dress rehearsals begin.

Detlev, a forgetful, rustling monster, drags himself through the whole play in costume and mask.

The property man is willing to hold Detlev's legs at the top, if only Detlev can get his legs up.

On Johnny's legs hang two bells from Our Ladies' Church in Scheyern, hang those who hanged themselves in the toilets of the labour exchange, oatmeal soup, chilblains, Creon's willy, grandad's axe, the seating plan of the High School for the Arts and a battered rib cage and photos of piles of children and two ladies' shoes with high heels.

These dress rehearsals are also only one attempt by Detlev among many — it could also be different; it could also no longer be an attempt — at killing as excitingly and originally as possible the time before complete destruction.

At the dress rehearsals when all the pieces of the piece are put together, the producer shouts at the overweight hero, the overweight hero shouts at the prompter, the prompter shouts at the lighting man, the lighting man shouts at the production assistant, the production assistant breaks down, the stage manageress cries, the stage hand gives notice, the director arrives with a bag of sugar.

Detlev begins to eat his way through the sticky algae. Detlev's head on the cushion and both arms in front of the cushion prop up Detlev's complicated legs — at stake is the attempt to play the leading role in the best theatre in Germany.

— How could we live without the extra money that I earn?

— I'm going to try it, even if I had to walk on my head for the whole play!

109

During Latin Detlev's satchel falls to the floor. Detlev drops down to the legs, the worn out shoes, tracksuit bottoms, trousers from uniforms, collects everything from his satchel together and shoves it back into the satchel.

He must keep up with Latin. He's been absent for a week again because of rehearsals. He must not fall behind, otherwise he'll get a 5 in Latin too and then he'll have to repeat.

— Then I'll kill myself.

The satchel falls down once more.

Detlev jumbles the mass of pages, books, paper covers, pencil box with little painted ducks, dry toast from among the legs of his classmates together again and stuffs it back into the satchel.

He must keep up with the Latin, otherwise Dr Storck will throw his spectacles case.

The satchel falls down again.

The next period Dr Prelle. Friendly fat Dr Prelle.

— Let me have men about me that are fat.

He had been in England once.

Detlev can't find his exercises.

— Let's both look for them, says Dr Prelle.

Detlev has to come to the front with the satchel and lay the jumbled mass on the front bench and Prelle reaches into Detlev's paper and cheerfully lifts a bundle up and lets it flutter down, past the faces of his classmates, down to the tracksuit bottoms and the wet feet.

6a laughs. Reports will be handed out soon. The class doesn't laugh very loudly at Dr Prelle's joke of letting the home-made exercise books fall from Detlev's satchel to the floor of the Arts Senior School, the still blank reverse sides of the folded field letters, the substitute paper, wood pulp paper, the home made sewn together exercise books. It takes approximately half a period and in the end Detlev has to collect everything together and stuff it into his satchel again. He's allowed to go to his seat, where Marion Böge, although she still loves him, doesn't dare look at him.

110

Before falling asleep Detlev designs useless machines, with ropes, electric bell systems, cogwheels and paddle wheels. The machines are not supposed to make anything work. Only to go, to buzz, to stretch and slacken again, to function. Pails rattle. Wheels spin.

Cranes swing round. It should all flash and flare up. Water streams.

Astonishing. Very small. No larger than the palm of the hand. Very graceful and mysterious.

Detlev would carve the mountings from the violet sandal-
wood of Uncle Emil's old cigar boxes.
Thread and silver wire.

111

Below sit the mayor, René Drommert from the *Free Press*,
the critics from the *Hamburg Echo*, from the *Hamburg
General News*, from the *People's Paper*.
After the final rehearsal of *My Heart's in the Highlands*
the director gave Detlev a sugar cube,
— Spaniels get big eyes with sugar cubes.
she was so pleased.
Curtain up!
Spotlight on!
America, the land of unlimited opportunity.
Johnny Sonnyboy sits in the sun.
Jump. Do cartwheels. Hupp! Happy! Joyous.
His hair with the verdigris from the *Trojan War* in the
dust of the stage, in front of the prompter, who would like
to prompt Detlev to a good headstand.
The arms push the body up. Johnny's arms, Detlev's legs.
A bubbling over headstand.
But now Detlev has to tremble for his father, in case he
suddenly forgets the part he's playing and begins to laugh
from the stress and the performance goes down the drain.
The overweight hero gets more and more bad-tempered,
he runs out of breath in front of the American Detlev, on
whom after four weeks of forgetfulness and half-hearted-
ness muscles of glue, dust, chalk, food ration coupons,
cane, cut out pattern sheets, flavouring and camouflage
water lilies grow under the premiere lights.
Johnny exits stage left with a plate of grapes. Now Detlev
runs round the outside, up, into the dressing room, where
the sex maniac kissed him on the shoulder, with the grapes,

out to the iron stairs, over the roof of the auditorium. He hears the voices of his father and of his Armenian grandmother and the soft gurgling from the hall, when the audience is amused, without laughing out loud.

Detlev is hungry and thirsty. He's shivering. Detlev is standing beside chimneys and fire escapes.

He puts a grape in his mouth. It's only an imitation grape made of old rolls, painted pale green. Detlev eats it hungrily anyway.

112

It was all as good as over.

Now Detlev doesn't know how to go on.

The father, the overweight hero, gives the cue.

Detlev sees his father slowly close his lips and push them open a little again, because he had breathed in too much air for the sentence.

Detlev sees the prompter below in the cellar, looking at him expectantly, as if he should be prompting her with the next sentence and not she him.

He sees the lighting man and the stage manageress and the Armenian grandmother, who is straightening her dress for her entrance.

The auditorium a black box with skulls.

113

I forget.

I.

Who I?

Detlev?

Johnny?

I see Detlev who's playing Johnny, standing on stage and the audience sees Johnny in front of his father, and if the right word doesn't come to Detlev, then Johnny has ceased to exist, without having died.

Ten, nine, eight, seven, six, five, four, three...

Detlev could turn to the public, as Hilde Krahl did in *The Skin of Our Teeth*; but then it was part of the play and everyone was enthusiastic, because it was modern; in *My Heart's in the Highlands* it would mean a scandal and the mayor would be very disappointed by the premiere and not a soul would give Detlev a part again. And what could they live on?

If I forget Detlev, I don't exist any more.

Ten, nine, eight, one, seven, six, one, two, five, four, three...

"Detlev stands apart from the others on the balcony. The orphanage children are waiting for Sister Silissa and Sister Appia to enter the dining room, look into the two deep soup pots, take two eggs, two white, two eggs out of the hidden pockets of their habits..."

Ten, nine, eight, seven, six, five, four, three, two..

— Forget, that you operated the gas oven in the camp, in order not to be gassed yourself.

— I have forgotten a proper S and lithp tho much.

— I have — ah — I hahahave... I have forgotten it — ah — I have forgotten the right word and say a wrong one instead.

Ten, nine, ah, eight, seven, six, five, bull, ten, egg, ah..

"Detlev stands twopart from the mothers on the ah. The ice men are waiting for Himalaya Time and Sister Appia to enter the didining room, that thieves, who cough into the chamber pots, take two weggs out of the hidden stop of the black habit..."

Detlev doesn't know, how he should desire the naked niece Suzanne.

Detlev doesn't know, that the unfathomable in Mr Gerstenberg is desirable to the naked niece Suzanne.

I have forgotten that Jeff is desirable.

I have forgotten to eat.

And starve.

— You wanted to forget that you operated the gas oven in the camp, in order not to be gassed yourself, and when after the liberation someone unknown drew a swastika on the window pane, you became — ah. .

I have forgotten, what Detlev forgot.

— mad, because you were afraid, to remember and you had to be locked in this time to be healed.

Ekthtinguish, Ekthtinguish. Ekthtinguish. Ekth. . Ekth. . ah. .

— You wanted to forget, that you operated the gath oven not after the liberation thwathtika on the window pa. .

Ekth. .

Ekthting. .

114

Everything continues once more.

The overweight hero did not crush me and carries me like dead from the stage.

His father has now shut his mouth and Detlev says what Johnny has to say.

The prompter down in her hole is in raptures, because she really never has to pass anything up to him.

I've forgotten what Detlev would have been within a hairs-breadth of forgetting.

My name comes first, before that of the father in the pro-gramme. Now I can die by chance.

Nothing. Imageless. Nameless. Unconscious.

I can never again be forgotten. Someone will know even for all eternity, that I played Johnny in *My Heart's in the Highlands*.

Applause.

Because Detlev plays the principal part, he's allowed to take a bow by himself. It's a success and that's why everyone's smiling.

Someone shouts:

— Bravo!

down from the balcony.

The first one to shout "Bravo!" always stands in the balcony and looks round very pleased with himself.

115

Afterwards there's the premiere dinner.

The director and dramaturg and the business director wait in the foyer until the actors have removed their makeup. The director is wearing a two tone turban. The latest thing. Green and black. Despite the shortages.

— How on earth do the overweight hero and the director manage to be relatively so extensive when there are so few calories around?

A large table has been laid in the studio theatre restaurant. A crystal glass and folded cloth serviettes for each person.

— Are the overweight hero and the director often invited to the character actor's home?

As she's sitting down the waiter pushes the chair into the back of mummy's knees.

The director makes a short, humorous speech which commands respect. She also mentions Johnny and raises a glass full of hot drink.

Then soup with garnish is served from the right.

Four largish eyes of fat and as garnish five little star shaped noodles.

The character actor's Swedish relatives send boxes of herrings and bloaters and smoked haddock rolls. Colleagues and friends and also important, lean personalities from the senate and other guests at the premiere count themselves lucky if they're invited to eat by the character actor; he offers piles of the vitamin-D rich fish, some Hamburg personalities can't help being sick, because their state of nutrition doesn't allow them to digest so much nourishment all at once and they disappear at intervals to the toilet. The others present, with the stronger stomach nerves, regret the uselessly squandered bloaters and smoked haddock rolls. Some have a fortunate natural constitution and can eat for a week ahead. And the character actor gives away bloaters with both hands.

The elegant artists and personalities in dyed and altered clothes, men and women of Hamburg, those who have returned and the denazified or those released from inner emigration have brought greaseproof paper with them and when the the character actor isn't looking or is far enough away, where he only sees everything as a blur because of his short sightedness, they all quickly grab bloaters and smoked haddock rolls and so on and wrap it all up in greaseproof paper and tuck it away in the evening bag from before the war or in the dinner suit that has now become too loose. It's not very refined and everyone avoids looking at the others doing it.

For the next course the director has served a delicate, thin slice of boiled fish and two pieces of potato and parsley.

The waiter takes position with the bottle behind the guests and pours in more hot drink.

As dessert a domino sized pudding with sauce made from the hot drink.

The character actor's guests don't want to take up any more of his time. They're afraid that the fat could soak through and make a mess of the gala wardrobe. They quickly take their leave. Smiling, the director fends Detlev off when his mother gives him a shove, as he is about to say thank you for the meat without coupons.

116

I'm too late again. I ran out of the rehearsal and still
hoped to catch the right no 22. But it was useless. I'm
the only one who gets out at Bornweg. Dr Noack as well,
who makes a lot of fuss when the pupils are late and writes
them down in the register. The school yard is empty.
Everyone can watch me from the classroom windows.
The concrete box is particularly lop-sided, when one
arrives late.
The noises from the classrooms sound like the scratching
of the supposedly dead against a coffin lid.
Pupils sprint out of the school hall in gym singlets.
The breathing, grunting spectacle case throwing, pooping,
admonishing, daft alsatians, gorillas, jelly fish, chimpanzees;
snot runs down onto their ties and when they talk white
threads stretch between upper lip and lower lip.
Goethe, Keller, Hesse, Brueghel, thanking, Europe, punish-
ment exercise.
Muli, who sings "At dusk, as it was cool" in the school
hall for hours.
In there now.
School trips. Class party. Gymnastics display. The school
ball. Co-education.
I would gladly see the concrete thing with all its occupants
struck by an atom bomb and disappear in a flash.
Dr Prelle!
One must not think that. Koch and Himmler are monsters.
We have nothing to do with that. As a matter of principle
not. I am being educated.
In there now!
But it's not that simple.
The janitor now punctually locks the door and only opens
it again a full quarter of an hour later.
Now I have to wait beside Dr Noack for a whole quarter

of an hour and on top of that Miss Vagt comes by and calls:
— Well, baby mammoth!

117

— But nevertheless with a touch of the routine and a self-consciousness, which should be grounds for the most careful guidance, writes René Drommert in the *Free Press* about Detlev.

118

The cleaning woman has connections and enters the director's office without knocking. She brings the sugar cubes, blubber, beef-suet and semolina.
For *The Post Office* and *The Skin of Our Teeth* Detlev gets five Reichsmarks per performance.
For *Peace* ten marks.
For the leading role in *My Heart's in the Highlands* the director doesn't want to give more than twenty marks per performance.
— The office staff have already complained, because a twelve-year-old boy is earning more than they are. Consider what small sums an office worker has to get by on these days. After all salaries are far below the pre-war level. You mustn't allow your boy to expect such star fees.
— But my son is on stage the whole time.
— It shouldn't be so special for him to appear on stage from time to time.
— I have tried everything to dissuade him. He would have come to you himself, if I hadn't spoken to you in the ladies' toilets when I did.
— Acting is in his blood!
— My son is acting here every evening. Twice on Wednes-

days, Saturdays and Sundays and on Sunday mornings a matinee as well.

Finally the director agrees to a lump sum agreement: Six months at 300 Reichsmarks a month.

— For 300 marks I can buy a pound of butter in Thalstrasse. He's a growing boy. How can I feed him properly?!

— But you can't go to Thalstrasse! You must cook the child some mash, says the director.

Mummy often repeats the sentence.

119

Anyone who has been successful is also allowed to perform on Northwest German Radio.

Older actors sit outside the casting office and wait for a part. Here Detlev meets Manfred again and Gerd, Gerd from *Frau Holle*, Manfred and Gerd from *The Post Office* by Rabindranath Tagore. They're wearing long trousers and want to look like grown up actors. Gerd's voice is breaking. He can only get a part occasionally.

— I'm about to go to Harburg for an engagement, he says.

— If I were in your place I wouldn't retire to the provinces, says Manfred. His voice hasn't broken yet — apart from that he's on good terms with Becker of Schools Radio.

— What are the provinces? Since Germany no longer has a capital, Düsseldorf is no less the provinces than Harburg.

— But Düsseldorf has Hoppe and Gründgens.

— In Harburg I shall probably play Hamlet.

— With you as thin as you are.

— The old story. It's a translation error and should be: He's sweating, and scant of breath.

— Were there really only ten curtain calls at the premiere of *My Heart's in the Highlands*?

— In the studio theatre they've never understood anything about raising the curtain.

— If no one's clapping any more, raising the curtain doesn't help either.

— I've taken on a small, but interesting commission: I'm playing the crippled boy in a Jesuit piece.

— Yes, that's fantastic! We need Jesuit plays! That's what the studio theatre has come to! In the best theatre in Germany a Jewess is putting on Jesuit plays!

— I'm withdrawing from the stage entirely. I think it's commercial to play the same part fifty times en suite. Today the important things are happening in radio. Ernst Schnabel, Günter Eich, Wolfgang Weyrauch, Schröder-Jahn. You mustn't forget, *The Man Outside* by Borchert was conceived as a radio play.

Manfred is to collect a Children's Radio manuscript from the casting office.

Gerd is allowed to audition for the waiter in *White Horse Inn*.

Detlev only quickly says — the moments are still not over — "Good afternoon" to Miss Trylow in the casting office.

120

Detlev continues to wear his mother's elegant high heeled shoes and because of that is afraid in the dark.

Lisa Bischoff was lured into an allotment by four boys from the Thorwart Gang.

— Come, the cat has had a litter! Do you want to see black, blind little cats?

In the hut the four of them held down Lisa Bischoff. She's twelve. The boys from the Thorwart Gang were maybe nine, ten. And tore off Lisa Bischoff's new shoes, which she had from the black market, in order to exchange them for cigarettes on the black market.

One of Detlev's high heeled shoes remains stuck in the mud in the schoolyard.

Jürgen Rühl doesn't very much feel like looking. It's already getting dark and Jürgen is beginning to feel cold.

The senior classes walk past and say:

— The baby mammoth has lost a shoe.

Miss Vagt has to catch the tram.

Muli calls with his melodious voice:

— At dusk, as it was cool!

Dr Prelle gives Detlev his frightful hand in encouragement. No one dares to tell Dr Noack anything. Everybody is pleased when he's passed by.

Dr Perlewitz is in a world of his own.

Dr Bahlmann makes exact inquiries. He would very much like to help; but anyone can see that with his hump shaped bones he really can't very well. Dr Bahlmann puts on a delicate smile.

Dr Timm almost gets stuck himself with his bicycle.

White threads form between Dr Gröger's upper and lower lip. His advice is to hurry home, because with the standing around they could all catch bronchitis, if not something even worse.

Lottchen Huger doesn't give up.

The whole of 6a is standing at the edge of the muddy puddle beside Detlev with his one muddy sock and admiring Lottchen Huger, who is systematically digging through the mush with a fence paling for Creon's pages, for Peace's, for baby mammoth's, Johnny's only second shoe.

— How would I get to rehearsals tomorrow? One shoe alone is worth 300 marks. A pound of butter. My monthly fee. But if she finds it, everyone will see that it's mummy's high heeled shoe.

Which Detlev has usually been able to hide in the schoolyard by thrusting his feet into the front or treading the shoes down on one side.

It's dark and Lottchen Huger is still raking around. Suddenly the mud squelches up and over the fence paling like a U-Boat that had been sunk lies Detlev's high heeled shoe.

Detlev sees clearly that Lottchen Huger has seen it's a lady's shoe, she quickly throws it over to Detlev, who can hurriedly tap off the dirt, and push it on and no one notices the high heel.

121

— I got in quite legitimately for six times the ticket price. I didn't even need to hand over your smoker's card, says Detlev, when his mother comes to collect him.

— On the black market the tickets for the guest performance cost 1,000 Reichsmarks, butter, beef-suet and bread coupons and carpets were offered.

If his mother had believed that he would get in with his pocket money — with or without smoker's card — she would perhaps have tried to put him off; it would have been pointless to forbid him.

— It's a beacon. It is the most important testimony of the French resistance. He is a philosopher and chose a classical setting, to deceive the German censors in Paris.

— Heinrich von Kleist chose an ancient German setting, to deceive the French censors

— Of course he is very influenced by Kierkegaard, Heidegger, Jaspers and Husserl.

Mummy looks at her son. Is it for this that she laid reproductions of Raphael and Leonardo da Vinci on his childhood bed? She realises that now he's going to begin to imitate the sentences of the educated, pronounce Kierkegaard wrongly like the educated, until no one can tell any more whether he himself has discovered the philosophers, to whom he refers and whom he hasn't read, or whether he only overhears their names from the educated, who haven't read them either.

— The leading actor wears a fluffy camel hair coat and the chauffeur has to push open every door in front of him

and close them behind him and the leading actor doesn't
even take his hands out of the big camel hair patch pockets.
But Mr Montag in the porter's lodge didn't want to let
him go past and called out: Excuse me, who are you, hallo?
— Isn't it unbelievable! The leading actor* fell into a rage
and smashed the glass pane in front of Mr Montag's nose
with the Knirps telescopic umbrella, which he carries hidden in the fluffy coat. Then he had his chauffeur drive him
back to his pension in the Colonnades and all the former
camp inmates and the professor of film in the Third Reich
and the overweight hero and the grandes dames pleaded
in front of his chaise longue for him to perform, because
after all the public had made such sacrifices for the tickets.
Eventually he gave in on condition that Mr Montag
was dismissed.
— And how was it then?
— On stage he's very young. There's something triumphant about him. Once he's begun, he doesn't let anyone
in again until the scene change. I had to stand outside the
door for the first act. But his triumphant voice carried as
far as the foyer.
— He was in an internment camp too like all the great
men of the Thousand Year Reich. Hamlet. In the mid
twenties. Large white hands on a black costume. Hamlet,
as he's tormenting his mother.
— But, mind you, if there were something I could do,
something to give me the freedom of the city; if even by
a crime I could acquire their memories, their hopes and
fears, and fill with these the void within me, yes, even if I
had to kill my own mother —
— What was the French resistance supposed to do with
the void within?
— Everyone stands and stares at the hole, out of which

* i.e. Gustaf Grüdgens (trans.)

the dead are supposed to come, in order to torment the living because of their sins. Orestes relieves the citizens of Argos of their remorse through his murder and their bad conscience. Freedom, mummy! The new age!

— And Ilse Koch?

— Orestes is tangled up in his destiny like a horse whose belly is ripped open and his legs are caught up in his guts. And now at every step he tears his innards.

Innards, says his mother. There was a torture among the ancient Germans. Who was it that wrote about innards? Did Thusnelda warm her feet in the innards of an aurochs? Horse slit open, winter campaigns, Ufa films, Christina Söderbaum warms her blonde feet in the blood.

— I went to put the city around me and wrap myself in it like a blanket.

— I want to put Mr Montag around me like a fluffy American camel hair coat. Detlev, don't forget where you come from!

— I am too light. I must take a burden on my shoulders, a load of guilt so heavy as to drag me down, right down, into the heavy ground of Argos.

— Heavy ground?

— Perhaps I've remembered it wrongly or it's the translation.

— Do you really think it comforts me, if you're constantly in raptures about matricide?

— Is it not meant perhaps in a symbolic way?

Detlev looks at his mother. Before, she used to take him to the theatre and fill him with enthusiasm and explained the meaning of the dramas to him. Now she has settled for the dusty hole and prompts the rest of the text, when an actor's memory fails. Detlev imagines that she only sees the footsoles now and the nostrils. Couldn't she at least have kept on playing walk on parts? On the same level as the big names and in the same light?

No lighting.

Hartungstrasse.

To right and left the mountains of rubble.

The hundreds of theatre visitors are marching along in a single black block. Everyone is whispering enthusiastically about the resistance in Berlin, about Albert Schweitzer and Heidegger.

A hundred yards further on someone is attacked.

Screams.

It's very unnatural and in the theatre no one would accept it. The many hundreds of theatre visitors march more and more slowly, finally they're almost stepping on the heels of the person in front and the very first, who don't have anyone in front, are almost walking on the spot and lean backwards a little as long as the screams last. During the moments of the attack several impressions are laid one on the other in Detlev's mind, scenes jostle one another, and he simultaneously thinks the beginnings of long chains of thoughts and their end. He can't taste anything. He doesn't become aware of smell and touch sensations either. The shivering only began later. In his ear the cries and steps becoming more and more cautious:

Electra pours American cocoa into the cup, Emmi Goering gave it to her for her birthday.

What kind of philosopher is that?

What kind of leading actor is that?

Who proclaims that we should kill our mothers without remorse.

The French philosopher flees from the camps of the Germans and crawls through the snowy undergrowth.

The French philosopher blows up bridges, shoots at the oppressors, without remorse. Does the French philosopher torture without remorse? The leading actor flees through parks past canals, Hermann Goering stands at the end of a long ditch and waits for him.

— I decide, says Hermann Goering and:

— You are under my protection. You protect!
A deed!
A deed, in the new age, which has begun to write and triumphantly to act.
Without remorse the French philosopher and the leading actor call up their dead.
Which ones appear there?
Which call to an act of violence did they not dispute without remorse?
Ilse Koch too wants to forget at the edge of the quicklime and without remorse with a heavy wicked deed around her neck again and again to the heavy ground of the people of Argos.
Ilse Koch and the French philosopher and the leading actor as giant embryos with shiny leather shoes tangled up in their umbilical cords, trampling out the innards of mothers in mixed marriages and wrapping themselves in them as in a blanket.
— He is a philosopher, I must take him at his word. He has experimented. Why should I kill my mother without remorse?
— Perhaps it's meant symbolically after all.
— Everyone was enthusiastic. Clapping. Stamping. Called out to the guest ensemble: Stay here! Stay here!
— He releases them. The audience has had mothers killed and profited from bombing and played cello beside the gas ovens. And he's saying to them: What I have done, I have done without remorse, in order to fill the void within me. And you should have done what you had to do without remorse and now forget everything, says mummy.
No one breaks away from the block of theatre visitors, runs forward, helps the man who has been attacked.
With the screams, both the scenes crowding into one another in Detlev and the sensation of very complicated thoughts spreading in different directions stop.
His mother turns round. She's afraid of the place where a

man has been attacked and walks against the faces of the premiere audience, towards Rothenbaumchaussee.

Here Detlev was allowed to join the Hitler Youth.

Detlev forgets the screams. He forgets the doubts that he felt. They sink away in the knowledge of having attended an important guest ensemble premiere with exceptional actors. All Hamburg was there. The very important perceptions of an existential philosopher were conveyed. He fought in the resistance against National Socialism, while the leading actor saved the life of many Jewish actors through his friendship with Hermann Goering.

At Dammtor they still get a 3 to Methfesselstrasse.

122

Wolli says that a girl gang crucified three girls against the back wall of the Star Club and Carla, wearing the Tyrolean hat, got into a fight in the Skandi with another transvestite at three o'clock in the morning; the latter's anus had been sewn up and he's running around with an artificial anus, plastic.

— A fight can be fatal for someone like that. But despite that, he or she, whichever you prefer, started a fight three times in one evening.

123

The crooked path is the worst of all.

— Don't go down it, Detlev, go up Kaiser Friedrichstrasse and then along Löwenstrasse.

— Then I'm a coward and then they'll come after me.

— But you're only twelve.

— Through murder I enter the abyss.

— But not through the murder, which is carried out on you.

— I don't condemn murder, so I cannot run away from it.

— Why do you have to go along the deserted crooked path at eleven o'clock at night, when not a soul is about any more and one can hardly see ten steps ahead.

— I don't want to make a detour.

— Now spring's coming. But that only makes everything much more terrible. In winter one can see through the bushes. It's easier to see if someone's standing there. Now the leaf buds hide the murderer.

— The victim is guilty, Franz Werfel said in the twenties, says mummy.

— The post box is the knife. His two legs. But that's only the muddy patch by the entrance to Violet Common.

— There crouches a barrel. A murderer.

The birds pursue Detlev. Detlev knows that it is a bird, but is frightened nevertheless.

— Don't run! Don't hide! Anyone can find you everywhere.

— If you hide, you won't ever dare to come out again and you'll have to remain sitting there till tomorrow morning and then granny will find you, when she goes to Remmel to fetch broth, and will cry.

— Don't run. He can run faster anyway. Walk very calmly and imagine what a murderer does. He cuts off your breast. He comes from behind with the cord and twists. Don't run faster! If you hear him behind you, turn round and talk to him.

— The blackbirds.

— This is a lamp post.

— If he comes from the front, force yourself to go right up to him. That confuses him. If someone walks towards the murderer, he's disconcerted.

— But if he's not disconcerted?

— He must be disconcerted.

— I don't want to kill mother.

— I would have to kill myself.

— He smashes the bones in the head.

— Don't walk faster.

— How are you going to convince him that he shouldn't kill you?

— I wouldn't be able to defend myself. I am convinced that a murderer should not be hanged.

— Löwenstrasse at last.

124

It's simpler in winter. There's no need to bother about the path by the little allotment houses from '68, because one can always see from a distance whether someone's still standing there.

Now the buds are coming out. So everything becomes obscured. It's too late. No one else is coming.

And suddenly at two o'clock at night one's standing in front of the violet Kielerstrasse Labour Exchange, where twenty-five years ago those of mixed race were allocated to the suicide squads. Turn round away from the labour exchange and back to the Alsenplatz hostel along the allotment gardens lane.

Still no one.

The Turks and Serbocroats are sleeping too.

No one anywhere, beside the barrel or at the little transformer station.

Now he's coming!

Go towards him.

Come a bit closer.

Suck at the cigarette. Red light on off on off on off.

Several.

— Going looking with your balls!

One smells of mattjes herring.

Why at night, when only god knows who's about and one can hardly see ten steps ahead, do you have to walk through the parks?

One smells of bone meal.

One has a tulip bulb for a sack.

One bleeds.

One goes mad as he comes. He utters very high pitched notes as it happens, almost like a child.

The crooked path is empty.

Run over there. There's one standing over there. That's the pole with the letter box.

There's one coming after all. Closer. Is it him, him, him at last? What kind of a man is he, the man alone, between the Alsenplatz tower block and the Kielerstrasse Labour Exchange.

The man is afraid and runs away zig zag.

Beside the little transformer station a foreign worker is taking his revenge and elegantly thrusting into someone's belly from behind. Who pays the foreign worker for it. Who leaves him elegantly standing there like a dead man. Don't run. You won't catch up with him any more.

Do you want to pay money for it too? on the crooked path by Kielerstrasse Labour Exchange at two o'clock at night?

Do you hear the cracking?

Now it's going to fall on top of you?

Noises, that's the end. Noisiness.

The heart breaks.

The one at the back there is only a bush. No one's standing over there any more either. You won't find one over there.

125

Back to the Provisioning Office again.

We're afraid in front of the Provisioning Office.

It's built of red bricks and was supposed to look cosy and homely and mark a new age, when it was built at the beginning of the Thousand Year Reich.

One goes to the Provisioning Office, when Hamburg has

been razed to the ground; then field grey ladies sit behind
the cosy entrance of brick colonnades and bull's eye glass
and dole out pea soup to us.

The Provisioning Office survives the carpets of bombs.

Brick is secure and the school pupils' records are stored in
the brick. One has to go to the Provisioning Office, if as a
half Jew one's not yet in the concentration camp and wants
to join the Hitler Youth; then Mrs Schürmann and Mrs
Lürs and Mr Lüders occupied the cosy brick building and
they received us snappily in leather, brown, with radiant
armbands; they're allowed to carry the torches to the East
before us.

Behind the homely Provisioning Office stand trucks and
cars ready for action.

Perhaps they won't let us out of the brick again and transport us to the edge of the newly ordered Europe onto
a slag heap?!

Today the new money is being handed out at the Provisioning Office. Hundreds of thin families stand in front
of the homely building.

We lean with weakness against the brick walls. A few have
brought folding chairs with them.

In Thalstrasse the Reichsmark is being offered on the
black market in washing baskets.

Now the Tommies are taking the plentiful Reichsmarks
away from us as well! Everyone is to have just 40 marks
to spend. Krupp and the people in the Ley House. All
national comrades are equal before the currency reform.

Not Krupp. Krupp is in gaol.

No one is allowed to own more than anyone else. It's
terrible. It's the end of individualism. But then what have
we got to lose?

— Will any theatre ever be allowed to pay me ten marks
for an evening again? Now we won't even be able to afford
what the food coupons could be redeemed for.

The heroes and the heroes' mothers and the blond lads and
lassies have suffered in the cold and damp, the muscle
families from the Aryan Reich.

In front of the brick, the thousand year monumental faces,
the Arno Brekers in the queue, the battle lips and the
Nordic ears — chilblains still in May and cracks and fissures
on the Führer types; the bags below the eyes beside the
denazified SS Life Guard noses.

126

It's crazy of course and typically mummy, but after the
disbursement she goes to the Siemersplatz restaurant and
treats us to a currency reform meal.

The waiter himself is quite astonished, but he is allowed to
serve the dishes without food ration cards. He still has the
scissors dangling from his apron and is already clicking
them, ready to cut the meat coupons and the cereal coupons
from the card. Astonished he drops them again and even
mummy — although she knows that today everyone is
equal in the German nation and that suddenly money is
worth something again — is astonished.

Detlev and his mother order ragout, noodles au gratin,
baked plums.

Crusty rolls, roast noodles. That's the taste of the new age!
Plentiful, filling, fatty — noodles au gratin!

Who would have thought, that there would be yet another
new age — with plentiful fat!

This enjoyment of the grilled and the sweet taste of the
swollen baked plums in the meat gravy!

The end and death from hunger draw further away from
Siemersplatz.

Slippery with fat it slides down behind Detlev's rib cage,
dented from the hunger years and the way he sits in
school, piles up in his stomach, makes his legs and his

arms firm, thrusts the dizzy feeling out of his head.

For a moment Detlev once again remembers the perception of Christmas tree and cripple leg, pink brick flour from the ruins and pink substitute flour made from hips, the smell of the corpses in the cripples' home — already softened by the egg dough and freshly melted ration coupon free suet.

127

The boxes made of shavings, ashtrays, postcards for the blind, the floating soaps, little hand carved dachshunds, the salted vegetables, celery salt, sham packages, rosehip flours, sweeteners, warming teas, hot drinks, field envelopes, baking powder, cigarette papers, ersatz coffees, dried egg powder, butter flavourings, maraschino flavourings, shopping nets, paper bags are exchanged overnight in shop windows for sides of bacon, pots, irons, school exercise books, rum, wood free paper, Antoine de Saint-Exupéry, summer coats, hats, shoes, handbags, briefcases, wool, mulpa couches, Rilke, fold up beds, three piece suites, Wolfgang Borchert's Collected Works on India paper, crêpe soles, pears, copper wire, cereal, Raphael, underwear, cauliflowers, an extra allowance of raisins, brandy, leather goods, kidney shaped tables. The sales staff stand in the doorway and smile invitingly at the heads of families, who have already squandered far too much of the new money.

128

Wolli is expecting customers from the Ruhr; perhaps the Persians are coming too.

The door man at the "Yoshilambodu" lets him know, that the murderer still hasn't put in an appearance yet.

Jäcki considers whether he should run up to the hot room again, the witness room.

— Should I not do something, that I want to do, only

because by chance I could be shot down as a witness?
And goes up.

Wolli is attending to the snakes beside the plush settee, to
the bushmaster with the handbag pattern, and to the anaconda, which has already bruised three striptease dancers.
Wolli erects the 8 mm film screen and looks the films
out of the hiding place:

School of Lesbos.

The Strict Tenant.

Wolli's art collection hangs between television and rubber
tree plant. The big men of St Pauli collect with their big
money Oelze, Max Ernst, Käthe Kollwitz, in order to
invest their money safely.

Wolli has an original idea. He would like Salvador Dali,
Paul Wunderlich, Magritte, Picasso, Bernard Buffet,
Generalizc to paint a portrait of his brown straight willy,
as well as Gold Hamster's dyed cunt. But the brothel isn't
making that much yet.

The doorbell rings.

Wolli receives the couple from the Ruhr with his submachine gun.

He winds *The Strict Tenant* onto a reel. Jäcki briefly looks
at the home movie screen again. He already knows *The
Strict Tenant*. Nothing is more boring than watching
the same moving randy pictures a second time. It's like
watching a documentary about athlete's foot.

He goes into the library with Wolli.

Wolli:

— I detest violence. I refuse to exercise even the least force
on my surroundings. You will never see me in a fight.

Jäcki:

— I rely more on the muscles in my legs too. Awareness
of one's own weakness is really the only security in St
Pauli. I don't need to concentrate on the endless possibilities of brutality, but only on the very small margin
of non-violence.

Wolli:

— I am ready to help everyone. I give every beggar two marks. I allowed a susie — a tenant — to live for nothing for two months in the hostel I lease and fed her on top of that. When I look in the mirror, god should look back at me, the pure, Jesus. Every Friday I go to the Altona Steam Baths and lay myself down for the old and the injured. They can get up to whatever they like with me, discharge themselves over me. Only when someone younger, more pleasant comes, do I withdraw. He's still got a chance with others. With me the dead beats should have Christmas for once too.

Jäcki:

— You're receiving every visitor today with a submachine gun.

— The film is over, calls the married couple from the Ruhr. Wolli winds *School of Love* onto a reel for them.

— Shall I turn up the heating?

— No, it's fine as it is, replies the married couple, who have undressed.

The man's stomach folds into three white Mercedes tyres, underneath a very stiff, crooked, red piston.

The woman's tits, smooth giant breasts with blue veins, swollen from the effort of hanging.

— The thighs form bubbles of fat.

Figures from *Simplizissimus* — living — even the fat and the ureter are wanked up antiquities from the twenties. Simplizissimus, the lean baroque youth, has to lend his name to all postwar bacon.

Wolli undresses in the library:

— They're expecting me under the projector. Oh, I'm mixed up in a nasty business, which I don't want to talk about. But if I don't immediately shoot his hand to pieces on the door handle, the guy who's supposed to blow me away for two air tickets and 500 marks, then I'm a sieve. I

am a god. Am I supposed to put my own and Gold
Hamster's future at risk, so that a hired killer can pocket
his bonus? What has Christina been working for all these
years? Look, anyone who annoys you in a bar, you talk to
him patiently for a long time. But perhaps he insists and
before he ruins you, you knock him down and when he's
down, you can't let him get up again and you give him a
proper kick in the gob, something he'll remember so that
he doesn't annoy you again.

The doorbell rings.

Wolli says to Jäcki:

— Read Trotsky, Bakunin, Trakl or the Encyclopedia of
Bullfighting. But put each book back in its place.

Wolli receives the business delegation from Persia with
erection, submachine gun, hair back combed, naked and
wearing makeup.

The members of the business delegation have come to be
voyeurs for 200 marks. Wolli wants friends to earn the
money and phones a beginner from Vienna to come up,
and the doorman from across the road. When it's all supposed to get going, the business delegation feels embarrassed
in front of the interpreter, Wolli feels embarrassed in front
of his card partner and plays uneasily with the submachine
gun, the girl from Vienna has never done it before and the
doorman says to Jäcki:

— I'm so embarrassed, because I've got a somewhat un-
usually long sack.

The bell rings.

Everyone heaves a sigh of relief.

Wolli forgets the submachine gun.

Shots, shouts, barking.

The married couple from the Ruhr imagine it's part of the
entertainment and are greatly amused.

Four policemen, followed by five German shepherd dogs,
lead Wolli in.

Two policemen go into the kitchen and divide the butter in
four. The nude photos are removed from the potatoes.
The gay series fall out from behind the Mao bible. Fuck
pictures flutter out of the de luxe edition of Don Quixote
with illustrations by Gustave Doré. Inside the card holder
of the student's edition of the works of Bertolt Brecht lies
half a kilo of hashish from Afghanistan.

So the German shepherd dog trained for hashish seizes the
half kilo from Afghanistan.

The other German shepherd dogs trained for hashish chase
him away from it again, the half kilo from Afghanistan.

Quick as a flash the policemen undress and try to restore a
degree of order again with "Heel!" and "Couchez!" "Ajax!"
Wolli lets the bushmaster snake out of the terrarium; the
members of the Persian business delegation also undress
quick as a flash and jump on top of the sofa. A German
shepherd dog eats the bushmaster snake, which eats its
way through him and peeps out by his bushy testicles.

Wolli has put *Punishment in the Pine Grove* on a reel and
the silent, grey, regularly moving sex organs of the short
film, the faces turning questioningly to the cameraman, the
colourless clitorises moved into the right light and the grey
rods squirting in the wrong direction at the wrong moment
slide over the black brown animal coats, red, shiny penis
tips, scabby ankles, tanned clefts and loose cheeks.

The next German shepherd dog gulps down the bushmaster
snake, which is protruding further and further and eats its
way through him too.

The German shepherd dogs now form the pyramid of the
police sports display tournament, while the bushmaster
snake threads one after the other.

Jäcki walks past the harbour hospital. The fog drifts upwards. The art nouveau jetties have already been almost
sucked in. The bushes disappear, also the railings and the

barbed wire along the embankments; Jäcki's shoes begin to
grow indistinct to Jäcki's eyes. In the fog Jäcki comes upon
three men. Each is standing several yards apart from the
others. They form, from each of their standpoints, a triangle.
They're settling up. They walk on a little. Jäcki has disturbed them. Perhaps it's something exciting!

One of them raises his hand. Jäcki recognises something
twinkling above the thumb, that's pointing at him.

What's going to happen now?

— Is it not more important to observe what's going to
happen now, than to go on living without the complete
observation?

Before the man performs a further movement with one of
his fingers, Jäcki jumps back into the fog, and the other
doesn't shoot at random, because he must be afraid of
unnecessarily drawing the attention of the watchmen in the
harbour hospital to himself.

Jäcki laughs:

— I escape from Wolli's, the hottest apartment on the whole
Freiheit and am almost shot down at a queens' rendezvous
in the twilight by an arms smuggler running amok.

Wolli is sitting alone on the plush sofa.

Reimar Renaissanceprince brings Gold Hamster back. First
she had necked around with Reimar as if to make love, but
then she got annoyed about the waste of time and went to
the Palais d'Amour to find customers. Was she annoyed by
the waste of time?

She understood:

The prince, over there, won't drag me out of here and so
in that time and with the same amount of effort I'd rather
earn some money.

Gold Hamster sits down beside Wolli on the settee.

Reimar Renaissanceprince stands in front of the table.

Jäcki sits in the plush easy chair.

Jäcki observes, how Reimar looks at Christina who is red from the cold, how Reimar notices her shivering, her silence, her patent leather bag with the money she's earned, which she, like a child, Reimar Renaissanceprince might think, pulls along on her hand and then puts on the table, how Reimar, who lets Wolli give him the money for the cheap hotel to spend tender hours with Wolli's woman and go for an expensive meal with her, how Reimar would like, but yet doesn't dare in front of Wolli — to lick Gold Hamster warm!

— Did you make a lot, says Wolli.

— It was ok, says Christina.

— I've earned a lot too, says Wolli. Four films sold, six hundred marks, two coloured originals, that's six hundred marks. Six customers, that's about another three hundred marks on top. Agent's commission, passing on stuff — if I subtract what I owe the porter and the drinks, then I've brought in two big ones, that is, two thousand.

— I earned four hundred marks, says Gold Hamster.

— We've just got to hold on until November, then we can expect two hundred big ones to be in our account in Switzerland. Then in the New Year you don't need to work any more. We shall purchase a villa on Tenerife or a farm house in Lower Saxony with lake and forest or a small chalet and spend our days walking out into the stillness of the woods and observing the structures which the water leaves behind in the sand. Then I won't set foot in St Pauli again. All I'll buy apart from that is a late night bar, which I'll lease to someone else right away, I'll let the lawyer collect the money from it and from the girls' hostel and live only for literature and painting.

Jäcki sees that Reimar Renaissanceprince notices, Gold Hamster expects, Wolli to put his arm around her, to be caressed, to have her ear bitten, to be licked, to be beaten. Jäcki and Reimar Renaissanceprince smile at one another.

— So we meet again. You've got a minor working for you in Berlin and I'm still bi and still living with Irma.

Reimar Renaissanceprince's smile broadens. He has four lips.

— The smile — some kind of submissive gesture of the orangutan — baring teeth. A white barrier in the face. Look, my teeth. I do not want to bite you. And now we strenuously use it at every opportunity, just as at every opportunity we use the expression: It has to be fun too. Top managers smile themselves crooked before the fatal board of directors meeting.

— He loves me you know, Wolli, says Reimar Renaissanceprince. He smiled at me for weeks and didn't dare to make me. That was still before my marriage.

— Loved you? What does that mean? says Wolli. Wanted to clean you out, profit from you, as Gold Hamster profits from you, for her sexual satisfaction, because she fancies showing you off as lover man around the district, profit, as I profit from Gold Hamster's body. And when she doesn't fancy you any more, that is can no longer profit from you, then she drops you and goes only with me again. You've got a larger penis than me, but à la longue a woman profits more from the shape of mine; apart from that I lick better than you.

— Don't I know what kind of cock Reimar has! says Jäcki.

— With whom, Christina, is it more complete fun? says Wolli.

— With you, says Gold Hamster impassively.

— On the day before my marriage, Jäcki and I considered whether we should live together. Because of me Jäcki would have left his woman, the best woman in the world, says Reimar Renaissanceprince.

— Do you believe, you love your Jeff? When you've got bored with his black prong, and how soon will that be, you'll love a white or red one, says Wolli.

— Then when my wife began to kill herself all the time, Jäcki spoke forcefully to her and said, that's repression, says Reimar Renaissanceprince.

— I had said *Erpressung* — blackmail — says Jäcki.

— Yes, you gave her a good talking to. And I thought that was so great and the act of a real friend. And it even had a very good effect. She stopped her suicide attempts for a while then. That was about the time that I brought Jäcki up here to you, Wolli, says Reimar Renaissanceprince.

— Now your Jeff is the most degenerate bum and whore. You love him. He has a way of turning his hips to penetrate you, that it makes your brain jump; and I tell you there's nothing more despicable in the world than a male prostitute and among male prostitutes nothing more despicable than a male prostitute who loves. Isn't that so, my little Gold Hamster, the worst tarts kiss! To take payment for a kiss! Every male prostitute lies, every male prostitute steals, every male prostitute murders; now she sits there and doesn't say a word, as if we would punish you, if you speak! Squeeze them out, you have to squeeze people out, as long as there's juice in them and then drop them. Don't tell me, you're more noble-minded. You too will only come up here, as long as you find something about me that you can profit from, says Wolli.

— But if you find the male prostitute so contemptible, then you must also find contemptible the customer, who makes the prostitute into a prostitute. Just as the prostitute runs around, for a whole afternoon, to find a customer, the customer runs around for days, to find a prostitute. The customer gives the same sum as the prostitute takes. They love each other for the same amount. The customer is only a prostitute with a minus sign, mathematically put, says Jäcki.

— Do you despise the susies just as you do the male

— A female prostitute is different. Most of the male prostitutes are normal, says Wolli.

— Normal, Wolli! Are you normal? Am I normal? Is Reimar normal? says Jäcki.

— Homosexuality is not normal, says Wolli.

— You're crazy, says Jäcki.

— The male prostitute does not only pretend to carry out a love act with someone, whom he doesn't love, like the tart, but he does something altogether abnormal with a man, that he would do with no other man without a profit, says Wolli.

— Reimar, are you normal? says Jäcki.

Reimar smiles again! Jäcki leans over his back and reaches a hand into each of Reimar Renaissanceprince's pockets.

— The worst are the customers, when they look at you from top to bottom. You have to put on high heeled shoes, because they expect that from a tart. They put their hands down your jumper in the contact yard and ask: For twenty marks — and is that nude? — Then upstairs on top of that they want it without a rubber. They lick you all over your face and say: Oh, how beautiful you are. Oh, how good it is! And in the end you have to fuck them in the arse with the rubber prick.

— Reimar, are you normal, says Jäcki, and feels the Renaissanceprince's cock grow thick again.

— I never offered you money for it. I treated you. I helped you out. I didn't have anything myself. I was a bum like Reimar. What I gave him, was never as much as the rate.

— How we tremble and struggle, run back and forward, redden with shame and want to choke on the sentence: Yes, I am a customer, says Wolli.

— Go on, put on a performance, says Gold Hamster.

— Would you let Jäcki have you? says Wolli.

prostitutes, says Gold Hamster.

— Everything, if I'm drunk and he pulls enough out for it, says Reimar Renaissanceprince.

— But Jäcki is your friend! Jäcki was the only one who wrote to you in prison. Jäcki entrusted his woman to you, the day before you were arrested. Jäcki advised you. With a friend I would do everything. Just the fact that he's aroused, arouses me. With a friend you have to do everything! says Wolli.

— For money I'll do everything. For money I'll even give somebody a blow job. And even a French kiss, says Reimar Renaissanceprice.

— Me too. For money I'll do everything. For money I'd let myself be covered in shit and for a lot of money I'll let myself be tattooed on the forehead afterwards: I was covered in shit! — Or have my arm chopped off. — But you can't take payment from a friend for giving yourself, says Wolli.

— Perhaps a male prostitute really is the most despicable thing in the world. Presumably I could have done nothing worse to Reimar Renaissanceprince than to help him out, and feed him and send him cigarettes in prison, give him money, which otherwise I wouldn't have done, and so forcing him, talking him into, doing something abnormal.

— I mean doing something with me, which he would not voluntarily have done with me, the most important thing, which he would never have with me — yes with me. He'll never forget that. I am a customer.

129

A tasteful, elegant, beige alpaca waistcoat is displayed at Prange's. Detlev would like to have it.

He already sees himself wearing it at premieres — although premieres are not what they used to be, before the currency reform; usually there are even still tickets for the night at the booking office.

He sees himself wearing the alpaca waistcoat at gallery openings — the painters and sculptors too are complaining that they can't bring in enough of the hard currency. The "Gallery of Youth" has got problems and will perhaps have to close.

Detlev cannot understand how he could have paid so little attention to waistcoats before.

Because a waistcoat is the main thing.

But he and mummy didn't have the money for it.

Apart from that it would have been far too big for him.

— And thirdly, what are you going to do with a waistcoat? A waistcoat is worn under a jacket, then at most a thin strip of the beige alpaca wool peeps out. Do you have a jacket? A waistcoat alone is nothing.

Cord velvet is becoming modern now and available in every colour at Horn's.

130

— I'm growing older. Soon I'm going to change the type of role I play. I can't be so choosy any more. I also have to accept roles that don't fulfil me artistically. People are buying themselves frying pans and not going to *Iphigenia* any more. I can still make a mark or two with dubbing, although fundamentally I'm against allowing my talent to be exploited in purely mechanical and technical activities. You have to imagine it like this: The English film is cut into small pieces by Eagle Lion and they're run in front of your nose again and again. You speak along with the silent lip movements of James Mason and Stewart Granger until it matches. It's nerve-wracking. But it's sensationally well paid — if you have a name. Nevertheless it's also true that completely unknown and moderately talented actors are pure geniuses at dubbing and can demand the top fees because they always finish the job very quickly. The most embarrassing thing is that you have to negotiate the fee with the director. — Now tell me, what were you thinking, he'll say to you. After that the course of the negotiations can take various and very different forms. If you mention a figure and say too little, he's onto a good thing. Not him, but Eagle Lion, because he's only an employee too, but he's made some extra he doesn't need to declare, because he's saved money. If you say too much, he can say: — But that's completely out of the question. And you feel ashamed and then he can really squeeze you, because otherwise he can give preference to someone else the next time. If you let him start, you keep the upper hand. He makes himself vulnerable, by naming the first figure. Now you can say: — But that's completely out of the question! Apart from that you've found out approximately how large his budget is. Of course — whoever has the dough, also has the power and at most you can prevent the director screwing you by another hundred marks. You won't force him up to four thousand, if he's intending to pay a hundred and fifty. But remember this: Never name the first figure in negotiations. He has to expose himself. And even if it takes half an hour: Never be first to name a figure! You really just are a proper half semite, said Jürgen Rühl.

131

After the currency reform the Dr Ross Children's Home, Westerland on Sylt, offers quite different board from the holiday home of the Bismarck Upper School during the hunger years.
Dieter Brinckmann, Marion Böge, Jürgen Kühl, Helga Fuchs, Uwe Lütkens, Ove Müller-Neff, Gert Harbeck, who had several bottles of face lotion with him, Eberhard Draheim waited outside the kitchen, to catch the increasingly strong smell of food.
The food was appropriate to the circumstances.

Detlev even got used to buttermilk soup.

Between meal times he picked cranberries with Eberhard Draheim. But they didn't give them a sense of intoxication nor did they provide that feeling of being full up.

By letter Detlev begged mummy for coupons for 300 gm of bread.

Mummy herself only weighed five and a half stone.

Dr Schneider spoke about china clay and terminal moraines. His prewar suit had also become too loose. For pedagogic reasons he could not allow himself to show signs of the stimulating effect of the sea air.

He made sure that the swimming regulations were strictly adhered to, because of the undermining influence in the stimulating climate.

The Dr Ross Children's Home is famous for the increases in weight achieved over seven week periods.

132

We eat raisin soup. Every third day there's raisin soup.

— Yet another new age!

And sandwiches.

We are curing the damage done by the postwar years.

The elite soldiers with the fat arses did everything possible to make us lose weight, and now, because we have a new currency, Aunty Karin and Aunty Inge and Aunty Katja are doing everything possible, so that we get fat arses.

We rest in the afternoon.

Under medical supervision we enter the healthy water of the North Sea.

We put on weight.

— Eat, children! There really is plenty!

Raisin soup. Bread and raisins. Sandwiches.

The first plateful is thin. Reddish soaked bread and a couple of raisins.

Put on weight!

A liver sausage sandwich.

We run to Aunty Inge at the pot.

— Don't be in such a hurry!

The second plateful is thicker.

— Don't be as impatient as in the Jews' School!

We eat a second sandwich.

— Lord, you act as if you were starving to death!

The third plateful is like the second plateful.

There are still sandwiches left too. Liver sausage spread thin for children's homes.

We eat the fifth and sixth platefuls.

— The little ones and those who don't want any more are allowed to leave the table now.

Some of the big ones are still eating.

Plateful of raisin soup, sandwiches.

The raisin soup is thick now.

Raisins are heavier than soaked bread and sink to the bottom of the pot.

Whichever one of us just manages to hold on long enough, gets them all at the bottom. All the fat raisins. Ladle full. Plate full.

Ten plates full of raisin soup.

After that we eat the last three slices of bread.

— It's been hard for you for years.

We want to put on weight!

133

Aunty Karin is cross-eyed.

Detlev loves Aunty Karin.

Because he's an actor, Aunty Katja allows him to go to see *Marriage in the Shadows* with Aunty Karin.

Cinema is shadows of varying darkness.

It is a long time ago that the couple had to kill themselves.

She was a Jewess.

— Five years age I was living in the orphanage.

Ilse Steppat and Paul Klinger perform movingly and with dignity the fate of a mixed marriage in the Third Reich.

Detlev feels how melancholy, a longing for Scheyern is released in him, quite illogically, after the repression in the orphanage, after Mater Cecilia and the gauleiter's corpse, after the SS uniforms, at the sight of which mummy began to cry. Serious, sensitive people, who walk through the stricken city. The leading actors are surrounded by unobtrusive elegance and, before their tragic fate overtakes them, spend a couple of days with friends in a tastefully furnished house by the sea. The audience in Westerland/Sylt leaves the cinema silently. Impressively blond Friesian men and women. Rather dead than slave. Right beside the North Sea. Blond as himself and Aunty Karin. Upset by *Marriage in the Shadows. Shadows. Shadows. Shadows.*

Some Friesian women wept.

The cross-eyed kindergarten teacher hugs him and Detlev wonders, before he's touched again, whether she's doing it to get rid of something or because she likes him.

134

Bernhard Waitzmann wheezes as he falls asleep.

Some boys creep into the girls' dormitory at night and play ghosts.

Walter Dirks lies down beside Harriet Moll.

Wolfgang Brettschneider climbs out of the window and hides in the little wood of the children's home, to smoke.

Detlev dreams about his watercolours with the Jews. He dreams that he has painted violet and orange next to one another, although they don't go together. He dreams, that his mother has died and SS men in silver vestments are standing at the graveside and weeping. It gets darker and Detlev finds himself in his mother's coffin and knocks, in order to get out. Knocks. The gauleiter ordered him to be executed on the Scheyern market place and as his last wish Detlev had wanted to have a boiled egg and had eaten it with a chipped zinc spoon. Detlev hasn't noticed that he has woken up.

The convalescent boys sleep in rows in their white beds.

In the next one Harald Wohlers knocks, knocks.

Detlev recognises the white wall of the dormitory and recognises in the white bed the somewhat less white, darkened by the sun body of Harald Wohlers. He sees how the whole body moves while knocking.

Detlev hears Fat Jürs' voice:

— Are you ready?

Harald Wohlers' voice:

— Yes.

Fat Jürs' voice:

— Then stick it in!

Harald Wohlers' voice:

— I can't do it. You're making it so tight.

Fat Jürs' voice.

— Is it more slippery now?

Harald Wohlers' voice:

— Yes. I'm in now.

Fat Jürs' voice:

— I can feel it now too. But I feel as though I've got to shit.

Harald Wohlers' voice:

— You have to move back and forward with me. Then I'll squirt the cream out more quickly.

Detlev recognises, very small under Harald Wohlers' ribcage, Fat Jürs' head.

— Now the cream is already tickling at the tip, Detlev hears Harald Wohlers' voice.

— The grocer took my friend's willy in his mouth.

I wouldn't do something like that.

The verse about Goethe goes round Detlev's head again.
Detlev says:
— Fatty, what are you doing in Harald's bed then?
— Catching flies, isn't that nice?
So he's homosexual and doesn't even feel ashamed as he
should do. Detlev feels his own prick become hard and
thick and the blanket stands up a little because of it — as it
did once before, when there was no war yet, before they
had travelled to Upper Bavaria, eight years ago.
Detlev imagines, Harald and Fatty come and tie him down
and touch his little pipe indecently, put it in their mouths,
bite a bit off, put it up their backsides.
— If Fatty and Harald would at least only stick their poles
into my behind. That's not so bad. I don't do anything and
don't move back and forward. It's superior force.
Detlev repeats softly:
— You must go down! You must go down!
Because that would be just too embarrassing, if Aunty
Karin and Aunty Rosemarie came and switched on the
light and Detlev's doodle was sticking up and Fat Jürs was
just about to stuff it into his behind.
— Then mummy would rightly put me into a reformatory
   if I wasn't just sent to a concentration camp.
Gradually it does become thinner and flexible again. But
Detlev doesn't trust Harald and Fatty any more. Detlev
puts himself to the test. He thinks about female figures by
Ernst Barlach and about Helga Fuchs' tits and about the
English elite soldiers, into whose white flesh under their
trousers Harald and Fatty want to shove their willies.
And Detlev forces his cigar to stay small and flexible.

135

A new batch of convalescent boys arrives.
Aunty Karin now prefers Günther Jäger, because he's

more of a leadership personality than Detlev.

In the report for the Public Health Office Aunty Karin writes:

— Detlev is a typical only child.

— That's not true. Don't leave it like that. Rub it out again. Write anything you like. But don't write "Typical only child".

— You don't need to be so disappointed about that! What's so important about it. Typical only child. I always write that, if I can't think of anything else. No one else has ever got upset about it before. Only you. There you go: You really just are a typical only child!

136

Wed. 21.7.48

Dear Heart!

I at last received your long awaited letter the day before yesterday! Your sweet postcard came the next morning as well. I was very pleased about both and thank you affectionately. The writing was good, punctuation bad. I did not care for the cinema story. You should be a child and play and sleep at night, instead of burdening yourself with marriage-in-the-shadows problems! Once is enough. But no repetition please. It was very nice of kind Aunty Karin to entrust you with a magnificent aquamarine ring.

Yesterday evening, tonight in fact — I've just come from Eidelstedt — I prompted at *The Baron Plays a Joke*. I enjoy it. I wouldn't like to be always getting musical plays or operettas. I think too, I'll get the classics next.

I now have rehearsals for *Head in a Sling* — a thriller and social problem play. Very interesting. With the boss and Kilburger. The director is Meyer-Oltens, who is also acting. I know him to look at from when I was in my teens. He's from Eimsbüttel and always used to run around the streets of Hamburg in a big cape and bareheaded with long blond hair. We always called him the lion man. Altogether I've been, touch wood, very happy in my work until now.

Saturday morning we had a staff meeting in Harburg again. I got up at quarter past six. Have to reckon on two hours by tram. At the meeting we were finally told that wages will have to be cut. Either cuts or closure.

Against that it was objected that, if the civil servants and local authority employees were getting their salaries, in fact on the contrary could expect a rise of 15 per cent, our wages should be conceded.

They kept saying: There's no money there!

The takings in Harburg are supposed to be very poor. On Tuesday, on the day of the premiere of *The Baron Plays a Joke*, not a single ticket had been sold yet for Thursday and Friday.

My pay will probably be cut by 15 per cent(!). That is 225 DM gross. A very distressing amount. Every possibility of buying something occasionally is gone. The idea of furnishing the room nicely is not to be realised.

Besides, the Thalia Theatre has also made an appeal to its staff.

On Friday evening I went to the Youth Stage and saw *Etienne or How Do I Bring Up My Father* with Hardy Kruger. It was very good.

I cannot even think of moving house at all now, since one doesn't even know if the theatre will still exist next year. Our operetta, which, in the prompter's opinion, is supposed to have a very good reputation, is going to make a guest appearance in the New Theatre, Curschmannstrasse, with *Three Old Maids*. Since it is running simultaneously with *The Baron Plays a Joke*, that's with Rönneburg also, with *Scampolo* three performances a day, I will probably keep *The Baron Plays a Joke* for the moment.

One day at the boss's invitation back to Hamburg in the truck with some others.

On Wednesday I went to Harburg on the steamer with Mr

Stillhofer. Stillhofer, who suffers from boils at the moment, on his posterior into the bargain, is a man who takes an interest in serious problems. We had a wonderful conversation. About art and artists, even about Dr Steiner.

Did I already write to you: Mrs Mischke has become an agent for a laundry? Early on Thursday I took my curtains and mangle washing — not washing to be dried — there. Apart from that I bought the plates you liked with the blue border in Epa. And I brought the old ones back to granny. A new soup ladle as well, the old one back likewise and three chrome plated soup spoons. I shall return the aluminium pot to her too, as soon as I've bought a set of three that fit into one another (shortage of space!). I've got a new mop with handle too. The blinds have been put up by Mr Krommes. I have the brown and coloured hat at last. I must have a good pair of shoes too. Then the only thing missing will be a pair of really elegant stockings.

When I saw your little blond head disappearing as the train went round the bend, I walked along the platform and took the elevated railway to Dammtor. On the way I realised that I needed 40 pfennigs, i.e. 4 marks in ten days for fares. From Dammtor till I ate at Möller and Weseloh's I looked at shops from 9.30 till 12 o'clock, until I was quite dizzy. Discovered beautiful things once again. I took my ring to be repaired. Costs about 4 marks and will be finished by the first of the eighth. Good, isn't it? I asked how much an amber ring was, about the same as the others. No cheaper. A majolica stove costs 155 marks with 2 marks for delivery. A bed-settee costs from 350 marks, depending on the number of rolls.

After the meal at Möller and Weseloh's I was as shattered as I can ever remember being, it was probably the thunderstorm. Always think of your mummy, then I can sleep better. A big kiss to you from your mummy!

You'll remember, won't you: Head up! Dentist tomorrow. Bye!

137

Granny lies beside grandad under the ground and has
become a matter of winter planting and summer finery.
The pointed grey detached house — thirty years parents
with daughter with illegitimate child, half foreign child —
has been sold. Mummy, who is going on for seventy,
moves near the High School for the Fine Arts, her State
Art School of half a century earlier.

Mummy:

Medea.

Clytemnestra.

Jocasta.

Antigone.

Lady in waiting to Queen Anne.

Widow with rectal syringe.

The Sleeping Beauty's spinning lady.

Dust woman under the stage floor.

One room flat with window box.

At the intersection the cars rev up recklessly.

Irma and Jäcki visit mummy.

The Persian lamb with the mink collar is hanging in
the hall.

This is how one makes oneself at home after fifty years
beginning a new age, Modern German Dance, Goetheanum,
beeswax crayons, Gustaf Gründgens as Hamlet.

Mummy has laid out a pearl necklace for Irma and for
Jäcki, a couple of books from before the currency reform,
yellowed ration cards and mail order catalogue socks.

— Although she isn't loaded despite the inheritance.
She should take a holiday or go to the opera and not buy
any socks.

— Mummy asks, whether Rosenthal have delivered the
Mexican candlestick yet.

— Has it arrived in one piece?

Jäcki has brought his mother wild roses. She puts them in
the beaten copper vase from Sweden. Irma has brought

her a couple of photographs. Paris. Rome. London.
Mummy doesn't know what she should do first.
Coffee.
— Here's cream.
— I'm sure you'd like a piece of apple tart.
— Yes. The piece with the currants.
— Raisins.
— Currants. Raisins. What does it matter.
It annoys Jäcki, that his mother said "raisins" again and
that he had to repeat "currants".
Mummy pours more coffee and lets them know that this is
filter coffee. Then she describes exotic sexual performances.
There was a theatre in New York, in which the sexual act
was performed openly on stage.
Since Jäcki says nothing, she says:
— It should all be swept away once and for all with an
iron broom!
And Jäcki says promptly too:
— We know all about the iron broom.
— Just tell me once and for all, quite honestly: Are you
still living in Othmarschen at all?
— Do you think I'm sleeping in the prop room at the
Thalia Theatre?
— Well, it's all right, if you're being honest with me.
Jäcki thrown out of the decent apartment, spending nights
in railway tunnels and allotment huts or living in stations.
Whether Jäcki still goes to St Pauli?
— Do you believe, the cream of Hamburg society is more
stimulating than the pimps. One eats better food with
Wolli than with shipowners and there's more inner nobility
in St Pauli than in the Elbe suburbs.
— You haven't gone and become a pimp yourself?
Jäcki sleeping in the suburban railway and organising orgies
for council house tenants.

— And tell me, you don't have anything to do with drugs, do you?

If Jäcki would concoct a confession:

— There's not a single pore on my body without a puncture mark!

She would pour out more coffee.

— Wait, there's a second tin of cream in the kitchen.

— I disappoint her. I have neither children nor LSD.

Jäcki's mother thinks that Irma's Cardin boots look like tart's boots.

And mummy twice considerately uses the word menopause with reference to Irma.

— How are your fat legs, mummy, says Jäcki solicitously.

— Pass the cake round again.

Irma's legs are the dream of any teenager.

Asiatics.

That's the word that does it.

How did it happen?

Perhaps a second superfluous remark by Jäcki about male prostitutes.

That brings Jäcki's mother round to the rockers.

— Which you read about them in the *Evening News*.

What you didn't read was that the reporters had nothing else to offer the rockers except crates of beer and even that only because the students weren't available for headlines because of the holidays.

From that to brutality.

Jäcki's mother:

— The brutality of the rockers.

Jäcki:

— The brutality of the...of the...of the...

Then the word:

— Asiatics!

Or:

Jäcki's mother:

— Just don't get involved in politics as well!

Jäcki:

— Why actually is politics reserved for an elite? Why does the word "political" still actually have a pejorative after-taste for people in Germany?

Jäcki's mother:

— What does that mean?

Jäcki:

— What?

Jäcki's mother:

— Pejorative?

Jäcki:

— Devalued.

Jäcki's mother:

— Politics is something dirty. Must be something dirty! People with power!

— Just don't imagine, you still have something in common with the people!

The newspapers!

The students!

We have!

You have!

Seat of the pants!

Third World!

Individual!

Cuba!

Chaos!

End!

Sun!

Bright!

Warmth!

Freedom!

Repression!

— They should go over to the other side!

— That's not an argument!

Is it an argument?

— Asiatics!

Jäcki loses his temper, as he's never lost his temper before. Yes, once, when Alex was visiting and mummy was probing like that all the time too and insinuating all kinds of things. But then he was still a lot smaller.

It's different from begging, sulking, screaming, because he's not allowed to go to the Kellinghausen Baths or because he's not allowed to go to the Yehudi Menuhin concert, different from bawling, even earlier, out of fear of the shiny men under the bed or the trembling and shouting, while reading *Orestes* in the half room with the sloping ceiling. Jäcki feels himself to be in a big scene — but that's only by the way. Something is filling him up, that he, if he was asked, would describe as a sweet blood pudding, sweet jellied — not sour blacksour. There's a dish like it somewhere.

He can feel it under his ribs.

It's all very heated and the words come from every direction:

— What does "Asiatics" mean anyway? What does "Asiatics" mean anyway? It means roast Asians. It means white tropical suits from Hongkong and insecticide.

Mummy tries to reason. She's afraid there could be further unpleasant consequences:

— The Asiatics have a quite different relationship to their body, she says in a controlled voice.

But her face —

— Mummy's face. The very first face. In some places it's become quite immobile. Some features I can't judge anymore, changes, loses colour. The suppressed carpet-of-bombs face emerges, the face from the cellar, the face between American parachute bombs.

— Yes, I know! The astral body and the ethereal body and the karma. I can't stand hearing that nonsense anymore!

Jäcki has said "nonsense" about the thing that means most to mummy — apart from himself. Jäcki means most to her. The arts means most to her; Jäcki takes it back:

— I can't stand hearing this whole reactionary nonsense any more: Don't stand out! Just don't say anything! Accept things as they are. All your *Evening News* and labour exchange!

Now Jäcki's mother says temperately:

— Have you gone mad? Why are you shouting like that?

Jäcki shouts:

— Yes, I've gone mad: In '45 you said: We didn't know anything! and now you know exactly and say: Asiatics!

Jäcki's mother:

— Who on earth is "you"?

Because Jäcki doesn't answer, he gets louder:

— And so you say "Negroes" and so you say "Russians" and so you say "homosexuals" and so you say "mixed race"!

Jäcki's mother:

— I didn't mention the word "homosexuals" in that connection at all!

Jäcki:

— In what connection?

Jäcki's mother:

— In the one you're talking about.

— But you did say "mixed race"!

— Who didn't say it?

— You with your terrible cowardice accused granny, because she sang "Daughter of Zion, Rejoice" at Christmas!

Jäcki's mother:

— And why did I do it? To save you! They would have taken us away! Did I not type deportation orders myself?

— Why did you type them?

— What else should I have done?

— You sat next door, while they cut their arteries in the Raboisen Labour Exchange toilet. Asiatics!

— And what do the students do today? Don't they say "Asiatics" and "pensioners" and . . . and . . . The workers can't even understand them when they open their mouths. The only thing we can understand is their eternal abuse and threats against older workers and employees! I had to work for a wage all my life and now I have to let my only son say "reactionary" and *"Evening News"* to me, just because I said "Asiatics" without thinking! What do you do then? You want to write a play about poor crazy Mr Cartacalo/la who has to work for a wage. What did you do for him then?

— I took him red wine and smoked sausage!

— Like in the fairy tale! I beat granny's upholstered chairs clean for him and wiped the cabinet and went to the phone and called the removal van and made sure that they got the whole lot there in one piece! I took the trouble. Smoked sausage. Asiatics. Have you ever given anything to the children in Biafra? Here, look at them, the twigs. I stuck all the letters of acknowledgement onto the little twigs. Have you given anything to Terre des Hommes? Or to the SOS Children's Villages? Or for Albert Schweitzer? Or for the blind, deaf and dumb? Or for Bethel? Look! I took it all out of my pension and even today still have to think twice before I take the train or the underground, while you spend all night at your studies in St Pauli!

Mummy takes the coffee pot out.

Irma says:

— Wonderful!

Jäcki's mother:

— Are you going already? I'll see you to the front door. It's locked from eight. I'll just quickly slip on other shoes.

She walks along the trellis-lined path with Irma and Jäcki. At the door Jäcki says:

— I'm sorry for shouting like that.

Jäcki's mother says:

— Don't feel guilty, for having said all that. Have you got everything?

138

Jäcki's walk cuts across the central railway station.
Insights into the layers of the irrepresentative:
The nature of the living conditions of the Turkish guest worker.
Health care in the case of the tubercular beatnik.
Non-allowance of convalescent leave for a sixty-year-old office worker with syphilis.
— Did you know, that you're held in solitary confinement for ten years, if you murder a woman at seventeen?
Jäcki wanders over to the festively illuminated Playhouse and meets many old acquaintances from the "Palette" there.
A crowd is gathering in front of the Playhouse.
Iphigenia is being stormed. The eight-year-old's festive cream cake.
Danton's Death with Erich Schellow as Camille Desmoulins, Jäcki's unconscious French Revolution scaled by the German revolution of the "Palette".
La Prise de la German Playhouse!
The old uniformed attendants command the little card pieces of the tickets and ladies and gentlemen in C&A — they no longer command these Paletticians, long haired and doped up, these excited dossers, gays, students, these rebellious ideologues and proponents of popular theatre.
On the unrivalled stage Gustaf Gründgens — discussion.
Duvinage photographs everyone for the *Evening News* and some actors deliver words of enlightenment now from the stage box, now from the stage.
Jäcki feels more sorry for the usherettes than the ushers. It was pointed out to the attendants at some time in their youth that they might perhaps have to defend *Iphigenia* against surprise attack. But the usherettes?

In forty years of employees' wage scales, health insurance scheme and employees' insurance to persecution of the Jews, terror attack, compulsory service and occupation, who has prepared them for the existence of a central station pouring itself into the foyer, and for a dress circle no longer counting for more than rows 20 to 23 in the stalls? An employee who's got used to sleeping with a gun under his pillow runs from box to box and screams:

— Fascists! Fascists!

and swallows the second syllable as he does so.

— Man, queen! Jäcki would like to call out to him expressionistically and in a deep voice. Grow above yourself! Make your own contribution to the destruction of the concentration camp, in which you're living much more than many others. Be less foolish.

And Jäcki doesn't call out to him.

Someone, who knows the man, whispers to Jäcki:

— He was in a camp.

Oh, so he really was in a concentration camp. Fascism is not a quasi-syntactical problem for him.

— Concentration camp. If I'm honest, I've forgotten everything about it. What I had to fear at nine and what I read about at ten, is gone.

A pale boy in the stalls shouts:

— It's five minutes to twelve. If the Emergency Laws get through everything is lost.

Someone waves the *Morning Post* over the expensive seats: "De Gaulle Flees Paris!"

The good old *Morning Post*!

Hardly have we stormed the German Playhouse here, than Madame and Monsieur de Gaulle are already fleeing Paris in a Louis XVI carriage! Despite that the stage hands want to go home, because they have to be out again at seven o'clock tomorrow morning.

Jäcki feels responsible.

Who was a worker?

Jäcki!

Who knows the stage hands?

Jäcki!

Danton lives in Jäcki too and flutters on his cheeks and twitters over his lips.

Jäcki tries to conciliate, to appeal and gets the stage hands to agree that they want to continue discussion in the university.

Jäcki tries to prevail upon St Just and Robespierre, who now dominate the stage, with the suggestion: Stage hands of the German Playhouse debate with the SDS at the University.

— Some different workers in the university apart from the three ubiquitous Communist shop stewards.

But it's difficult. What's going on here? Jäcki doesn't prevail with: The wage slaves are tired. Our mass base has to get up early tomorrow morning and will get into a bad mood, if it can't go and doss now.

Nobody listens.

— The workers want to debate with you at the university.

St Just in front of the curtain declares:

— The workers have a deformed consciousness!

— The workers don't want you to lower yourselves to them at Blohm and Voss or in the Malersaal hall. The stage hands want to come up to you on the platform at the university.

— I have a deformed conscience? says a stage hand, whom Jäcki has known since *Liliom* and *A Glass of Water* and whom Jäcki sometimes meets in a toilet.

— Consciousness, they call out to him.

— Deformed consciousness, shout twenty-year-olds at him, whose consciousness could no longer be deformed by the word "conscience", because they weren't born until 1945, when this stage hand was already having to push sets around for *Liliom* and *A Glass of Water*.

But he doesn't let himself be put off his stride.
— I have a deformed conscience? Why then? Why do you
tell me that then?
Why do I have a deformed conscience then?

139

The Flower of Sharon is dead.
Jäcki last saw him in front of a chemist's. The Flower of
Sharon said he was playing in living theatre.
He was saved at the first suicide attempt.
When found after the second, he was turned blue by the
overdose of a narcotic, that he had injected into his veins.
He was just twenty.
He was found too late or perhaps late enough.
He had never shouted "Why does no one stand by me!"
but "Why don't you leave me in peace!"
Sauna Greasestreet tells a photographer that he had loved
the Flower of Sharon.
Shortly before his death two hippies took several kilos of
hashish from him, without paying the agreed price.
— Violence, that's what is decisive, says the Flower
of Sharon.
— You mustn't proceed against marginal phenomena
and puppets, complain about conseqences. You must kill
ideologists, officers, politicians, industrialists. Many. Still.
Youths brush past Jäcki and the Flower of Sharon. With
naked shoulders, naked torsos, a bath towel tied round the
waist, their long Hanseatic legs uncovered; white plastic
sandals on their feet. They pass from the tiled showers to
the WC, past the lockers, through the cabins, panting
arrogance with their long strides and feeling embarrassment
at their own hated desired nakedness, streaming with sweat
they tug the bath towel over the puncture marks of the

syphilis treatment in the small of the back, protect anal gonorrhoea as an intimate secret with plastered down hair-styles, try to compensate for bow legs by the angle of the chin. Thoughtlessly the youths pass on their athlete's foot in the white plastic sandals. Behind the tall harmonious bodies follow shorter older ones, those successful in the world of the law or of the theatre, who can get away with it, they worship the commanding sweaty figures between two cabin doors, silently slide trembling hands into the towelling of the silent refusers.

Rolf Lüders, the thin assistant producer, has put on weight and it's with satisfaction that he sees Jäcki, the Christ Child from *Frau Holle*, in the same steam bath.

The Flower of Sharon takes naked Jäcki's arm and walks with him towards the big common room with its three couches. The Flower of Sharon's feet click as he walks. The enamel, the cornelians and turquoises mounted in gold and silver fall like a net over his Mongolian legs.

Since resin has been injected under the skin, the muscles have been held at their dilation and remind Jäcki, despite the coarsening through the bandages, of the legs of the boy in duffle coat and jeans who came floating down the little violet steps of the "Palette".

The garment becomes firm at the hips, stiff up to the armpits and across the shoulders. Golden, silver, turquoises, cornelians, glass beads, enamel.

The Flower of Sharon raises his ring and metal band covered hands, whose fingers are tied and immobile, full of traces of the flesh scorching oil; he wipes the mask, which has been divided into streaks of gold, from his face.

— The situation is favourable, says the Flower of Sharon.

— There are only a few countries, in which we are allowed to exist and spread our views. In the end we will destroy the system of these countries too, in order to set up the only one we recognise as right, under which we ourselves can no longer live of course. But that is neither necessary nor desirable. The only use which you and I — petty bourgeois intellectuals, afflicted by all the vices of our class, which places a stigma, that of conversion, even on revolt itself, capable of beginning the process of liberation, incapable of existing in the state of freedom, we can only set the ground beneath our feet alight; when redemption arrives we are inevitably already annihilated.

We must destroy the enemy positions starting with the few countries which do not grind us down beforehand. In independently targeted actions, two, or three men, cut pipelines, rob banks, put printing presses out of action, violate consulates, shut down power stations, disrupt, always, but above all kill statesmen and their business and intellectual allies. Everything else is revolutionary Mallarmé. To break Adorno's heart — ludicrous.

We must hurry. Soon the security systems will be so perfect, that it will no longer be possible for minorities who can communicate with the masses for the purpose of their liberation to exist.

— Would you torture, says Jäcki.

— That question doesn't concern me.

— But I'm asking you. Would you torture?

— It's clear, that during a transitional period we shall have to make use of the enemy's methods. Victory is close, in a few months it may already have become impossible forever. Should a few plane crashes or hostage shootings prevent us from bringing it about?!

— Don't you think, that a gentle subversion of the unconscious, which can no longer be undone, produces a deeper transformation? If I'm honest, I can only conceive of freedom as a gigantic worldwide homosexualisation, says Jäcki.

— We haven't got time for that.

— Or Neckermann instead of Robespierre. Tourism as a universal wall newspaper.

— Tourism! If you are not prepared to use methods that are not part of the system, you won't change the system.

— Say you, stamped by the system that you want to transform. Would you torture?

— I will not be the one who has to torture.

— So some with gloves on and some without after all?

— I already said so.

— I don't want to torture or have torture carried out. I refuse to give the order to shoot.

— Seven million Jews said that too. Then you'll go on sleeping, while people are being tortured next door. Then soon, and that will be tomorrow, you will be overwhelmed by the masses.

Gradually the cabin doors have shut and, to the thunder of the bodies smacked to the ground in the karate course on the floor above and with fluttering lips behind the white lacquered pulp wood shutters, can be heard called the

"Horst"s,

"Rolf"s,

"Dieter"s.

The plastic tiles are made completely wet by those licking one another, holding on to the partition beams, pressing into one another, until they shake themselves with disgust at the discharges and the tongue quickly abandons the other face with its black, round toothless mouth, the sagging eyes and the slobbery nose.

The skin on the Flower of Sharon's face has turned very red. The skin on the right cheekbone is unravelling in a spiral. The eye sockets crammed with milky jewels. The makeup sticks to the shrunken lids behind the artificial eyes. Remains of old pink makeup. A few lashes sticking to one another.

Reddish hair in the nostrils. The face swells up and is driven apart as if by a white crumbly mass.

— The tongue is firmly lodged between the right hand side teeth, shrivelled, hard, black.

— A few crawling maggots and cocoons are found among the pieces.

The carefully woven wig has come away from the scalp and is caught on the headband.

140

Not violence.

Only unviolence.

Only tenderness.

Would you not defend yourself, if you were being put into the truck for the oven.

If the Turk, the negro, the one from Casablanca slowly crushed your balls and said:

— You are a white homo!

I smile. I let my coat be stolen. I lie on the floor and let my teeth be kicked out, said with blood pouring out:

— I'm your brother.

I give him one, hit him in the face, kick him back in the balls.

I remain motionless and wet the wound and lie on the ground under the brickie, who says

— Well, you bloody queer!

kick him in the teeth, till he shuts up.

I remain motionless.

Don't ever start it.

If Irma betrayed me.

I imagine her climbing up to the bachelor apartment at Stephan's Square with the conductor or the commercial artist and I throw him through the cross bars of the window in the middle of the rush hour and kick, torment her.

Smile on the ground, remain motionless.

I would be armed with knuckle duster, fuse, bottles, gun, could do karate, would fight my way up to be the Untouchable of Grosse Freiheit and laconically arouse admiration in the salons. Explosion. Blood for the oppressed. Kicks. Cause slipped discs and cracked testicles. Beat out the kidneys of relevant personalities, who were still standing me drinks only yesterday.

Where does it come from, my admiration for Gandhi, who rubbed his clothes for hours, to remove an orange spot.

Cowardice? The fear of feeling pain oneself? Non-violence as easy chair?

Comfort and tiled stove out of fear of getting my hands, my beautiful, sensitive hands caught?

Am I to blame for my non-violence?

Where does my idea of a certain kind of gaping wound come from?

Lately it all has to be fun.

Liberation must be fun too. The holy liberator. Kick out teeth as asceticism!

Don't ever start it, because then you're lost.

Revenge.

Like Uli, who has beaten a couple of people until they were cripples; who dreams of slowly knocking his teacher to death in a state between unconsciousness and extreme awareness at the top of St Michael's church tower.

Nail the navel to a tree trunk and force the one who's guilty to run round the trunk, till the whole intestine has been wrapped round the bark in retribution.

Dr Prelle for example.

Don't think like that! One must not think like that! We are not Ancient Germans. We are not potential Ilse Kochs. Unmen. Outside of men. We should not consider it. There is no possibility of identification. Not you. Smile!

To torture, for the sake of the cause. Hammer in nails. I am a man at last.

To be beaten at last by the wonderful policeman with the long black rubber truncheon.

That's why listening to torture is so much worse than suffering torture oneself — the complicity of torturer and tortured falls away, all the small tender gestures with which the pain is heightened and the facial expressions exchanged after the success of a new torment.

Remain motionless and smile and you don't need to soil your thoughts with thoughts like: I'm a man at last! and with all the superfluous adjectives.

Don't want to divide Jeff down the middle, the most desired body. To the right a foot, to the left. Divide the testicles, the intestine, the lungs, the larynx. To see him lying before you. The two halves of his brain. Spit into his normal words, his normal thoughts, his whole normal innards.

You didn't do it. Stay calm. It doesn't happen.

The temptation of violence. Splinters. Forward!

I fished the fly out of the milk and guided the frog safely across the street. Lain in every position. Felt each sex and imitated each one.

Something new!

I don't know that yet. Violence!

One screeching queen more, who cuts the figure of a good officer out of boredom and declares her emotional backwardness to be an exemplary operation of consciousness.

141

Along the shore are natural signs, tide marks, small cliffs, produced by water draining away, waves left behind in the sand by waves, signs by children from the home, sentences, hearts, aeroplanes, lines, for hopping round, impressions of toes and hands.

Detlev loves nature of himself, the violence of the ocean, the sublimeness of the sunsets — and because he has read

so much about the beauty and sublimeness of the North
Sea islands.

With the other convalescent boys he walks to the newly
established "Abyssinia" and watches the nudist camp
members climbing the dunes.

Detlev and the others spy on lovers in the beach grass.
Detlev sits with Harriet Moll on a section of the beach
fenced in for children from the home.

Here the sand is fairly untouched. Only a few claw marks
and spurts of sand from seagulls flying up into the air.

Harriet Moll loves nature too and takes an interest in
serious problems.

They both faultlessly inhale the healthy air, till everything
goes black before his eyes. Broad bands of foam toss on
the waves.

— The equinoxes, says Harriet Moll solemnly. She read
the word in North Sea stories.

— There was nothing, says Detlev.

— Apart from salted vegetables and a few opera libretti.
The Swing Youth, so like:

He rides in his troika

Mr Moneybags with the balalaika

Down by the Black Sea

Beside his Betsy

And sings the Song of Broadway.

But they hanged themselves in the lavatories of Raboisen
Labour Exchange. The liberation! We got army coats from
the flak shelters and I found a few books. *The People of
Seldwyla*. That was the liberation. All those who had
tormented us before remained. There was less to eat than
before and the bread became yellow, because the interpreter
had mixed up the American word for maize with the English
word for wheat. In the newspapers you saw the piles of
bodies and in the allotments sixty-seven comrades of the
people starved to death. The theatre was the new life.

Painting too. In *Listen Now!* there was a picture by Chagall
of a man who had six fingers on one hand. We subscribed
to two art magazines — but mummy locked the *Abstract
Work of Art* away from me, because she was afraid that
abstract art could jeopardise my development. The Hitler
Youth leaders all read Hermann Hesse now. I was dragged
along behind the tram car for the first symphony concert
after the war. But the theatre! *The Unfathomable Mr
Gerstenberg* by Axel von Ambesson. Wolfgang Borchert
was still alive and cried: Mothers, say no! He died yellow
with fever in Switzerland. He's only just five thousand
years old, cried Ida Ehre. Moses appeared in a play with
modern paper costumes and at certain points the producers
and the actors talked to the audience. For freedom and free
theatre life we paid six times the ticket price, smoked
sausages, smokers' ration cards, woollen carpets. Sartre
called out to us, that even for the Germans self-denial is
not the attitude, which they are free to choose after the
military collapse, and that his play *The Flies* should not
only point us towards the future, but also help us to
achieve it. Freedom, Harriet! To shake free of one's mother
through a grave crime and sink down into the abyss of the
people of Argos. We all read it and stamped our feet and
shouted: Stay here. The whole of Hamburg was there.
Harriet Moll is the girl who listens to him, does not just
play forfeits with him or breed snails! She doesn't reject
him because of Ove like Helga Fuchs.
— Can you imagine it?
Harriet Moll nods quickly.
— But that's all threatened now. People are only interested
in alpaca waistcoats and frying pans now. But a waistcoat
by itself is nothing. The theatres are empty. The "Gallery
of Youth" may perhaps have to close.
Sometimes I myself have the feeling that I'm becoming
shallow. I rummage through walls of shoes at Citreck and

Timm, until I've found the right blue pigskin shoes with the stinking crêpe soles to match my blue Norwegian pull-over. If my film contract comes to something, we want to buy some furniture again.

— Perhaps you've only overexerted yourself a little and need to recover now, says Harriet Moll.

Detlev begins to scratch in the sand with a piece of cuttle fish: "*Iphigenia in Tauris.*" "*Nathan the Wise.*" "*Liliom.*" "*Medea.*" "*Frau Holle.*" "*Antigone.*" "Rabindranath Tagore." He avoids the bumps in the sand. He encircles the remains of wicker beach chairs, which have almost been covered up, with letters. If a Nivea tin is lying on the surface, he pulls it away and fills the depression with sand and wipes the new surface smooth.

"*The Unfathomable Mr Gerstenberg,*" writes Detlev and "*The Skin of Our Teeth*" he writes curving round a beer bottle stopper, between pieces of cuttle fish and the eggs of the horned ray.

Harriet Moll is afraid that the triangles of foam, which whip ahead of the large waves, will make her feet wet.

142

Writers must — in 1944 come from the east and return to the east again, be mown like a full ear of corn by the sword of death, hearken to the silence, silently preserve, be calm and sparing of words, grow ever taller in the memory of posterity and finally proffer the crown of life to the people as most holy heritage — 1945 — not only point the Germans towards the future but help them to reach it, despair in anguish, if no one gives them a pencil, hoarsely sob out hot emotions, thread pearls and cultivate their handwriting — 1946 — shed light on the paths of others, turn against calligraphers and begin to root out the slave language, start from the beginning and make a clean sweep in language, substance, ideas — 1949 — work for the reduction of evil in man, mark a truth with every sentence, circle and circle like hawks — 1950 — tear off man's mask, hold up the mask before us — 1951 — display existential backgrounds or lack them, assemble them fascinatingly — 1952 — steal collectors' editions for their friends, be good seismographs of spiritual catastrophes — 1955 — be in form, like a sprinter on his starting blocks, allow the paradox of human existence to emerge, work suggestively on prerational strata, but also start the secret zones of concepts oscillating, alienate them, deform them — 1957 — set the continuously creative never complete open ended interpretative process in motion, express insights gained from skating on thin ice, assimilate technological civilisation and its problems to the content — 1959 — give whole generations of academics nuts to crack — 1960 — confront the audience with the incomprehensibility, the questionableness of life — 1961 — plead for the positive, discover that a cold is harder to describe than cancer — 1962 — be suspicious of the word, transfer to the twenty-first century — 1963 — understand the second law of thermodynamics, require contradictory sequences of sentences, register the situation, investigate grandfathers in the kitchen, try out points of view — 1964 — be precise, solve sectional problems according to specific demands, hold starvation to be the appropriate dish for a writer, continue the report, force language to express itself, enjoy being kitschy — 1966 — not work without openly taking an explicit political position, destroy political theatre, take language at its word — 1967 — lay down a possible end point of literary development, write badly, in order to be really good, put language itself at the centre — be of unfathomable integrity, shoot their critics, call the audience arseholes at every reading, prepare their contributions to the working out of fundamental positions — 1969 — be in front — 1970 — produce commodities, be artworks, have dry hands.

143

Outside the entrance to the "Grünspan" psychedelic club Jäcki remembers the gold dust, which turned into verdigris — *Grünspan* — on his head, when Detlev played "Peace" in *The Trojan War Will Not Take Place*.

Derwisch is the manager of the "Grünspan".

In post "Palette" times Derwisch ran the Schmilinskistrasse Tearooms, served complicated teas to Bach, chess, Go and nostalgic jazz, opened the "Oblomov" on Glockengiesserwall, went downhill, the bar with the name of the Russian censor was to be shut down by the police because of drugs, minors, down and outs, male prostitutes.

Derwisch critically consciousnessed himself up to the still hot end of Grosse Freiheit and opened — putting down how much in slush money? — his new consciousness garage; to end capitalism he pocketed capital with the psychedelic, had the firewall decorated with a modern tiled picture and at the weekend dubiously coaxes one mark admission from hippies, bums, winos, students, New Leftists and is said to have forbidden Jeff, hired as film projectionist, to piss during working hours.

The disc jockey rides on her high stool.

Two dance floors.

A film screen.

Three projection surfaces along the balcony parapet.

Two stroboscopes.

Four automatic slide projectors.

Two film projectors.

A lot of decibels.

Between two slides coloured inks and alcohol, which begin

to pulsate from the warmth of the projector. The projectors tremble from the soundwaves and affect the pulsing of the coloured drops and the alcohol, pulsing, which throws the light across the dance floors and projection surfaces in giant waves across the dancers, pulsing to the same beat, unrecognisable under the projections.

Comparable to trees.

Comparable to Faust II.

Comparable to record covers.

Comparable to burning people.

Comparable to shrivelled burnt corpses.

— Capri! says a gentleman with the grey felt hat and points at a layer of part of a projection.

Two

Stro

Two

Stro

Two

Bo

Bo

Two

Stro

Bo

Stro

Sco

Bo

Sco

Pe

Pe

To the eye the smallest parts of movements are not movements, but fixed.

There

Da

Jeff

In the

Whi
Smo
Of
Pa
Flees
Step
Bu
Dance
Bends
Laugh
An
Hi
Bald
Head

— It signifies a great liberation, says the mild looking ash blond young man. Only we mustn't let ourselves be satisfied with dancing beneath slides of snow covered fir trees mixed with car races and Mickey Mouse films. I would wish that it went further under the skin as far as sections of brains, brain surgery, spattered brains, operations on the brain, smashed, bloody brains with splinters of bone sticking out at accidents.

— Brothers, are we then closer to love?

Banks from Liechtenstein and Luxembourg are recruiting agents among the pimps and boy prostitutes of St Pauli, to arrange loans to workers who can no longer keep up their hire purchase instalments and to whom no bank in Germany would give another loan, at an interest rate of 30 per cent.

— The Drog Squad, says Igor, and the CID are feuding with one another.

— If the Drog Squad lays a trap, says Igor, then the Customs gives it away and a large number of the threatened drog dealers escapes. Half the SDS in Frankfurt were drog dealers anyway, who were only released by the police, because they were prepared to be informers and act as agents provocateurs, says Igor.

— The CIA wanted to make contact with the big Hamburg drog dealers. A CIA agent was shot by the police at a meeting of big Hamburg drog dealers.

— And not just one either, says Igor.

— In Red China the imperial drog fields continue to be cultivated, says Igor, and the harvest smuggled into the USA. That earns hard currency and weakens the class enemy. Of course it also weakens the revolution in the USA and that's probably why the CIA now carries on the drog trade together with the Red Chinese, says Igor.

That's what Igor says.

An then greets Akhnaton furr the seedbed an says:

— Your loins well known to me from countless embraces. Gold shall ah lay doon that they do pump nae cedar oil intae yer hole an yer tender passage dissolves an not naethin is left o yer innermost. Carefully shuid they cut oot yer passage an wash an pickle an stuff wi rosin an upricht stick atween yer legs. Ma seedbed!

A punta do Janeiro

Pra fazer um tabaquciro

Akhnaton grieves for the seedbed:

— No cedar oil shall I let in, that your innermost burns up. Your sex they should cut off, pickle, stuff and place upright between your legs again.

— The brain preserved in toto.

— For the journey through the night.

An auld teacher Dutch, teacher Dutch, teacher Dutch

Maks frac the udder a bacco pouch, bacco pouch, bacco pouch

Frae the meenister's coo.

Spray Estée Lauder's Super Youth Dew on the body satiné.

And Michel puffs himself up in the Étapes Touristiques Africaines and claims the French press baron personally let him into the secret of the LSD reports: Racists from the Deep South got together because they wanted to do something as private persons about the unrest in the universities.

They launched reports about LSD and paid for them to be placed like adverts full page or double page in the big magazines in New York, Paris, Hamburg, Rome — shocked reports, each one with a concealed reference to the use and acquisition of synthetic drugs. This bought indignation would cause such a spread of LSD and such a crippling of the enemy that the racism of the Deep South can safely survive the seventies.

Out of the shabby fashions of the bums from the "Palette", Leather Uta has flowered into a black orchid. Satins in varying degrees of brightness encase her thighs and chains, wafer thin nappa leather, comparable only to charred paper, cling to her breasts, and her head with the glowing eyes is crowned by the Gongora sonnet biretta of gorilla fur.

— Is Cartacalo/la's suffering pain then?

Stroboscope.

— Is Detlev's orphanage pain then pain?

— Stroboscope.

— His lantern stick hunger hunger?

— Stroboscope.

— The pain of the Hamburg-Hamm cellar fire shrivelled corpses pain?

— Stroboscope.

"Guidelines for the Chemical Examination of Fats and Cheeses". J. König, *The Chemistry of Human Foodstuffs and Beverages*, Springer 1937.

— Should I let Cartacalo/la come on stage as she is when she goes to bed with Wolli? It's cold in the prefab house. Cartacalo/la, the witch, the magician, wears long baggy underpants with black garters, an unironed shirt with tie and ski-cap.

"Portrayed in the style of a stereotypical Soul-Musical-Ballad operetta is the exemplary story of the bloody repression and the struggle of the seer and drag queen Cartacalo/la to erect a fulgurite garage and for the right to

live in his solid very small detached house No 237 Lily
of the Valley Allotment Gardens, together with some digressions on the possibilities of love for the eccentric solitary,
wardship, an unusual involvement with the fortunes of
the German press and the ultimate apotheosis despite
the demons."
I don't want to write the play about Cartacalo/la. I've lost
faith in Wittgenstein, Tarski and the operetta.
It's become smart to be amused by gay plays from England
in all the theatres of the Hanseatic city.
I am going to concern myself with a theory of sensitivity,
read Ernst Mach, Nicolas Bourbaki, visit Proust in the
library of the Duc de Guermantes.
Brothers.
Whose brothers?
Brothers? Brethren?
Do marriages break up therefore, because too many take
part or too few?
Are we
First person plural.
closer to love
Are there then no longer any schools of torture in Brazil in
which how to make the eardrums burst with blows on both
ears is taught?!
Is no one hung up by the testicles any longer?!
Does Mercedes Benz no longer sell any armoured vehicles
to Venezuela?!
Is the USSR no longer building any power stations
in Greece?!
Does the International Red Cross have access to the political
prisoners in Lisbon?! Are they allowed to snatch some
sleep in their unlit flooded cells?!
Are they still not allowed to sleep, for weeks on end?!
Are then Moroccan children no longer being beaten in the
cellars of the royal police stations?!

Is no homosexual being thrown out of an aeroplane in Yemen any longer, as punishment?!

Are no Russian intellectuals being injected with amazin, sulfadiazine and sodium aminate in psychiatric special hospitals any longer?!

Does no one force a needle under the thumb nail any longer and play on the needle with a ruler during the interrogation?!

Does no one anywhere remove an eye from the eye socket of a prisoner any more?!

Are the breasts and the knee caps of Indian women no longer sliced off with a machete blow?!

Can the head clerk from Fuhlsbüttel be given a goodbye embrace by his lover in front of the office, without being fired?! then closer to love?!

Your good is not my good.

Your beautiful is not my beautiful.

Your true is not my true.

Everything is beautiful.

Everything is true.

Everything is good.

— Brothers, are we then closer to love?!

There is no more True, Good and Beautiful.

No more Iphigenia.

No *No More Invocation of the Great Bear*.

Everything finished.

Even Hans Henny Jahnn?

Even Marcel Proust's Library of the Duc de Guermantes?

— Clean him out!

— Him clean out!

Left over is the ocean of green-violet — orange-violet is over too! — plastic, over which the naked man staggers and paints himself with the eye of a fish, so that there are beautiful flowing lines.

Not I.

Sensitivity.

— Brothers, are we then closer to love?!

Jeff.

He has shaved his head and taken off the white patent leather tuxedo.

I feel how my nipples begin to burn from the ever repeated rubbing of his hard hands.

I feel his cock very early, very deep, deep below.

My cock very early, far below, deep into his arse.

His hands on my nuts.

My hands on his eggs.

My almonds against his eggs.

We look at one another through our eggs.

My teeth burst.

— Brothers, are we then closer to love?!

Both the damaged step up to one another, Jeff the Negro, Jäcki, the bi.

Each remembering his injuries through the other.

— Je ne le fais pas que pour des raisons économiques.

And Jäcki's agreement to that.

Jeff, the weakness of the injured, again and again to have been dependent on payment.

Forth into your shadows, restless treetops

Of this ancient, sacred, verdant grove,

As in the goddess' own silent shrine,

Do I yet step with shuddering awe

As though my foot did enter for the first time,

And here my spirit finds no rest.

— Brothers, are we then closer to love?!

— The skin on the head, as of the rest of the body, felt hard as glass, is completely desiccated, discoloured brown to black and can be broken off like a thin, awkward piece of wood, still somewhat elastic in places.

— The Drog Squad and the CID are feuding with one another, says Igor. If the Drog Squad lays a trap, then the

Customs let the cat out of the bag and large numbers of the drog dealers escape, says Igor.

Mrs Schwerdtner copies out the essays of the nine-to-ten-year-olds:

Hashish.

Hashish is a drug. One can smoke it, take it as a pill or inject oneself.

If one takes it often one can become addicted.

Drugs are also (used) by doctors.

If one takes it, one has beautiful dreams and sleeps — is prescribed

so that one doesn't feel pains — tight.

Michel is showing off in the Étapes Touristiques Africaines. The French press baron had personally let him into the secret of the LSD reports. Racists from the Deep South got together, to do something with private means about the unrest in the universities.

Information theory is not sufficient.

It doesn't include the misunderstanding and the lie.

The decisions are made before the forming of signs.

For from the friends I love the sea divides me

And day by day I stand upon the shore,

Seeking with all my soul the land of Greece!

— Brothers, are we then closer to love?!

— In Red China the imperial drog fields continue to be cultivated and the harvest smuggled into the United States. That earns hard currency and weakens the class enemy. Of course it also weakens the revolution in the USA and that's probably why the CIA now carries on the drog trade together with the Red Chinese, says Igor. They had full page or double page reports about LSD placed in the big illustrated magazines, which all contained a hidden reference to the use and acquisition of synthetic drugs.

Drugs come from the Southern States. They are very dear, because one has to pay a lot of customs duty on them.

There are many drugs. Usually they are smoked. It's really forbidden to take drugs, because one, as has been said, becomes addicted. They're usually taken by young people (delinquents). They smash everything up, if they don't get them. If they're caught, they're loked up in the youth detention camp. The bed is made of iron. The wall is stone without windows. He can't break out of it. They want to bann the sale of drugs now. But it is still sold. Someone always smuggles drugs across the border. Usually with fishing boats. This is how it hapens. Hashish at the bottom fish on top. Nobody pokes around there. It'll always be like that.

— The liver feels very hard all over, can be cut like very fatty firm cheese.

Shocked reports, each with a hidden reference to the preparation and acquisition of synthetic drugs. This bought indignation would cause such a spread of LSD and such a crippling of the students, that the racism of the Deep South can safely survive the seventies.

— Brain preserved in toto.

"My Dream."

I was alone at last and could prepare for my journey to M. Otto met me and I invited him of all people to come with me. I would not have a single free minute. Of course, he could sleep with me at the pension or in the room that Horst wanted to put at my disposal.

Otto usually slept late and in the breakfast room I discussed with the others, whether Otto really loved me, "valued" is what this "loved" in my dream meant.

I doubted it.

But they assured me, he had frequently expressed himself favourably about me to them.

There follow obscure passages in the memory of my dream. Perhaps a new dream, but probably the continuation of the old one.

Otto took me to the airport with the others. The two of us went into a cafeteria and the waiter asked me for my student card.
— Is it no longer possible to drink a cup of coffee in this country without proving one's identity?!
He could see that I was a foreigner. Why should I have a student card.
Then my passport.
I didn't have the faintest intention of showing it. He should bring me my coffee or prove his own identity.
An elderly man, to whom the other customers in the airport cafeteria were showing identity cards and student cards, came and stood beside him.
He held out his police badge and demanded my passport.
Opening it I discovered, that it was Uwe's passport.
Why, when for once I'm by myself at last, do I have to share my room with Otto or Uwe?
As I looked closely at the police badge, I remembered that I had dreamed of Uwe a few days before. We had been in a pension together and they had mixed up our passports.
We had wanted to sort it out right away, but then Uwe, without thinking any more about it, had left and now I had to pay for it in this dream in the airport cafeteria.
The policeman looked at me and remarked:
— But you looked fuller in the face then.
I gave him a kind of driving licence — I had left my identity card at home — a folded piece of card with a photograph of me, just as Youssif had really shown me a kind of driving licence yesterday, a folded piece of card with a photograph of himself, in the dunes. The policeman didn't notice the discrepancy between the photographs and the names in the two documents. That would also have disturbed me less than I was disturbed by the fact, that a confusion of passports in a dream a few days previously could, as I knew, have consequences now, in this new dream, in the airport cafeteria.

But if I think about it now when I'm awake:
Did I really dream a few days ago, that my passport and
Uwe's got mixed up?
Or did I only dream it?
Did I dream, what I'm reporting of my dream?
How much of it enters my consciousness?
Did I dream nothing more or less and now that I'm awake
do I make up new connections to it?
About which dreams did I really dream and what can I
report of them — strictly speaking — about me or about
Uwe or Otto?
In Red China the bought indignation Someone smugolds
the young people always would will and on the bank imperial drog fields an drug from through continue to be
cultivated which says Igor the upper classes and the harvests
such borders is spread usually of the with in the USA
LSD I am cause smuggle exist and fishing boats it one The
the in comes hapens such hard currency form of and so
crippling chewing gum three the enemy It the enemy's
weakens or four times that naturally the hashish long days
the country without payment at too also the the racism
revolution fishes in below underclass of the to the USA
Deep South because above safely carries on there investi-
gates the CIA yes which no one drug trade seventies after
years survive. After that they demand payment from the
youths can It'll always be like that with the Red Chinese
together of the Greeks searching with the soul, says Igor.
— Capri!
Brothers Libi Dro LSA Breth passes Libéconomique
1 2 3 4 5 6 7 8 9 10 11 12 13 14 15 16 17

144

Detlev stands in the half room with sloping roof. He has
remained thin despite the currency reform. But he no
longer has any verdigris on his head.

Detlev is surrounded by the utensils and the rest of the
furniture. He stands in front of the mirror. It hangs on the
damaged chimney wall. Perhaps mummy's headaches in
the mornings come from the carbon monoxide escaping.
Something new is beginning.

The familiar afternoon light produces a novel sensation.
The sounds from Hagenbeck's Zoo give rise to new cor-
respondences, even the sight of the dark red brick water
tower with the green copper top, which Detlev has been
looking at for as long as he has been able to see. Detlev
stands in front of the mirror. He looks at his nipples —
puffed up and not at all boyish. Because of them Detlev no
longer likes doing gymnastics with the others. But Karl-
Jörn, who used to be his friend in the Dörnstrasse school
and took his pictures of cars, has swollen nipples too and is
not embarrassed to appear at gym without a vest.

Karl-Jörn is stronger.

Detlev looks at his chest hollow because of the poor food;
perhaps it also comes from his incorrigible posture while
reading.

Detlev breathes with his diaphragm in the prescribed way,
as the physiotherapist taught him.

His cigar, his little pipe, his diddle, doodle, dibble, his
willy sticks out, not because of dreams, as in the Dr Ross
Children's Home.

Granny and grandad would notice it immediately, if they
interrupted their lunchtime rest and came upstairs.

As a young man grandad was a policeman and one of his
colleagues died, because during a visit by Emperor Wilhelm
the Second, he didn't dare break ranks and go to the toilet
and do a big one.

Detlev sees a different Detlev in the mirror.

What should one do about it?

Detlev leans against the mercuried glass. The mirror turns
milky, where his lips touch it.

Detlev wants to try it.

— It's not certain, whether peace will even last beyond the New Year. We shan't survive the next war.

Detlev talks to his mirror image with the cigar between its legs:

— I am now going to rape you.

Detlev puts his hand around his willy. His balls look out of the mirror at his balls; they look back.

Detlev imagines, his hand is an unconscious woman's body. But no semen at all comes out of him and flows into the unconscious countess.

The sounds from Hagenbeck's Zoo become recognisable again.

Fewer sunbeams spray through the curtains.

Detlev reflects that he is now no longer only a child actor, but that he could play the Marquise of O., he means, as Hermann Lenschau could play the Russian officer in the *Marquise of O*.